Prescribed by the University of Delhi for the Higher Course in Subsidiary English (Course A) for B.Sc. (Honours) and B.Sc. (General)

English for Students of Science

Board of Editors

A. Roy

P.L. Sharma

Co-ordinator

R.K. Khanna

Orient BlackSwan

ENGLISH FOR STUDENTS OF SCIENCE

ORIENT BLACKSWAN PRIVATE LIMITED

Registered Office
3-6-752 Himayatnagar, Hyderabad 500 029 (Telangana), INDIA
e-mail: centraloffice@orientblackswan.com

Other Offices
Bengaluru, Bhopal, Chennai, Guwahati, Hyderabad, Jaipur,
Kolkata, Lucknow, Mumbai, New Delhi, Noida, Patna, Vijayawada

First published 1991
Reprinted 1992, 1994, 1995, 1996, 1998, 1999, 2001, 2002, 2003,
2004, 2005, 2006, 2007, 2008
First Orient Blackswan impression 2009
Reprinted 2009, 2010, 2011, 2012, 2017

ISBN: 978 81 250 0395 3

Printed in India at
Yash Printographics
Noida

Published by
Orient Blackswan Private Limited
3-6-752 Himayatnagar,
Hyderabad 500 029 (Telangana), INDIA
e-mail: info@orientblackswan.com

Preface

This course in English has been designed to cater to the needs of undergraduate students of science while they are studying as well as after they have obtained their degrees. The main objectives of the course are: (a) to improve the students' ability to comprehend their class lectures, text books and articles in journals, etc.; (b) to give the students the ability to write accounts of their laboratory work and to report on scientific materials and processes; and (c) to equip them with enough English to enable them to enter the usual professions open to them.

The course contains a varied selection of reading passages of prose, poetry and drama. While many of them are of special interest to students of science, care has been taken to also include passages of a more general interest which would help extend their intellectual horizons beyond the limits of their specific disciplines. Each reading unit is accompanied by exercises and activities that would develop the students' language and writing skills. An extensive glossary and notes section gives explanations of vocabulary and other items with reference to the context. The Reading Comprehension exercises are of two kinds — the first kind checks understanding of the main ideas and the second calls for a more intensive study of the text. Each reading passage is a source of contextualized examples of a rich variety of language points and the Language Study section that follows each unit contains exercises that enrich vocabulary and sharpen general language skills.

The section on 'Composition' and the Appendix on 'Writing Skills' concentrate on helping the student write the kind of clear expository prose required for work relating to their discipline or their professions.

Appendix II deals with problem areas in grammar and contains exercises which give practice in using them in actual communicative contexts. It also provides insights into the fundamental structures of the languages.

To achieve the objectives of this course it is essential that the students work their way intensively through the book, reading the passages and working through the exercises at the end of each lesson.

Acknowledgements

Theodore J. Gordo, 'The Year 2050'. Reproduced with permission of author.

A. Bandhopadhyay 'The Mushroom of Death' from *The Statesman*, August 6, 1987. Reproduced with permission of *The Statesman*.

Joseph Wood Krutch, 'The Miracle of Grass [pp 66–71] from THE BEST NATURE WRITING OF JOSEPH WOOD KRUTCH by Joseph Wood Krutch. Copyright © 1952...1970 by Joseph Wood Krutch. Reprinted by permission of HarperCollins Publishers.

Louis MacNeice, 'Prayer Before Birth' from COLLECTED POEMS by Louis MacNeice, published by Faber and Faber Ltd. Reprinted by permission of David Higham Associates Ltd.

W. R. Niblett, 'Experiment and Experience' from *Melbourne Studies in Education*, 26 Jan 2010. Reprinted by permission of the publisher Taylor & Francis Ltd, http://www.tandfonline.com

Aldous Huxley, 'Benares' from JESTING PILATE: THE DIARY OF A JOURNEY by Aldous Huxley. Copyright © 1926, 1953 by Aldous Huxley. Reprinted by permission of Georges Borchardt, Inc. for the Estate of Aldous Huxley.

Manohar Malgonkar, 'Bachcha Lieutenant'. Reproduced with permission of Mena Malgonkar.

Ogden Nash, 'Bankers are Just Like Anybody Else, Except Richer' Copyright © 1938 by Ogden Nash. Reprinted by permission of Curtis Brown Ltd.

Hermon Ould, 'The Discovery'. Reproduced with permission of English PEN.

Appendix I

Neil B Sadwelkar. Reproduced with permission of author.

Every effort has been made to trace copyright holders and to obtain their permission for the use of copyright material. The publisher apologises for any errors or omissions made, and would be grateful if notified of any corrections that should be incorporated in future reprints or editions of this book.

Contents

The Year 2050 — Reflections of a Futurist

THEODORE J. GORDON

One of the most remarkable features of 2050 will be that most of the 1960 babies will still be alive.

Why do I think that more than 50 percent of the "boom babies" will survive to age 90 when today only 18 percent do? Because of a biomedical revolution which is under way.

In the last 20 years spectacular and unexpected changes have been taking place. Deaths from major cardiovascular diseases have dropped 20 percent; hypertensive deaths by two-thirds; stroke deaths by 20 percent and death due to rheumatic heart disease by 50 percent. Recent availability of drugs which offer control of hypertension explain part of the improvement, but not all. Whatever the reasons—availability of antibiotics, better health care, attention to diet, jogging, exercise—the effects in the United States are clear-cut and lasting.

It is also possible that by the middle of the 21st century some progress will have been made toward extending the human life span beyond 110 years.

But increased longevity and improved health are likely to have several drawbacks:

- World population will be larger than it might have been. The most optimistic forecasts of demographers would place world population in 2050 at about 10,000 million (as compared to our current 4,200 million); with increased longevity, population is likely to be about 12,000-13,000 million.
- Low birthrate and increased longevity combine to raise the average age of the population. In 1980 it was 30.1 years in the United States; by 2050 it will be almost 40.

- There is likely to be a period of difficult social adjustment as longevity increases. For example, most pension funds and annuities in the United States have been computed on the basis of higher death rates than we will achieve. This means that the funds will be paying out longer than expected, and this extra burden, added to other problems of pension funds, will undoubtedly put additional strains on them in the 1990s and early in the next century.

With these 12,000-13,000 million people, the world of 2050 is apt to be much smaller than it is now: less space per person, more rapid spread of ideas through instantaneous, inundating media.

On the "up" side are nascent technologies and infrastructural changes which improve distribution, reduce spoilage, bring new foods into wide use, improve productivity and increase the amount of arable acreage under cultivation. There is a really good chance that huge increases in food production can come from such developments as:

- new plant varieties, obtained through genetic engineering, which are photosynthetically efficient, use less water and tend to be self-fertilizing;
- improved uses of the ocean, including domestication of sea animals and aquaculture; and,
- tropical agriculture, which will open to the world many billions of acres of land currently unusable. This requires development of fundamentally new farming techniques that utilize the patterns of heat and rain to advantage.

By 2050 or so, our conventional petroleum reserves will have been substantially exhausted. The price of what remains will be so high that it will be impractical to burn it.

Between now and the end of the 20th century, before nondepletable alternatives are commercially developed, new synthetic fuel industries for the conversion of coal to gaseous and liquid fuels and the extraction of petroleum liquids from oil shale are likely to arise.

No one is sure, of course, how the energy picture will ultimately evolve, but the probability is an electricity scenario. All of the advanced energy technologies that we hear discussed today—solar, geothermal, wind power, fusion—are electricity producing. Given a breakthrough or two, it seems to me that the time of the electric automobile is almost here, perhaps even in the 1990s.

Furthermore, by the year 2050 we should be well along towards utilizing two virtually inexhaustible energy resources: solar electric power and nuclear fusion. Today neither possibility is very far advanced—both are expensive compared with existing systems; both require a great deal of basic and applied scientific research development, large-scale engineering and capital. But given these systems, we will have supply, not only of electricity, but of transportation fuels as well, since their output is convertible to mobile energy sources via hydrogen or through the use of yet-to-come energy storage technologies. The promise of these systems lies in providing means for generating power using essentially unending energy sources. Thus, they promise abundancy, if not low cost. Their cost, of course, depends on how the technologies evolve.

Technology seems to come in waves. In the field of energy we are witnessing the plateau of the fossil wave; solar and fusion are to follow. Between now and 2050 there are, it seems to me, three other technology waves which will blossom, plateau and, to a large extent, determine what life will be like for the boom babies and their progeny. These technologies are electronics, genetics and psychology.

Electronics is blossoming now and will plateau in the first or second decade of the next century. This means that essentially anything we can conceive of doing electronically can be done: go-anywhere telephones; fingertip information on nearly any topic; machines which speak and listen; three-dimensional life-size television; complete automation of appliances.

Well before 2050 progress in artificial intelligence will certainly have caused us to re-examine what it means to be human. When machines which augmented human mechanical capability were first introduced at the onset of the industrial revolution, the Luddites, fearing the machine age, asked the question, "What's left for humans?"

The answer at that time was that the human role is intellectual. Now there is the real possibility that machines will be able to perform intellectual tasks as well. Take any measure of human intellectual performance—IQ, recall, attention span, creativity. By early in the next century machines will be available which perform better in these dimensions than human beings. The Luddites' question will be asked again.

Two possible answers occur to me. First, we might view the machine as a colleague, working with us to augment our own sensory and reasoning capacities. Second, we might view ourselves ultimately as the framers of appropriate questions, the organizers of automated intellectual capacity in the pursuit of human needs, institutions and pleasures.

Genetics is a science about to become a technology. Early in the next century when developments in electronics are slowing, developments in genetics will be accelerating. This technology will lead to the ability to "design" plants and animals to perform human functions. In agriculture, scientists will be able to produce plants which have improved photosynthetic efficiency, minimum water requirements, self-fertilizing characteristics and a desired spectrum of nutrient qualities. In mining, organisms will metabolize desired metals and thus concentrate them for later "harvesting." In the production of pharmaceuticals, micro organisms will be used as factory workers to produce chemicals normally found only in natural body and plant processes.

Finally, in medicine, scientists will intervene in the process by which genetic diseases—such as sickle cell anaemia, Tay Sachs disease and mongolism—are passed from parents to progeny, to cure these diseases before conception. They will also address other diseases currently suspected of having a genetic origin, such as propensity to cancer or heart disease, and perhaps even the rate of aging itself. Ultimately, perhaps before 2050, this science of genetics, which will prove so important, will give us the ability to design animals, including ourselves.

By 2050 the technology of psychology may be ready to take off. The "trigger" discovery will be understanding how memory is recorded and retrieved. Today there is no clear understanding about whether memory is chemical, electrical or physical. Knowing how memory is stored and retrieved will improve education, persuasion, rehabilitation, personality development, knowledge itself, and open the huge and exciting possibility of expanding mental capacity closer to the limits of human potential.

Finally, by 2050, space may again offer several frontiers: in orbit, on the moon and elsewhere beyond the earth. A small town may be in orbit to take advantage of the unique characteristics which the orbital environment offers. Perhaps by 2050, observers in the orbital city could follow world food supply and predict harvest size and crop disease. Fishery surveys could be conducted to determine the quantity and location of meat-fish herds. Plankton and other small organisms could be detected from orbit and hazard warnings issued to shipping and coastal cities. Weather observation and prediction may be a primary business in this orbital town: air pollution measurements and contamination warning systems can be operated from orbit.

By the next century it may be possible to accomplish careful and limited weather manipulation from orbit. For example, large-scale cloud feeding might utilize orbital bombing with silver iodide. An orbiting mirror might be used to heat certain portions of the atmosphere to deflect atmospheric currents and thus divert rain-laden clouds or storms. The mirror might also be used to illuminate portions of the earth to speed crop maturation, or perhaps to aid in night time rescue operations.

In the next century, space may provide an alternative to war. Space, after all, offers the potential for a non warlike political arena where political advantage may be obtained without killing. As it may permit nations to develop advanced technologies without building weapons, it could thus provide new chances for international co-operation.

Space discoveries will tend to place man in diminishing perspective with respect to the cosmos which surrounds him. This realization—coming over decades—may help to illustrate the futility and purposelessness of conflict on earth. And as the earth becomes smaller as a result of its growing population, the limitless boundaries of space will begin to open to infuse in imaginations the spirit of exploration that otherwise would be denied all of the generations that come after ours.

The boom babies will face significant challenges in the years ahead. From our present perspective, 70 years is a very distant-time horizon, but from the perspective of history, it is a mere blink of an eye. And yet the challenges and opportunities for the generation we spawned are staggering in their potential.

NOTES

biomedical: in pharmaceutical terminology a biomedical product is a serum, vaccine, etc., used in the diagnosis, prevention, or treatment of a disease.

cardiovascular: affecting the heart and blood vessels.

rheumatic: a disorder or pain or stiffness in the joints of the body.

annuities: a specified income payable at stated intervals for a fixed or contingent period, often for the recipient's life.

infrastructural: the basic underlying framework or features of something, especially of a technological kind.

genetic engineering: the science of heredity, dealing with resemblances and differences of related organisms resulting from the interaction of their genes and the environment.

photosynthetic: (esp. in plants) the synthesis of complex organic materials, especially carbohydrates, from carbondioxide, water, and inorganic salts, using sunlight as a source of energy and with the aid of a catalyst, as chlorophyll.

shale: a rock of fissile or laminated structure formed by the consolidation of clay etc.

scenario: an outline of a story or a phenomenon.

basic and applied science: skills that reflect a precise application of facts or principles of science.

fusion: also called nuclear fusion; a thermonuclear reaction in which nuclei of light atoms join to form nuclei or heavier atoms, as the combination of deuterium atoms to form helium atoms.

boom babies: members born in the 60s have been named "the baby boom" by demographers.

industrial revolution: the complex of social and economic changes resulting from the mechanization of productive processes that began in England about 1760.

Luddites: a member of English Workmen (1811-16) who destroyed industrial machinery in the belief that its use diminished employment.

micro organism: a microscopic plant or animal.

sickle cell anaemia: a hereditary form of anaemia occurring chiefly among African Blacks.

Tay Sachs: a rare, fatal disease (mainly of the eye) occurring chiefly in children, especially of Jewish and of Eastern European origin.

mongolism: the abnormal condition of a child born with a deformed skull and slanting eyes, and generally mentally deficient.

frontiers: the limit of knowledge or the most advanced achievement in a particular field.

orbit: to move or travel around in an elliptical path.

plankton: the aggregate of passively floating or drifting organisms in a body of water.

iodide: compound containing iodine.

spawn: to produce in large numbers; to give birth to.

staggering: astounding; bewildering.

COMPREHENSION

1. Why does the author hope that the human life span will extend beyond 110 years by 2050 A.D.? (30 words)
2. What are the drawbacks of increased longevity? (50 words)
3. What makes the author believe that by 2050 A.D. there will be adequate increase in food production? (50 words)
4. What, according to the author, will the energy picture be in the 21st century?
5. Which technologies are likely to develop between now and 2050 A.D.? Mention the impact on our lives of one such technology.
6. Assess the impact of space discoveries on international relationships.
7. What other areas would you like to include in the picture of life in 2050 as outlined by the author? (about 100 words)

LANGUAGE STUDY

1. Give one word (from the text) for each of the following: The first two have been done for you.
   a. Pertaining to compounds formed by chemical reaction as opposed to those of natural origin (synthetic)
   b. effecting organic changes (metabolize)

c. pertaining to preparation of drugs, medicines etc,
d. to recover or regain
e. of or pertaining to internal heat of the earth
f. the science of mind or mental states or processes
g. medicine used in the treatment of infectious diseases
h. a person pursuing the science of vital and social statistics, as of births, deaths, marriages etc.
i. land capable of producing crops or suitable for farming
j. having or seeming to have the dimensions of depth as well as width and height
k. a broad range of varied but related ideas or objects that form a continuous series or sequence
l. a natural inclination or tendency
m. generations yet to come

2. Match the words in Column A with their synonyms in Column B.

Column A	**Column B**
progeny	increase
enhance	strain
inundating	flooding
currently	presently
burden	war
armed conflict	offspring

3. The words *science* and *technology* have been repeatedly used in the text. Find the difference between these two words. Similarly there is a difference between the meanings of *frontal* and *frontier*. Look up these two words in a dictionary to find out what the difference is.
4. Use the following words in sentences of your own so as to bring out their meaning:

   herd, blossom, nascent, conventional, staggering.
5. The expression *a mere blink of an eye* means a moment. Find out the meanings of the following idiomatic expressions and use them in sentences of your own:

   to keep an eye on, to see eye to eye with, eye-wash, an eye for an eye, in the twinkling of an eye.

COMPOSITION

1. On the basis of your knowledge of science and technology in India attempt a word-picture of the state of scientific and technological development in the year 2050 A.D.
2. "Knowledge comes but wisdom lingers". Expand this statement into about 400 words.
3. Will people be happier than our forefathers by the middle of the next century? (about 400 words)
4. Write a dialogue between two persons Ashok and Ramesh. Ashok believes that youth is better than old age but Ramesh holds the opposite view. He believes that old age is better than youth.

The Mushroom Of Death

The World After A Nuclear War

AMALENDU BANDYOPADHYAY

The bombing of Hiroshima and Nagasaki provide our only direct experience of the consequences of nuclear explosions on cities. Those events have taught us a great deal about the potential physical and biological impact of a nuclear war. But it must be remembered that the cities of Hiroshima and Nagasaki experienced only a single explosion each of a weapon much smaller in yield than many of those stockpiled in world nuclear arsenals today. The bomb dropped on Hiroshima released energy equalling 20 kilo-tons of chemical explosive.

It must be remembered that the environmental impact of the Hiroshima and Nagasaki bombs were geographically limited, and survivors were almost immediately able to obtain medical and other assistance from outside. Thus the impact of those bombs, though devastating for the people directly affected, was much more limited than might be expected in a full-scale war.

The deployment of increasing numbers of powerful weapons since Hiroshima and Nagasaki prompts the question: "What will happen if many modern nuclear weapons are exploded?" It is obvious that the consequences will be far more severe than in 1945. The most important fact is that the consequences can be of a kind that were not even contemplated until recently, i.e. the possibility that smoke from massive nuclear-ignited urban fires can cause a worldwide disruption in the planet's weather and climate.

What are the effects of an air burst of a nuclear weapon? Nearly all the energy of the explosion is added to the surrounding air in the form of an extremely strong shock wave which propagates outward, rendering the air luminous and creating a fireball in the immediate vicinity of the burst. If the explosion occurs close to the surface, there will be a shock wave coupled to the ground and a crater can be dug in the ground. The main material damage of a nuclear explosion is caused by the blast or shock wave. The light emitted from the fireball causes thermal effects that depend upon the amount of thermal energy incident on exposed material or skin of man. Also an air burst produces initial radiations of which the most harmful are the gamma rays and neutrons. Fall-out nuclear radiation becomes increasingly important as the relative height of the explosion decreases. Lethal fallout from a large-yield surface burst surpasses the range of all other effects, especially in the downwind direction.

Although the actual inventories of nuclear weapons are secret, authoritative unclassified estimates of existing and projected weapons systems indicate that world arsenals contain about 50,000 weapons, with a combined explosive yield of nearly 12,000 megatons. Most of these weapons are almost evenly divided between the USA and the USSR, with a smaller number in Britain, France and China. These estimates were made in 1984.

It may be better to consider the effects of a large scale exchange of weapons which is plausible in the context of the current stock-piles. Within a millionth of a second after a nuclear weapon is detonated, enough energy is released to heat the surrounding air to tens of millions of degrees Celsius, forming a hot, buoyant bubble of gases or a fireball. There is also a very intense thermal pulse which appears as a brilliant flash of light lasting for a few seconds. As the fireball rises, it spreads out to form the distinctive mushroom cloud and its ascent creates strong suction at the ground level. This updraft, containing dust, smoke and radioactivity created by the explosion, forms the stem of the mushroom cloud. The fireball cools as it rises and expands and in the case of explosions in the megaton range, the top of the mushroom cloud stabilizes within the stratosphere. It has been estimated that for weapons exploded between the surface and an altitude of 30 km, about one-third of the energy is released in the thermal pulse, half as a blast and the remainder as nuclear radiation.

The thermal pulse of a nuclear fireball can ignite fires over an area of covering 200 to 600 sq. km. Near the central point of the explosion, even buildings of heavy construction will collapse. Within this zone, the thermal radiation will be so intense that many materials may be simultaneously ignited in fires. The potential burn-out urban areas can be as extensive as 1,000 sq. km. for a one megaton explosion. The spilling of flammable liquids, fuels and petrochemicals will contribute greatly to the spread of the fire.

Scientists have suggested that the smoke produced by the burning of cities in the aftermath of a nuclear war may significantly affect the earth's climate for long periods of time. Lofted into the upper atmosphere, this black smoke can have a serious climatic effect by blocking the sun's light and causing a severe cooling of the earth's surface. The blacker the smoke, the higher its content of elemental carbon and the more strongly it absorbs solar energy. As a result, the amount of solar energy that reaches the earth's surface can be greatly reduced. The absorption of sunlight at high altitudes by soot particles also causes a reduction in the greenhouse effect at the earth's surface, causing ground temperatures to be much reduced.

The effect on the earth's land surfaces of a severely reduced incoming solar radiation is to alter drastically the normal heat balance of the atmosphere and continental surfaces. The oceans play an extremely important role in influencing the earth's climate. If ocean conditions are significantly altered, this can have a profound effect on the global post-war climate. It is known that monsoons are large-scale atmospheric circulation patterns driven by seasonal differences between land and sea surface temperatures. There is little doubt that in an atmosphere altered by a nuclear war in the northern summer, normal rainfall patterns over the monsoon regions of tropical Africa and southern Asia (which includes India) will be drastically affected.

Studies with models that generate their own precipitation indicate that there can be substantial reduction in precipitation over most of the world in a post-war environment. One model has predicted a 25 per cent drop over the oceans about three months after the smoke is injected into the atmosphere. A question remains to be answered: "Will the earth's climate be permanently changed by the after-effects of a large-scale nuclear war?" At the present state of scientific knowledge, it is considered probable that there will be serious global climatic and environmental disturbances for at least weeks and months and that the effects might linger for years.

A large-scale exchange of nuclear weapons will produce unprecedented amounts of radiation that can penetrate and damage biological tissue. The most intense radiation will be contained in the early or local fallout which can be deposited within the first 24 hours up to hundreds of kilometres downwind from the burst point of a surface or near-surface explosion. This radiation is sure to cause sickness and death in exposed humans and other organisms that may otherwise survive the blast and fire.

Global fallout will occur over longer periods and will be more widespread but less intense than a local fall-out. It will not cause serious immediate damage in living organisms, but can result in a statistical increase in the incidence or cancer and genetic mutations over many years. Some of the radioactivity may remain airborne for years and since this radiation decays rapidly with time, the larger the radioactive particles remain airborne, the less damaging they will be to biological systems when they fall to the ground. Lethal dose levels can be produced by local fall-out over an area of 1,000 sq. km. around a one-megaton surface explosion.

In the aftermath of a nuclear war, air, water and food supplies will be heavily contaminated with radioactivity in the local fall-out areas. During the first few months, surface waters may be severely polluted. Lakes, reservoirs and rivers will gradually become less contaminated as water flows through the system. Ground water supplies may remain unpolluted for years, but can be contaminated in the years after the war and will not return to pre-water conditions for perhaps hundreds of years.

It is known that photosynthesis in green plants is the basis of the food chain in all natural and agricultural ecosystems, including those on which mankind depend. If light is to be reduced considerably after a nuclear war, plant photosynthesis will be reduced in the same proportion.This can have serious consequences for the entire food chain.

It has to be admitted that one of the major difficulties in studying the environmental and societal after-effects of a nuclear war is that there are no historical precedents. We have the evidence from the nuclear bombings of Hiroshima and Nagasaki, but multiple bursts over many cities, can produce qualitatively different effects, for which the 1945 bombing provides no precedent. Moreover, it has to be remembered that for Hiroshima and Nagasaki, there was an "outside" world capable of providing some assistance, but in a large-scale nuclear war, there will be no outside help, since there will be virtually no "outside".

NOTES

thermal: pertaining to, or caused by, heat or temperature.

incident: something that occurs casually in connection with something else; an episode in a story; an occurrence or event.

gamma rays: a high frequency, highly energetic, penetrating radiation emitted from the nucleus of a radioactive atom.

inventory: a detailed, often descriptive, list of articles.

unclassified: (data, documents etc.) not belonging to a category that is restricted for reasons of security; not secret.

buoyant: capable of keeping an object afloat, as a liquid; cheerful.

megaton: one million tons.

profound: intellectually penetrating (a profound theory); pervasive (profound influence); originating in or pertaining to the depths of one's being (profound anxiety).

precipitation: falling products of condensation in the atmosphere, as rain, snow or hail; a casting down or falling headlong; the act of precipitating.

COMPREHENSION

1. What lesson does the bombing of Hiroshima and Nagasaki have for humanity?
2. What are the effects of an air burst of a nuclear explosion?
3. Which countries have the maximum number of nuclear arsenals?
4. Assess the effects of a global exchange of stockpiled nuclear war-heads.(400 words)

5. Will the earth's climate be permanently changed by the after-effects of a full-scale nuclear war? (50 words)
6. The 1945 bombing of Hiroshima and Nagasaki "provides no precedents" for calculating the after-effects of a nuclear holocaust. Why? (150 words)

LANGUAGE STUDY

1. Use the following words in sentences of your own so as to bring out their meanings:

   potential, stockpile, arsenal, devastate, contemplate, vicinity, emit, lethal, plausible, ignite, aftermath.
2. The following words in the text have more than one meaning. Use these words in different sentences that bring out the difference in their meanings:

   yield, propagate, incident, buoyant, profound, precipitation.
3. The following words/phrases are often used as connections, to effect a transition of thought, for emphasis, or to stress a contrasting point:

   although, however, nevertheless, but, on the other hand, despite, yet, notwithstanding, indeed, still.

   Use them to make sentences that illustrate their meanings. Can you add to the above list?

COMPOSITION

1. Should India make the nuclear bomb? (300 words)
2. Enumerate the peaceful uses of nuclear energy. (250 words)
3. What can scientists do to forestall a nuclear holocaust?
4. What can students do to keep the world safe from nuclear war?

The Miracle of Grass

JOSEPH WOOD KRUTCH

Of all the green things which make up what Goethe called "the living garment of god," grass is one of the humblest, the most nearly omnipresent, and the most stupidly taken for granted—a miracle so common that we no longer regard it as miraculous.

To some (poor things) it is merely what you try to keep the dandelions out of, or what you strike a golf ball across. But even such are paying some tribute to it. To those of us a little more aware of the great mystery of which we are a part, its going and its coming, its flourishing and its withering, are a sort of soft ostinato accompaniment in the great symphony of the seasons.

Even in the arid Southwest it springs up bravely for a few short weeks. In California the brown hills turn to emerald almost over night. And in the gentler, more circumspect East, one hardly knows when the great awakening took place. So imperceptible, but ineluctable, is its progress that those of us who watch for it never quite catch the very moment when the transformation occurs. While our backs are turned it is alive again, and no other phenomenon of spring is at once so quiet and so all-enveloping. If there are astronomers on Mars peering at us as our astronomers are peering at their planet, they must see, much more dramatically, what is usually observed there by earthly astronomers. Martian vegetation is perhaps only a dry lichen much like what we see clinging on the bare rocks near the summits of our highest mountains. But ours is a green carpet, soft to the feet, restful to the eye, and announcing to all living things that spring is here again.

What is this thing called grass? "Why," say the botanist, "that is a question easy to answer. Grass, properly so-called, is any one of the numerous genera and species which compose that family of monocotyledonous flowering plants long known as the Gramineae. Unfortunately, its early evolutionary history (like that of all the flowering plants) is obscure since the fossil record is scanty. But at least we can say with reasonable certainty that no grass carpeted the earth in that long ago when the first air-breathing animals crawled out of the water. Also that it was not until the cool weather of the Miocene (say a mere forty million or so years ago) that it became a dominant plant and thus made possible the flourishing of the herbivorous mammals over a more peaceful earth where the bellowing of the dinosaurs had given way to the lowing of herds. Then, only yesterday as world history goes, grass conferred upon our own species that tremendous blessing called wheat."

For a less dusty question and answer we must turn to the poets, many of whom have had their say, though only Walt Whitman put grass at the center of a magnum opus.

A child said, " What is the grass?" fetching it to
me with full hands.
I guess it must be the flag of my disposition, out
of hopeful green stuff woven
Or I guess it is the handkerchief of the Lord,
A scented gift that Remembrancer designedly dropped,
Bearing the owner's name somewhere in the corners,
that we may see and remark, and say, "whose?"

Few today have time for such meditations or for such quiet pleasures. Most of us are too desperately busy seeking recreation, entertainment, and amusement ever to experience substitutes—as essentially ersatz as plastic for china, neon lights for dawn and sunset, or the corner grocer's cottony horror offered us in place of that other great gift of grass called bread.

"Joy be with you," people used to say when parting from a friend. Now the modish farewell is, "Have fun!" Sometimes those thus sped away actually do have fun; often they do not; and even the most successful in this enterprise are not too much to be envied. Those of us who want something more than fun, whether it be the exaltation of great art or the mystical experience of "belonging" to something greater than one's self, are a little afraid of being called highbrows or "nature lovers" because neither grass nor Wordsworth's meanest flower that blows are what we call "fun things." They can be something much more rewarding, nevertheless.

Henry David Thoreau once explained that he did not drink wine because he was afraid it might "spoil his taste for water." Henry loved to shock by "going too far" in defending what he wanted to defend, and perhaps he was going too far when he said that. If ours were an age tending toward the puritanical and the ascetic, he might be a dangerous influence, persuading us to surrender in the name of simplicity things much worth having. But since our manners and our morals are not, whatever else they may be, puritanical or ascetic, his voice is more worth hearing than that of those who call for more complexity, for madder music, and for stronger wine. Both of these last pay diminishing returns.

We boast that this is the age of abundance, and the proudest achievement of our best-intentioned men is that, for the first time in history, abundance has been democratized or, to put it somewhat sourly, that now as never before nearly everybody can have rather too much of many things not worth having. Deprivation can kill joy, but so, almost as certainly, can superfluity, for though we always want more, the limiting factor is ultimately what we can take in. More toys than he can play with are a burden, not a blessing, to any child be he five or fifty. It is disastrous to own more of anything than you can possess, and it is one of the most fundamental laws of human nature that our power actually to possess is limited.

In 1989 Louis XIV ordered the following for his garden at Versailles: 87,000 tulips, 800 tuberoses, 400 lilies, and 83,000 narcissus. In this egalitarian age there are not very many individuals likely to be able to be quite that absurd. But there are many who can and do make the same mistake for the same reason. You just can't take in or possess that many tulips, and if you are foolish enough to try, you will miss the violet by the mossy stone, and even more surely the "thought too deep for tears" which one violet or one tulip might inspire.

"The happiness of the great," wrote Francis Bacon, "consists only in thinking how happy others must suppose them to be." In Bacon's time the term "status," so beloved of present-day sociologists, had not been invented, but Bacon had grasped the concept behind it. The desire for status is the same desire to be envied which Bacon had in mind, and it was what Louis XIV also was aiming at. "It will be evident to all," so he said to himself, "that no one else in all the world can have as many tulips as I can, and they will envy me—though, God knows, the whole eighty-seven thousand of them look dull enough to me."

When grass becomes merely "a lawn," it is in danger of becoming what that sour economic Puritan Thorstein Veblen said it always was, namely, a "status symbol," a display of conspicuous expenditure meant to demonstrate that its owner can afford to waste in mere display what might be used to produce wheat or vegetables. Veblen was wrong, because a lawn can also demonstrate a great truth which economists are prone to forget, namely, that beauty may be its own excuse for being. But a lawn can be what he called it, and there is no greater paradox than this transformation of the humblest and most unshowy of green things into a status symbol. Of course, neither your lawn nor mine (when in Connecticut I had one) is that. But just to be sure that it isn't, a salutary experience can be had if we ask ourselves from time to time what our real reason for having it is.

If we have any doubts an experiment might be worthwhile. Lie down upon your lawn to see what happens. And while I would not advise that all lawns be surrendered to dandelions, I would suggest that you ask yourself, when one of these gay little miracles raises its flower toward the sun, whether you reach for the weed killer without first remembering Whitman's tribute:

> Simple and fresh and fair from winter's clothes
> emerging
> As if no artifice of fashion, business, politics,
> had ever been
> Forth from its sunny nook of sheltered grass—
> innocent, golden, calm as the dawn,
> The spring's first dandelion shows its trustful
> face.

"All flesh is grass." For once the apostle and the scientist seem to be in agreement though they were not saying the same thing. To St. Peter all flesh is grass because man, too, "withereth and the flower thereof falleth away." To the biologist all flesh is grass in a more literal sense. No animal, man included, could exist if it were not for the fact that green plants mediate between him and the inanimate materials of the earth. They alone have the power of rising by one step the relative simplicity of the mineral to the complexity of the proteins indispensable to him. Where they leave off his mysterious metabolism takes over. What was mineral but became protein now becomes that even more mysterious thing called protoplasm. And protoplasm is the base of all man's life, thought, imagination, and ideals.

In time, a man passes away, he also withers and the flower thereof falls away, protoplasm descends the scale again to the merely mineral, and grass picks it up once more to repeat the cycle. The process began some billions of years ago and must continue as long as life lasts.

Which of the two truths is the most profound and the most important? The moral truth of the apostle, or the strange, in human truth of the biologist? One is as old as civilization, the other almost as new as yesterday. And perhaps just because it is uniquely ours we tend to value it most highly. But we may be wrong. Many civilizations, some of them glorious, were created and then destroyed by men who were innocent of chemistry. But they could not have been what they were had they not known what Peter and what Whitman knew. It is just possible that our civilization will fail because we do know one kind of truth and, in our pride, forget the other.

And now it seems to me the beautiful uncut hair
    of graves.
It may be you transpire from the best of young
    man,
It may be if I had known them I would have loved
    them.
It may be you are from old people, or from offspring
    taken soon out of their mother's laps,
And here you are the mother's laps.
This grass is very dark to be from the white heads
    of old mothers,
Darker than the colorless beards of old men,
Dark to come from under the faint red roof of
    mouths. (From *The Leaves of Grass*)

NOTES

The author presents science in an allusive style, mixing the magic of nature with the marvels of scientific investigation, skilfully interweaving the poetry of Walt Whitman with the facts of the theory of evolution.

Goethe (1749-1832): a German writer.
dandelions: yellow-flowered wild plants.
ostinato: (Italian) bass melody.
symphony: an elaborate musical composition for an orchestra.
South West: South West American desert region.
circumspect: careful; slowly-moving.
lichen: flowerless small plants of different shades that grow like a patch of skin on stones and tree trunks.
genera: kinds; classes; plural of genus.
monocotyledonous flowering plants: flowering plants with a single seed-leaf.
Miocene: an epoch of Tertiary (the third geological period) when the high mountains like the Alps and the Himalayas were formed.
dinosaurs: large but now extinct reptiles.
Walt Whitman (1819-1892): a great American poet. His Magnum Opus (masterpiece) was *Leaves of Grass.*
Remembrancer: one who reminds; (here) God.
ersatz: (German) imitation.
grocer's cottony horor: mass produced bread of the texture of cotton in contrast to home-baked bread.
William Wordsworth (1770-1850): English Romantic poet and a great lover of nature.
Henry David Thoreau (1817-1862): American writer well-known for his masterpiece *Walden.*
puritanical: of extreme strictness in religion and morals.
diminishing returns: the law of diminishing returns in Economics: (here) fails to produce more pleasure for the additional effort.
Louis XIV (1638-1715): the extravagant king of France.
Versailles: French town, known for its beautiful gardens.
meanest flowers...too deep for tears: see Wordsworth's *Immortality Ode.*
violet and tulip: names of flowers.

Francis Bacon (1561-1626): English essayist and thinker.

Thorstein Veblen: U.S. economist and social scientist.

"All flesh is grass": a quotation from the First Epistle of St. Peter (Ch. 1, v. 24). The saint was one of the disciples of Christ.

metabolism: the process involved in the building up and destruction of living matter.

protoplasm: essential semi-fluid living substance of cells.

COMPREHENSION

1. Why does the author say that grass is "a miracle so common that we no longer regard it as miraculous"?
2. "Deprivation can kill joy, but so, almost as certainly can superfluity." Elaborate with illustrations.
3. What do the apostle and the scientist mean when they say "All flesh is grass"?
4. Bring out the different perceptions of grass in science and grass in poetry.

LANGUAGE STUDY

1. The prefix *omni* means *many, infinite, all, everywhere.* Mention four words beginning with the prefix *omni*. To help you, the meanings of these four words are given below:
   a. all powerful or having infinite power.
   b. knowing everything or having infinite knowledge.
   c. eating all kinds of food; reading all kinds of books.
2. Look up the following words in a dictionary and use them in sentences of your own that bring out their meaning: Herbivorous; mammals; circumspect; conspicuous; paradox; apostle, sociologist, arid, highbrow, ineluctable, ascetic.
3. Match the words having similar meanings. Select one word from each list:

List 1	List 2
mysterious	ridiculous

prone	see
peer	likely
plenty	strange
absurd	abundance

4. Match the words having opposite meanings:

List 1	**List 2**
deprivation	simple
plenty	inanimate
abundance	scarcity
animate	scanty
complex	superfluity

5. Differentiate between words in the following pairs. Make sentences to illustrate your explanation.
   a. envy — jealousy
   b. advice — advise
   c. practice — practise
6. In English there are certain words that indicate sounds e.g. the *bellowing of* bulls; the *lowing* of cattle.
   Fill in the blanks in the following sentences with apprpriate words indicating sounds. Choose the words from the box given on the next page.

a. the ______ of babies	b. the ____ of drums
c. the ______ of coins	d. the ___ of a camera
e. the ______ of trees	f. the ____ of speakers
g. the ______ of water	h. the ____ of winds
i. the ______ of chains	j. the ____ of leaves
k. the ____ of a trumpet	l. the ____ of arms
m. the ____ of a snake	n. the ____ of footsteps
o. the ______ of wolves	p. the ____ of teeth
q. the ______ of birds	r. the ____ of engines

> thundering; singing or twittering or warbling; howling; hissing; blaring or blowing; clank; blare; whirr; beating; whistling; clattering; sound; clanging; creaking; rustling; whispering or rumbling; rustling; whistling; rippling or gushing; sighing; jingling; lisping; etc.)

7. The pre-fix *trans-* means *through* or *across*. If light passes through an object, that object is transparent. Give one word for each of the following. All these words require the prefix *trans-* .
   a. To carry something, usually in a vehicle
   b. To send messages or waves etc. from one object or place to another
   c. To cause a change in shape or position.
   d. To re-write a passage in another language.
8. The suffixes *-ion* and *-ence* are added to verbs to form nouns e.g.,
   Carrying goods by train is a form of transportation.
   Complete the following sentences. All these sentences require nouns for completion.
   a. Rewriting a passage in another language is called ________.
   b. Causing a change in position or shape is called ________.
   c. When the speed of anything is increased, it is called ________.
   d. Study of past events helps us draw an ________.
   e. At the end of a well-argued composition or an experiment we state our ________.
   f. When we shorten a word we use an ________.

   (*Hints*: Infer ___, conclude ___, abbreviate ___, accelerate, transorm ___, transfer ___, transmit ____, translate ___)
9. We know the literal meaning of *grass*. But there are also a number of idiomatic expressions in which this word figures. Look up the meaning of the following idiomatic expressions in a dictionary and use them in sentences that bring out their meaning:
   to let grass grow under one's feet; grass widow; at the grassroots level; a grassroots movement.
10. There are a number of idiomatic expressions using the key words *back* and *heart* e.g.
    to back up; to take a back seat; to have a backbone; to back out; backseat driving; to take to heart; to take heart.

Miscellaneous idiomatic expressions:

an eye-wash; to pay lip-service to; to pay through one's

nose; with one's tongue in one's cheek.

Look up the above expressions in a dictionary. Find out their meaning and use these idiomatic expressions in sentences of your own.

COMPOSITION

1. Attempt a description of two miracles of nature, namely, rain and the rainbow.
2. "Dust thou art and to dust thou shall return" is a well-known religious statement.
   Write a dialogue between two characters concluding with one of them making this statement to the other.

Human Environment

INDIRA GANDHI

I had the good fortune of growing up with a sense of kinship with nature in all its manifestations. Birds, plants, stones were companions and, sleeping under the star-strewn sky, I became familiar with the names and movements of the constellations. But my deep interest in this our "only earth" was not for itself but as a fit home for man.

One cannot be truly human and civilized unless one looks upon not only all fellow-men but all creation with the eyes of a friend. Throughout India, edicts carved on rocks and iron pillars are reminders that 22 centuries ago Emperor Ashoka defined a king's duty as not merely to protect citizens and punish wrong-doers but also to preserve animal life and forest trees. Ashoka was the first and perhaps the only monarch until very recently, to forbid the killing of a large number of species of animals for sport or food, foreshadowing some of the concerns of this Conference. He went further, regretting the carnage of his military conquests and enjoining upon his successors to find "their only pleasure in the peace that comes through righteousness."

It is sad that in country after country, progress should become synonymous with an assault on nature. We, who are a part of nature and dependent on her for every need, speak constantly about "exploiting" nature. When the highest mountain in the world was claimed in 1953, Jawaharlal Nehru objected to the phrase "conquest of Everest" which he thought was arrogant. Is it surprising that this lack of consideration and the constant need to prove one's superiority should be projected on to our treatment of our fellow-men? I remember Edward Thompson, a British writer and a good friend of India, once telling Mr. Gandhi that wild life was fast disappearing. Remarked the Mahatma— "It is decreasing in the jungles but it is increasing in the towns!"

On the one hand the rich look askance at our continuing poverty—on the other they warn us against their own methods. We do not wish to impoverish the environment any further and yet we cannot for a moment forget the grim poverty of large numbers of people. Are not poverty and need the greatest polluters? For instance, unless we are in a position to provide employment and purchasing power for the daily necessities of the tribal people and those who live in or around jungles, we cannot prevent them from combing the forest for food and livelihood, from poaching and from despoiling the vegetation. When they themselves feel deprived, how can we urge the preservation of animals? How can we speak to those who live in villages and in slums about keeping the oceans, the rivers and the air clean when their own lives are contaminated at the source? The environment cannot be improved in conditions of poverty. Nor can poverty be eradicated without the use of science and technology.

It is an over-simplification to blame all the world's problems on increasing population. Countries with but a small fraction of the world population consume the bulk of the world's production of minerals, fossil fuels and so on. Thus, we see that when it comes to the depletion of natural resources and environmental pollution the increase of one inhabitant in an affluent country, at his level of living, is equivalent to an increase of many Asians, Africans or Latin Americans at their current material levels of living.

The inherent conflict is not between conservation and development but between environment and the reckless exploitation of man and earth in the name of efficiency. Historians tell us that the modern age began with the will to freedom of the individual. And the individual came to believe that he had rights with no corresponding obligations. The man who got ahead was the one who commanded admiration. No questions were asked as to the methods or the price which others had to pay. The industrial civilization has promoted the concept of the efficient man, he whose entire energies are concentrated on producing more in a given unit of time and from a given unit of man-power. Groups or individuals who are less competitive and, according to this test, less efficient are regarded as lesser breeds—for example the older civilizations, the black and brown peoples, women and certain professions. Obsolescence is built into production, and efficiency is based on the creation of goods which are not really needed and which cannot be disposed of, when discarded. What price such efficiency now, and is not reckless a more appropriate term for such behaviour?

All the "isms" of the modern age—even those which in theory disown the private profit principle—assume that man's cardinal interest is acquisition. The profit motive, individual or collective, seems to overshadow all else. This over-riding concern with self and today is the basic cause of the ecological crisis.

Pollution is not a technical problem. The fault lies not in science and technology as such but in the sense of values of the contemporary world which ignores the rights of others and is oblivious of the longer perspective.

There are grave misgivings that the discussion on ecology may be designed to distract attention from the problems of war and poverty. We have to prove to the disinherited majority of the world that ecology and conservation will not work against their interest but will bring an improvement in their lives. To withhold technology from them would deprive them of vast resources of energy and knowledge. This is no longer feasible nor will it be acceptable.

The environmental problems of developing countries are not the side effects of excessive industrialisation but reflect the inadequacy of development. The rich countries may look upon development as the cause of environmental destruction, but to us it is one of the primary means of improving the environment for living, or providing foods, water, sanitation and shelter, of making the deserts green and the mountains habitable. The research and perseverance of dedicated people have given us an insight which is likely to play an important part in the shaping of our future plans. We wee that however much man hankers after material goods, they can never give him full satisfaction. Thus the higher standard of living must be achieved without alienating people from their heritage and without despoiling nature of its beauty, freshness and purity so essential to our lives.

The most urgent and basic question is that of peace. Nothing is so pointless as modern warfare. Nothing destroys so instantly, so completely as the diabolic weapons which not only kill but maim and deform the living and the yet to be born; which poison the land, leaving long trails of ugliness, barrenness and hopeless desolation. What ecological project can survive a war?

It is clear that the environmental crisis which is confronting the world, will profoundly alter the future destiny of our planet. No one among us, whatever our status, strength or circumstance, can remain unaffected. The process of change challenges present international policies. Will the growing awareness of "one earth" and "one environment" guide us to the concept of "one humanity"? Will there be more equitable sharing of environmental costs and greater international interest in the accelerated progress of the less developed world? Or will it remain confined to a narrow concern, based on exclusive self-sufficiency?

The first essays in narrowing economic and technological disparities have not succeeded because the policies of aid were made to subserve the equations of power. We hope that the renewed emphasis on self-reliance, brought about by the change in the climate for aid, will also promote a search for new criteria of human satisfaction. In the meantime, the ecological crisis should not add to the burdens of the weaker nations by introducing new considerations in the political and trade policies of rich nations. It would be ironic if the fight against pollution were to be converted into another business, out of which a few companies, corporations, or nations would make profits at the cost of the many. Here is a branch of experimentation and discovery in which scientists of all nations should take interest. They should ensure that their findings are available to all nations, unrestricted by patents.

Life is one and the world is one, and all these questions are interlinked. The population explosion, poverty, ignorance and disease, the pollution of our surroundings, the stockpiling of nuclear weapons and biological and chemical agents of destruction are all parts of a vicious circle. Each is important and urgent but dealing with them one by one would be wasted effort.

It has been my experience that people who are at cross purposes with nature are cynical about mankind and ill at ease with themselves. Modern man must re-establish an unbroken linkwith nature and with life. He must again learn to involve the energy of growing things and to recognise, as did the ancients in India centuries ago, that one can take from the earth and the atmosphere only so much as one puts back into them. In their hymn to Earth, the sages of the Atharva Veda chanted: I quote "what of thee I dig out, let that quickly grow over, let me not hit thy vitals, or thy heart". So can man himself be vital and of good heart and conscious of his responsibility.

NOTES

Indira Gandhi (1917-1984), daughter of Jawaharlal Nehru, was the Prime Minister of India. She delivered this speech on June 14, 1972, at the U.N. Conference on "Human Environment" at Stockholm, Sweden.

edicts: orders proclaimed by the ruler

Ashoka: (264-228 B.C.): the King of Magadha in ancient India; renounced war and violence after his victory over Kalinga, and embraced Buddhism. Archaeologists and historians value his pillar edicts found all over the country.

highest mountain: Everest (29,028 ft.)

Jawaharlal Nehru: Prime Minister of India from 1947 to 1964; the author of *Glimpses of World History* (1973) and *The Discovery of India* (1946).

Edward Thompson: (1886-1946) an Anglo-Indian poet; responsible for making Tagore popular in the West.

Gandhi: (1869-1948)known as the Mahatma; the architect of India's independence.

to look askance at: to look with suspicion, mistrust or disapproval.

Atharva Veda: one of the four Vedic scriptures—the other three being Rig-Veda, Sama-Veda, and Yajur-Veda.

COMPREHENSION

1. "No ecological project can survive a war." Discuss.

2. What are the consequences of the exploitation of nature?
3. How are the resources of nature being used up in advanced countries?
4. Mention the chief causes of environmental pollution.
5. "All creation is one." Does India measure up to this principle?
6. What do we have to give back to the earth?

LANGUAGE STUDY

1. Use the following words and phrases in sentences of your own so as to bring out their meaning clearly:

carnage	eradicate	in spite of
righteousness	enjoining upon	assault
pollution	slums	affluence
synonymous	anthropologist	contaminate

2. Choose a word from your text for each of the following:
   a. destroying the purity or healthiness of
   b. identical or similar in meaning
   c. claim unduly
   d. aloofness from earthly cravings
   e. giving up material desires
   f. to become out of date
   g. a branch of biology that studies the relation between life and its environment
   h. to gather at one place
   i. human beings belonging to the same family and sharing common traits, basic desires and the same habitat
   j. to destroy utterly
   k. the branch of knowledge that deals with industrial arts, applied science, engineering etc
   l. anything or event for which there is no parallel in history
   m. to improve the quality of life of the people
   n. the economic theory that disfavours private ownership of property or the profit principle
   o. the prosperous exploiting the needy
   p. people who are imbued with compassion and concern for others

3. Look up the following words/expressions in a dictionary and use them in sentences of your own:

obscure
discard
feasible
survive
cardinal
diabolic
conservation
overshadow
accelerate
patents
sustain
directions
eradicate
implication
vociferous
spectrum
suffice
fossil
ecology
perseverance
nutrition
contemporary
inadequate
desolate
breed
oblivious
ironic
vicious
miracle
inbued with
interlink
upsurge
stockpile
simplistic
reckless
perspective
alienate
deplete
design
insight
renew
disposed of
inherit
ensure
apportion
culminate
motivate
evaluate
coerce
civic
spontaneous

4. Give the antonyms of the following: (antonym – a word that has an opposite meaning, eg. hot—cold)

human
regret
pollute
compassion
succeed
diabolic
military
synonym
abstract
isolate
efficiency
prolong
conquest
superior
detachment
visible
private
punish
progress
civilized
peace
object
impoverish
conflict
present
righteous
arrogant
spiritual
effective
theory
protect
poverty
present
approve
deplete
survive
successor
affluence
preserve
beautiful
equality
official
concentrate
recent
mute
prejudice
majority
fraction
poison
forbid
prosperity
justice
marginal
freedom
fortune
malnutrition
limited

5. Give definitions of the following:

anthropology	contemporaries	philanthropist
bigot	neurotic	vegetarian
ornithology	entomology	sociology
fanatic	atmosphere	egoist
panacea	gregarious	cannibal
hereditary	biology	museum
aborigines	egotist	parasite

6. Fill in the blanks with appropriate prepositions:
   a. to look ______ somebody as a benefactor
   b. to abide ______ a contract
   c. to endeavour ______ fulfil one's obligations
   d. to evolve ______ a theory
   e. to triumph ______ one's handicaps
   f. to abstain ______ food
   g. to abstain ______ indulgence
   h. to abstain ______ luxuries
   i. to accede ______ a request
   j. to complain ______ something
   k. to comply ______ somebody's orders
   l. to feel proud ______ one's accomplishments
   m. to dispose ______ the work in hand

COMPOSITION

1. Write an essay in about 300 words on:
   a. Agents of pollution
   b. The Ganga and pollution control
   c. Nuclear pollution
   d. Indiscriminate deforestation
   e. Wild-life sanctuaries in India
2. Write a letter to your friend about the quality of drinking water being supplied. Tell him what suggestions you have made to the Municipal Corporation to supply pollution free and treated water.

Prayer Before Birth

LOUIS MACNEICE

I am not yet born; O hear me.
Let not the bloodsucking bat or the rat or the stoat or the
club-footed ghoul come near me.

I am not yet born, console me.
I fear that the human race may with tall walls wall me,
with strong drugs dope me, with wise lies lure me,
on black racks rack me, in blood-baths roll me.

I am not yet born; provide me
With water to dandle me, grass to grow for me, trees to talk
to me, sky to sing to me, birds and a white light
in the back of my mind to guide me.

I am not yet born; forgive me
For the sins that in me the world shall commit, my words
when they speak me, my thoughts when they think me,
my treason engendered by traitors beyond me,
my life when they murder by means of my
hands, my death when they live me.

I am not yet born; rehearse me,
In the parts I must play and the cues I must take when
old men lecture me, bureaucrats hector me, mountains
frown at me, lovers laugh at me, the white
waves call me to folly and the desert calls
me to doom and the beggar refuses
my gift and my children curse me.

I am not yet born; O hear me,
Let not the man who is beast or who thinks he is God
come near me.

I am not yet born; O fill me
With strength against those who would freeze my
humanity, would dragoon me into a lethal automaton,
would make me a cog in a machine, a thing with
one face, a thing, and against all those
who would dissipate my entirety, would
blow me like thistledown hither and
thither or hither and thither
like water held in the
hands would spill me.

Let them not make me a stone and let them not spill me.
Otherwise kill me.

NOTES

Louis Macneice (1907-1963), a British poet, was a liberal humanist.

The yet unborn, in this poem, has insight into the abject human condition. Wanting to be born, he prays for the respect and integrity of the human personality, and for protection against all man-made ills that would dissipate his being.

stoat: weasel; a small furry animal larger than a rat.
ghoul: (in stories) spirit that feeds on corpses in graves; a gruesome person.
rack(s): an instrument of torture.
rack me: torture or ruin me.
dandle: move (e.g. a child) up and down on one's knees or in the arms.
white light: the light or pure knowledge.
engender: give rise to, arouse.
beast and God: the beast and the angel are equally bad companions. A normal human-being is preferable to both.
dragoon: force.
The last stanza is a protest against the dissolution of the individual in modern society.

COMPREHENSION

1. "I am not yet born; O hear me." Explain this paradox. (*Note*: A paradox is a statement that seems to say something opposite to common sense or the truth but which may contain a truth.)
2. What are the main fears expressed in the first two stanzas?
3. What things does the unborn crave for in the third stanza of the poem? Why does he leave out human society from the charter of his demands?
4. What types of men and what aspects of nature make the unborn circumspect? (Hint: Read the fifth stanza).
5. What are the forces against which the poet wants to be filled with strength? Why? (Hint: Please refer to the seventh stanza).

LANGUAGE STUDY

1. The word *bat* has different meanings. Find out the meaning of the expression *as blind as a bat* and use it in a sentence of your own.

   Similarly there are a number of idiomatic expressions in which the word *wall* figures e.g.,

   with one's back to the wall — in a position in which retreat or escape is impossible;

   to bang/run one's head against a wall — to attempt to do something that is clearly impossible.);

   to go to the wall — (to be pushed aside as weak or helpless).

   Similarly a number of compound words can be formed with the word *wall* e.g., wall-flower, wall-painting, wall-paper, etc. Use the above idiomatic expressions and compound words in sentences of your own that bring out their meaning clearly.

2. Use the following idiomatic expressions in your own sentences:
   a. to be a cog in the machine (fig. to be an unimportant part of a large enterprise)
   b. hither and thither (here and there, in all directions)

c. stone blind/cold/dead/deaf (to be totally........)
d. stone-walling (to obstruct the business of parliament or other body by making long speeches)
e. to have a heart of stone (hard-hearted)
f. to leave no stone unturned (to try every possible means)
g. to throw stones at (to attack the character of)
h. within a stone's throw (very near).

COMPOSITION

1. "What man has made of man!" lamented Wordsworth. What is Louis Macneice's chief lament in this poem?
2. "Poets are the unacknowledged legislators of the world", said Shelley. To what extent do you agree with this view. Base your answer on this poem.
3. "Lives of great men all remind us,
We can make our lives sublime." (Longfellow)
Mention the works of a few great men which can inspire us, (You can write about Lincoln, Gandhi, Martin Luther King, Tagore, or Mother Terresa) and who contributed to the improvement of the quality of life.
4. What kind of life do you hope for in India?

Computers

I

Essentially, a computer is a machine that can process, store and retrieve information. It can perform only three basic functions: 1) Add, substract, multiply, divide. 2) Compare values. 3) Store, search and retrieve.

It possesses no intelligence of its own. Its I.Q. is zero, at least till today. Only the user can determine what tasks a computer will perform.

Computers can only perform tasks that a human being can. The difference is that they perform these tasks with unthinkable speed and accuracy.

A medium-sized computer executes over a million instructions per second: over and over again, without a single mistake.

The world's first modern computers were built by the Allied forces in World War II. They were used, successfully, to crack Nazi coded messages, and to perfect artillery calculations.

The second generation came around 1960. A few years later, transistors made way for integrated circuits ushering in third generation computers. These were less expensive and much more compact. People began using them on a 'time-sharing' basis.

Further developments in integrated circuits brought us the fourth generation in the late sixties. A whole computer circuit was soon available on a single chip, the size of a postage stamp.

It was the start of a social revolution. Overnight, computers became incredibly compact. Overnight, they became inexpensive to make. Suddenly, it became possible for any one and everyone to own a computer.

Scientists are now at work on the 5th generation...a promise, but not yet a reality. They aim to bring us machines with genuine I.Q., the ability to reason logically, and with real knowledge of the world.

You must have heard the words 'Bit' and Byte' used in connection with computers: '8-Bit computer', '32 Kilobyte memory' and so on. These words are so often mistaken for each other. What exactly do they mean?

Imagine a highway with eight lanes, and a heavy flow of traffic. If it is expanded to sixteen lanes, the flow of traffic speeds up considerably. '8-Bits' refers to the number of 'lanes' on a microchip. Greater bits means a more rapid flow of electronic signals — in other words, a faster computer.

Early microchips were 8-bit devices. And like everything else in computers, they evolved at lightning speed to 16-bit, and now 32-bit. What an 8-bit computer took one minute to do, a 32-bit computer can do in one second.

'Byte' refers to one unit of memory on a computer. Each byte holds one typed character (a, b, 7 or +). 1024 Bytes make 1 Kilobyte, or 1K. 1024K equals 1 Megabyte, or about 500 closely typed pages.

Memory in a computer comes in two forms: working memory and a secondary memory. Working memory is what people loosely refer to as 'capacity'. When someone asks. "How large is your computer?" He really means "What is its working memory?"

This memory is just a working space for the program in operation. Larger tasks obviously require larger working memories. Office computers generally have a working memory between 32 KBytes and 256 KBytes.

What happens when you have to store vast amounts of data (employees' payroll, for instance) on a permanent basis? For this, there is a secondary memory using a number of storage devices like tapes and floppy disks. They occupy very little space, and hold huge amounts of information.

A single floppy disk, the size of a 45-rpm record, can hold the contents of several thousand typed pages. A computer can scan through this disk in a matter of seconds—to retrieve a particular letter, for instance.

II

Versatility. That's one of the most wonderful things about the computer. One moment, it's speeding up your accounting. The next moment, it's racing through a complex inventory. In between, it's helping the MD's secretary trace an important letter in seconds. All you have to do to change its talents is slip in a new program.

Office modernisation is now an important part of computer technology; developing new and better ways to do work. Pushing out drudgery, pushing up productivity.

Your accounts department need not waste precious days compounding income tax, provident fund and take home salary for every employee.

A computer can carry out automatic checks on the stock of a particular item: see when it is getting low, and decide how much to re-order depending on your current cash flow position.

A law firm can use a computer to keep a record of important cases — and recall the details of a particular case instantly.

Architects can display their scale models on a computer, and study them from various angles and perspectives. Structural problems can now be solved with unprecedented speed and accuracy.

Hotels can use computers to greatly speed up billing and check-out, and provide instant information on room availability and room status.

Word processors are fast replacing typewriters ... and giving a whole new definition to paperwork. No more erasing or retyping for errors and changes. No more messy carbon copies. No more cumbersome filing and retrieval systems.

Basically, a word processor consists of a typewriter-style keyboard, a printer, and a screen that displays whetever you type. The screen is like a magic slate: words appear, disappear and rearrange themselves to your command.

If you have to add a sentence in the middle of a paragraph, the other words move automatically to accommodate the change.

If you want to change a letter from left aligned paragraphs to indented paragraphs, do it by pressing a single key.

Certain word processors even have a built in 'dictionary' Words you mis-spell are corrected automatically.

Letters and documents generated on the word processor can be stored on floppy disks. Just imagine the saving on storage space: one floppy disk, the size of a 45 rpm record, holds several thousand typed pages. You can recall a letter instantly even after months or years, and print out a fresh, crisp copy.

Factory automation has come a long way in the last few years. Computers have taken over monotonous and dangerous jobs like welding, as well as highly complex jobs like process control.

Drills, lathes, saws and entire assembly lines can be computerised. So can quality control tests, and the manufacture of items that have very fine tolerances — such as cutting and moulding steel.

In process control, the time lag between two important events may be just a fraction of a second. Thermal power plants, oil refineries and chemical industries virtually exist on computerised control systems. A total elimination of any possible human error.

Network is the latest buzz-word in computers. It is now possible for computers at different locations to function to gether as a single system.

Computer networks can be used to co-ordinate activities in distant places —without the delays that distances create.

Airlines will offer instant information on bookings for flights originating in other cities. From Delhi, for instance, you will get a confirmed ticket or an emphatic 'No' for a Bombay-Pune flight.

Banks can clear outstation cheques in minutes, instead of the days they currently take.

On a more widespread scale, computers are now talking to one another on the telephone (with the help of a common device called a 'modem'). This opens the road to all kinds of miracles. For instance, you feed a letter into a computerised Xerox machine in Madras — and out comes a copy from a Xerox machine in Delhi!

Homes, too are fast becoming better places with computers. Housewives use them to plan their monthly budget. Some even use them to store recipes. You can ask the computer: "What can I cook with capsicum but without mustard?" The computer will scan all the recipes in a few seconds, and recommend a dish.

III

Anyone who knows English can use a computer. It's not necessary for you to know how to write a program. Leave that to the specialists.

User-friendly is the phrase of the eighties. It means exactly that: computers that assist the user, and never intimidate.

Computer-aided instruction (CAI) is a wonderful example of computers 'talking' to people. How many times have you seen a teacher over-loaded with work, rushing to cover everything in the syllabus? She has very little chance to ensure that her pupils have absorbed even half of what is being taught.

CAI programs, available even on home computers, ask questions as often as they give information. If you don't comprehend what they feed you, they display more information: or the same information illustrated with a different example. And then ask you a question again.

They let pupils learn as fast or as slow as they can ...testing at each step to ensure that the instruction is effective. Letting the pupils know where he stands after every step he takes. They are patient and systematic teachers.

Programs make all this possible. What exactly are they?

A program is a pre-determined plan of action — a set of instructions to be carried out by the computer.

Languages used to program computers are getting better every year —and more and more simple. Modern programming languages use common English words like Repeat, Until, Print, Read, and so on. Look at this simple bank program for printing out the names of clients with overdue loans.

```
OPEN FILE (F, 'CLIENTS');
DATE TODAY = DATE;
REPEAT
READ (F, CLIENT);
IF (CLIENT. DUE DATE < DATE TODAY) THEN WRITE
(CLIENT. NAME, CLIENT. ADDRESS, CLIENT. PHONE NO);
UNTIL END OF FILE (F).
```

This program instructs the computer to open a file called 'Clients' and read all client details from it. It notes today's date and pinpoints those clients with overdue loans: printing their names, addresses, etc.

Another line can be added to the program to see if the client owes more than Rs. 1 lakh — and listing such big fish on a separate file.

That's all there is to it. A paragraph of carefully prepared instructions, and the computer will search a file of several thousand names every day. Taking just a few seconds for the work each time.

In the beginning, writing programs was a big headache ...till the first programming language was invented.

FORTRAN, originally thought of as a 'formula translator', came along in 1958. A few years later came COBOL, common business oriented language for business data processing. Then came BASIC, such an undemanding language that it runs on computers cheaper than scooters. Practically all home computers offer BASIC as the main fare.

The computer world has raced on to newer and newer languages, acknowledging some old debts on the way. PASCAL is named after the man who first thought of the adding machine.

ADA is the newest language: named after the world's first programmer, the daughter of Lord Byron, who supported the quest to build the world's first stored-program computer. In addition, it honours the women who play a major role in computing today, often outshining men as programmers and software designers.

A pity, though, that ADA will be the language used to program nuclear missiles and satellites; it is the officially recognized language for developing 'defence' systems. If there is ever a nuclear holocaust, ADA will be playing a major role in the last one hour of mankind's existence.

What will you be doing ten years from now? No one can say for sure. But one thing is certain: there will be a computer ir your life. No one can ignore the tremendous potential of the computer to make our world more organised, more confortable, a better place to live in.

We all need to look ahead, see the changes coming, and profit from them.

I

NOTES

I.Q.: Psychological measurement of the degree of intelligence.

Nazi: (member) of the National Socialist Party founded by Hitler.

microchip: the tiny 'chip' — the heart of an electronic computer. The chip is electronic circuitry, patterned on a silicon base with thousands of transistors and other components linked by 'wires' etched from extremely thin film metal.

COMPREHENSION

1. How are computers different from human-beings?
2. What are the characteristics of fourth and fifth generation computers?
3. What exactly do the words *bit* and *byte* mean in computer language?

LANGUAGE STUDY

1. Give synonyms of the following words:
   unthinkable, usher, execute, incredible, accuracy, genuine, crack, occupy.
2. Use the following words in sentences of your own so as to bring out the difference in their meanings:
   a. lose - loose
   b. fair - fare
   c. accept - except
   d. affect - effect
   e. advice - advise.
3. "They store huge amounts of information". Replace *amounts of information* with another suitable expression.

4. Some nouns are always used in the singular. Scenery is one such noun.
   Make a list of at least four other such nouns and use them in sentences of your own.
5. The prefix *re* means:
   again ... as in re-combine
   back ... as in reverse
   together ... as in react.
   Find words with the prefix *re* which have the following meanings:
   a. to argue against (ref ... te)
   b. to look at again, to point out (ref ... r)
   c. to give back (ret ... n)
   d. to mean, to be a sign of (rep ... t)
   e. to go back (re ... n)
   f. to move round an axis (re ... ve)
   g. an image in a mirror (ref ... ion)
   h. the act of turning (rev ... ion)
   i. a chemical change during synthesis (rea ... ion)
   j. the act of doing or saying again (rep ... ion)

II

COMPREHENSION

1. What is one of the most wonderful things about the computer? (one word only)
2. Describe the main areas where computer application is very useful. (about 300 words)

LANGUAGE STUDY

1. Each of the following words has more than one meaning. Use these words in sentences so as to bring out their different meanings:
   compound, single, mess, screen, command, hold.

2. Words like *accommodate* and *beginning* are commonly misspelt. Correct the spellings of the following words:
   enemity, recieve, neumonia, carear, publically, skillful, wellcome, vacum, beneficient, illitrate, reccommend

III

NOTES

BASIC: (Beginner's All-Purpose Symbolic Instruction Code) a high-level computer language for programming.

software: sets of instructions known as programs written for a computer.

COMPREHENSION

1. What is computer programming?
2. What is the terminology of computer programming? Give only the main terms.
3. The newest language in computer programming poses a threat to human existence. How?

LANGUAGE STUDY

1. Use the following words in sentences:
   pupil, comprehend, patient, carry, debt, quest, defence.
2. The phrase *to carry out* means to execute or to put into practice; the expression *to carry* means to win a motion e.g. The motion was carried unanimously;
   Use the following prepositional phrases in your own sentences:
   a. to carry off (to win)
   b. to carry on (to manage, to resume)

c. to carry through (to sustain)
d. to carry a thing too far (to go beyond a reasonable limit)
e. to carry the day (to win in a contest).

COMPOSITION

1. Should computers be used in a big way in this country? (300 words)
2. Prepare a project report for starting a computer centre in your college.
3. "The computer, like science, is a good servant but a bad master": Elaborate. (300 words)

Experiment and Experience

W.R. NIBLETT

Every educated man or woman who belongs to the mid-twentieth century is something of a scientist, whether he means to be or not. He will, that is, have learnt how to put himself into an experimental frame of mind, and how to keep himself for appreciable periods in that state. He will be interested in discovering hard facts yielded by evidence.

Long ago in a school laboratory, if he has been properly taught, he will have been faced with questions meant to make him observant in an exacting and precise way. Exactly what does happen when burning magnesium is plunged into a flask of nitrogen? What precisely is the result when two solids of different weights are dropped at the same instant from a height of ten feet onto the ground? Later on he becomes aware of experiments or tests, performed by others, which have vital relevance to his life. What was the rate of atomic fall out in Victoria — in Collingwood — last month? How many people (in any hundred in a given period in Melbourne) who watch TV for more than an hour a day still listen to the sound radio? What was the Roman Catholic birth rate in Australia compared with the Protestant in 1959? How accurate is this newspaper report or that?

For experiments and the experimental approach certainly do not any longer belong only to laboratory subjects. The modern historian has an appetite for facts; he tries to find out authentic data by delving into original sources and perhaps visiting, for himself those remains and that battle sight, even digging up the ground to find more about, say, a primitive people who formerly inhabited the land, and their ways of life. The study of literature, of painting or music all have an important experimental side.

Finding and proving what was the order of the canvases painted by an artist during his productive years, testing surprising facts about note vibrations, collating texts so that we know what an author really wrote; such quests in every case demand an experimental, analytic frame of mind. And experiments or research investigations carefully carried out do undoubtedly, and confortingly, yield firm knowledge. Moreover, if you carefully repeat an experiment in the laboratory, or anywhere else, it will yield exactly the same knowledge the second time, the third time, any number of times — until you get bored stiff with it. Tne experimenter must, of course, be detached. He arranges the apparatus, it is true; he weighs the stuff on the balance; he lights the bunsen burner; but essentially he is the observer, simply watching what will happen, not interfering, but hoping that the result will come out all right; not getting in the way at all if he can help it, and recording the result scrupulously. For self-deception, or attempting to deceive other people, is unscientific. In other words, the scientist is as far as possible acting impersonally, looking with concentration for items of knowledge which, when they have been obtained, can be added to all other knowledge to make the whole pile of knowledge bigger.

It is astonishing to recollect that in the seventeenth century the word experiment and the word experience meant very nearly the same thing. Even now, as a matter of fact, the French use the same word — experience, for both. But, all the same, in France, as in Australia or England, men have learned to differentiate sharply between experimenting and experiencing. To have an experience is not by any means the same thing as to perform an experiment.

Experiences that are vivid come to all of us. Six years ago I visited New York for the first time, crossing the Atlantic in a big Cunarder. No doubt my feelings on that voyage have been shared in some degree by many another man and woman. I was impressed by the vast loneliness of the sea. Once we had left the fishing grounds off the western coasts of France and England and were three hundred miles out, we neither saw not passed a ship until we were nearing the American coast, with New York as a magnet drawing the ships to itself. Such are the so-called 'busy' lanes of human commerce amid the immensity of the ocean. New York itself, approached as twilight was deepening, with its filigree sky-scrapers lighted and soaring delicately up into the sky, seemed a fairy-like place — with the low roar of the traffic, a dim, impressive background to everything. New York for me had magic about it.

In 1958 I flew over the deserts of Northern Africa to the sun-drenched Sudan. The journey from the airport, in a creaky, out-of-date bus, along the dozen miles into the city of Khartoum, was an unforgettable introduction to what for me was a strange land. We went bumping amid clouds of dust in the very early morning along a road that was hardly a road at all, with sand stretching away, nothing but sand — and the sun rising, a visible ball, away on the horizon. We passed donkeys laden on both sides with produce for the markets of the nearing city; and then, rounding a corner, we crossed, by a modern bridge of girders, the wide Nile.

My time in the Sudan, though short, was full of experiences. But neither the experiences I had on that first visit to Africa nor on my first visit to New York will ever quite be repeatable. For one thing, if and when I go again, I shall be older and therefore a little different myself, and, for another, I shall be visiting cities I have already begun to know. It is of the very nature of an experience, unlike an experiment, that it is unique.

Nor can we arrange to perform an experience as we arrange to perform an experiment. An experience is a response to the world and all that is in it. We are not detached when we are having it; eager, perhaps, looking forward with zest to the next minute and the one that is after that, keenly alive to what we see and hear and feel. For an experience, unlike an experiment, is a very personal affair. An experiment leads to our learning facts. An experience leads to our learning — what? What did I learn from my time in Khartoum or that voyage to New York, or from watching Peter Fleming as Iago at an O.U.D.S. performance long ago? (What an actor was lost when Peter Fleming decided to become a writer)! How is it possible to define such essences? Something about human nature, about the beauty of the world, about the possibilities of man? Yes, but this is an inadequate, irrelevant catalogue.

The fact is that whereas what we find out from an experiment causes knowledge to grow (adding it bit by bit to the pile), the knowledge we get from an experience causes us to grow. For it is very real knowledge, though so personal, and it can have powerful effects.

Now some people, especially in our own day, want to maintain that the only real knowledge is the impersonal, objective sort of knowledge obtained from experiments; knowledge, that is, which is open to logical, demonstrable proof. That certainly is knowledge, but it is not the only kind that comes to men, even to children. For example, it is extremely difficult to define precisely the kind of knowledge given us by music. Who can write down in so many words what he had gained in knowledge about things by hearing and being moved by Mozart's wonderful Pianoforte Concertos 17 or 25? But something nevertheless has been given him that he did not know before. We use the verb 'know' in a wider sense than we use the word 'knowledge'; and to extend the range and sensitivity of our appreciation of music will involve finding out not merely more about music, but more about life too. It is difficult to define precisely what kinds of knowledge are given us by reading literature. Of course it is possible to learn a Hamlet soliloquy or a Shelley lyric by heart. But that in itself may have hardly any connexion with knowing it or getting inside its meaning. Such knowing involves understanding it at a different level. Appreciation of poetry is not proportionate to capacity to learn it by rote. Really learning with the heart is a different process from learning by rote. The same is true, of course, of the study of the Bible or the Koran. Studying Christian theology is not equivalent to being Christian. One can indeed know about Christianity or Mohammedanism or Buddhism without knowing from the inside any of those religions.

The academic, university mind is perhaps particularly liable to assume that research is the one way through to knowledge — to real knowledge, that is. The arts subjects have followed the sciences in demanding for a higher degree that a man shall have routed out new facts — about the Elizabethan Theatre, for example, or the life of Pliny, or the differing attitudes of nineteenth century scholars to the significance of the Battle of Hastings. Perhaps this is all right. How otherwise can we be sure that Smith and Robinson, Miss High and Miss Low deserve the degrees they are working for? Or have they been working? Their digging up of massive, rocky facts so that they can arrange and exhibit them is the test. And solid, demonstrable, there they are, to be held in the hand and weighed in the balance into which they are put. Research is necessary and indispensable, even though many a Ph. D. thesis, as Sir Eric Ashby says, caste, but a 'fitful and intermittent light on non-existent problem'. Ability to do good research is an important ability in the modern world. But it is not the possession of this sort of knowledge alone that is important to modern man.

There is certainly more than one way of knowing. To deny the knowledge given by the heart which loves or suffers is to cut ourselves off from much of life altogether. And to try to convey the knowledge which comes from experience, in terms that are analytic, is to deprive it of most of its meaning. As Michael Polanyi has pointed out in his remarkable book *Personal Knowledge*, 'strictly speaking nothing that we know can be said precisely'. And he glosses the statement by quoting Ohitehead's. 'There is not a sentence which adequately states its own meaning. There is always a background of presupposition which defies analysis by reason of its infinitude'.

The infinitude which is in experiences, the overplus as it were, is their vitality. The magic of a great city, as of a person, lies, in its incapacity to be precisely known, to be defined. comprehended, completely analysed.

Experiments then are not a substitute for experiences, but neither of course on the other hand are experiences, a substitute for experiments. A good deal of the misunderstanding by ordinary people of what art is all about and a great deal of the misunderstanding by artists of the purpose and function of science springs from a lack of this realization: that both the experimental attitude (which is objective, patient, practical, analytical) and the experiential (which is personal and subjective, often intuitional grasping events as wholes instead of dividing them up into parts) are necessary. Experimenter is experiencer too.

NOTES

Professor Niblett (b. 1906) is a distinguished British educationist, and has a number of books on educational problems to his credit.

Knowledge gained through experiment and analysis — the approach in science should not be regarded as the only true knowledge. Our own experiences, both of life and literature, provide us a kind of knowledge which is equally valid. An experiment in science may help knowledge to grow; but the knowledge from our emotional or purely subjective experiences, though analytically indefinable, help us to grow. The experimental and experiential attitudes are not antagonistic but rather complementary.

Roman Catholic: people belonging to the church headed by the Pope of Rome.

Protestant: (member) of any of the Christian bodies that separated from the Church of Rome at the time of the Reformation (16th century).

authentic: genuine.

delve into: to make researches into.

collate: make a careful comparison between (copies of texts, manuscripts, books etc.); to learn the differences between them (to collate a new edition with an earlier edition).

scrupulous: careful to do nothing morally wrong; paying attention to small points (esp. of conscience).

Peter Fleming: British author and journalist.

Iago: a character in Shakespeare's play *Othello*.

O.U.D.S.: Oxford University Dramatic Society.

Mozart: a famous Austrian musician (1756-91).

Pliny: the celebrated Roman writer, statesman and orator.

Battle of Hastings: fought in 1066 between the King of England and the Duke of Normandy.

Michael Polanyi: British scientist and philosopher.

Whitehead (A.N.): English philosopher and mathematician (1861-1947).

intuition: the power of gaining immediate knowledge of something without conscious reasoning or study.

COMPREHENSION

1. In what way, according to the author, is every contemporary educated man or woman a scientist?
2. Bring out the experimental side of the study of literature or art.
3. What is the cardinal virtue of the experimenter?
4. Differentiate clearly between experimenting and experiencing.
5. An "experiment causes *knowledge* to grow ... an experience causes *us* to grow." Elaborate this statement by providing examples.
6. "There is certainly more than one way of knowing. The experimenter is experiencer too" Expand on this statement in about 200 words.

LANGUAGE STUDY

1. The word *observe* has different meanings i.e. to notice or watch carefully, to celebrate, to say by way of comment. Use the word *observe*, as also the following words, in sentences to bring out their different meanings:
   appetite, productive, detached, essence(s),
   academic, gloss, appendix.
2. Distinguish between the following pairs of words by using them in sentences of your own. (Use a dictionary, if necessary).
   canvas, canvass; jest, zest; compliment, complement.
   Make a list of ten more such pairs of words which are similiar in sound but different in meaning.
3. Substitute one word for the following:
   a. digging up the ground to find more about primitive people and their ways of life.
   b. the study of ancient things especially remains of pre-historic times, e.g. tombs, buried cities etc.
4. The word *delve* is followed by the preposition *into*. Certain words and phrases in English are followed by specific prepositions. There are, on the other hand, words that are

not followed by prepositions in certain contexts e.g. *He entered the room*. The sentence *He entered into the room* is not correct. The following are a few more examples of such sentences:

I request *to* you to consider my case. (omit *to*)
He demanded *for* an answer. (omit *for*)
The temperature rose *up* to 45 degrees celsius. (omit *up*)
He ordered *for* a drink. (omit *for*)

Correct the the following sentences:

a. We discussed about the matter.
b. I shall inform to your brother.
c. She resembles with her elder sister.
d. The police inspector carefully investigated into the matter.
e. Darkness pervaded over the entire landscape.
f. He meditates upon revenge.
g. This class comprises of forty students.
h. He commands over the sympathy of all who have heard the story of his sufferings.

5. Note the use of suffixes *ist* and *ian* in the following examples:

A person who studies and applies *science* is a *scientist*.
A person who studies and applies *phonetics* is a *phonetician*.

a. A person who studies and applies technology is a ______.
b. A person who studies and applies ______ is a geologist.
c. A person who studies and applies biology is a ______.
d. A person who studies and applies ______ is a chemist.
e. A person who studies and applies psychology is a ______.
f. A person who studies and applies mathematics is a ______.
g. A person who studies and applies statistics is a ______.
h. A person who studies and applies ______ is a theologian.
i A person who studies and applies electricity is an ______.

But

a. One who practices engineering is an ______.
b. One who practises medicine is a ______.
c. One who practises architecture is an ______.

'The suffix *ion* changes a verb into a noun e.g.
act — action.
apply — application.
relate — relation.

Change the following verbs into nouns:
to imagine, to attract, to destroy, to construct, to connect, to observe, to fluctuate, to obstruct.
In some cases some other changes may also have to be made, e.g.,
to join — junction.
Make nouns from the following:
to destroy, to query, to transmit, to receive, to magnify, to simplify, to determine.

6. Find words which have the following meanings. Choose the words from the box below:
   a. The ability to think creatively (im______)
   b. To increase or decrease unsteadily (fl______)
   c. The state or process of pulling e.g. as in magnetism (att______ion)
   d. To look at and note the behaviour of (ob______)
   e. To cause to move, to control. (di______)
   f. The act or state of being joined (con______)
   g. To mix or to cause to mix in a controlled way.
   h. The act or the result of mixing.
   i. To finish.
   j. The act or process of finishing
   k. The relationship between two things.
   l. To maintain unchanged.
   m. To group together or to increase the amount of an element or compound in a solution.
   n. Something which is made up or formed or the act or making or forming.
   o. The act or process of exchange.
   p. To build or to put together parts to make a whole.

attraction, imagine, direct, conjunction, connect, condense, conserve, concentrate, construct, constitute, complete, compose, communicate, combine, fluctuate.

COMPOSITION

1. "Without science life is primitive; without the arts life is poor." Comment.

2. Assess the role of the arts in our age of science and technology.
3. "If music be the food of love, play on". Write an essay of about 400 words on this topic. (This is the opening line of Shakespeare's famous comedy *Twelfth Night*.)

The Cloud

PERCY BYSSHE SHELLEY (1792-1822)

I bring fresh showers for the thirsting flowers,
  From the seas and the streams;
I bear light shade for the leaves when laid
  In their noonday dreams.
From my wings are shaken the dews that waken
  The sweet buds every one,
When rocked to rest on their mother's breast,
  As she dances about the sun.
I wield the flail of the lashing hail,
  And whiten the green plains under,
And then again I dissolve it in rain,
  And laugh as I pass in thunder.

I sift the snow on the mountains below,
  And their great pines groan aghast;
And all the night 'tis my pillow white,
  While I sleep in the arms of the blast.
Sublime on the towers of my skiey bowers,
  Lightning my pilot sits;
In a cavern under is fettered the thunder,
  It struggles and howls at fits;
Over earth and ocean, with gentle motion,
  This pilot is guiding me,
Lured by the love of the genii that move
  In the depths of the purple sea;
Over the rills, and the crags, and the hills,
  Over the lakes and the plains,
Wherever he dream, under mountain or stream,

The Spirit he loves remains;
And I all the while bask in Heaven's blue smile,
Whilst he is dissolving in rains.

The sanguine Sunrise, with his meteor eyes,
And his burning plumes outspread,
Leaps on the back of my sailing rack,
When the morning star shines dead;
As on the jag of a mountain crag,
Which an earthquake rocks and swings,
An eagle alit one moment may sit
In the light of its golden wings.
And when Sunset may breathe, from the lit sea beneath,
Its ardours of rest and of love,
And the crimson pall of eve may fall
From the depth of Heaven above,
With wings folded I rest, on mine airy nest,
As still as a brooding dove.

That orbed maiden with white fire laden,
Whom mortals call the Moon,
Glides glimmering o'er my fleece-like floor,
By the midnight breezes strewn;
And wherever the beat of her unseen feet,
Which only the angels hear,
May have broken the woof of my tent's thin roof,
The stars peep behind her and peer;
And I laugh to see them whirl and flee,
Like a swarm of golden bees,
When I widen the rent in my wind-built tent,
Till the calm rivers, lakes, and seas,
Like strips of the sky fallen through me on high,
Are each paved with the moon and these.

I bind the Sun's throne with a burning zone,
And the Moon's with a girdle of pearl;
The volcanoes are dim, and the stars reel and swim,
When the whirlwinds my banner unfurl.
From cape to cape, with a bridge-like shape,
Over a torrent sea,

Sunbeam-proof, I hand like a roof, —
  The mountains its columns be.
The triumphal arch through which I march
  With hurricane, fire, and snow,
When the Powers of the air are chained to my chair,
  Is the million-coloured bow;
The sphere-fire above its soft colours wcve,
  While the moist Earth was laughing below.

I am the daughter of Earth and Water,
  And the nursling of the Sky;
I pass through the pores of the ocean and shores;
  I change, but I cannot die.
For after the rain when with never a stain
  The pavilion of Heaven is bare,
And the winds and sunbeams with their convex gleams
  Build up the blue dome of air,
I silently laugh at my own cenotaph,
  And out of the caverns of rain,
Like a child from the womb, like a ghost from the tomb,
  I arise and unbuild it again.

NOTES

Shelley's beautiful lyric expresses the airy and joyous spirit of the cloud. The cloud, with a sense of delight and achievement, describes its life and work. The poem is concerned with the elemental life of the cloud.

The poem is based on a scientific observation of the cyclical; process of birth, life and death as symbolised by the cloud.

I: The cloud is telling its own story

noonday dreams: In the heat of the windless noon the leaves fall asleep and dream of the advent of the rains.

rocked: swayed gently.

wield the flail: *hail — a flail* (a wooden stick) used to thresh corn.

whiten: after a hail-storm the fields look white.

dissolve it: melt the hailstones.

'tis: 'the snow is'.

at fits: at fitful intervals.

genii: spirits.

he dream: he may dream.

The Spirit he loves: i.e. the spirit of water, scientifically, water is a conductor of lightning.

sanguine: blood red.

my sailing rack: my wind-driven mass.

shines dead: is no longer visible.

jag: sharp edge.

alit: having alighted (on the jag).

the light of: in the joy of, proud of possessing.

my fleece-like...strewn: we are to imagine that as the cloud is driven along by the night air, its edges and surfaces blow about like strands of fleece.

woof: texture.

peep behind her: look over the moon's shoulder, as it were.

And I laugh ... moon and these: the idea seems to be that as the cloud breaks, or moves onward, widening the rent in its mass, the stars appear to move in the opposite direction and, thus, to turn and run. As the cloud looks down, the moon and stars are reflected in the stretches of water on the earth below.

bind: envelope.

girdle: encircle, encompass, enclose.

the volcanoes .... banner unfurl: clouds and the dust raised by the whirlwind obscure the volcanoes, and the stars too only can be seen fitfully and seem to be moving.

cape: a piece of land jutting out into a large body of water (sea).

sunbeam proof: impenetrable by sunlight.

the triumphal arch: the rainbow.

fire: lightning.

the sphere-fire above: the sun's radiance.

nursling: an infant under the care of a nurse.

I pass .... and shores: i.e. when precipitated as rain.

pavilion of heaven: the sky is imagined as a pavilion.

for after ... blue dome of air: after the rain the cloudless sky appears like a blue dome over the earth.

convex gleams: the sky is like an inverted cup, it is convex in shape.

my own cenotaph: the blue dome of the sky looks like the grave or the place where the cloud now lies buried. The cloud, even after the rain, continues its existence in the form of water in rivers, lakes etc. and looks up at its own cenotaph in the sky.

caverns of rain: ponds, lakes, seas, etc.

like a child ... build it again: when the sky is again overcast with clouds, it no more looks like the cenotaph, described earlier. The cloud destroys its own cenotaph. The rebirth of the cloud marks the destruction or its cenotaph. The rebirth of the cloud is very much like the birth of child and this marks the beginning of a new life.

COMPREHENSION

1. Describe the benign work done by the cloud as described in the first stanza of the poem.
2. Describe the different aspects of the cosmos that are influenced by the sweep of the cloud.
3. "I change but I cannot die." Describe in a paragraph the scientific truth recorded in this statement.
4. Explain the expression, "I silently laugh at my own cenotaph."
5. Which line in the poem gives the central idea of the poem?

LANGUAGE STUDY

1. Match the words in the left hand column with their synonyms in the right hand column:

unbuild	monument
stain	parching
cenotaph	demolish
thirsting	spot
area	vanish
swim	flag
pass	glide

dissolve
dim
banner
unfurl
torrent
column
chained
change

zone
spread
gloomy
float
pillar
turbulent
transform
fettered

2. Read the text of the poem and give the antonyms of the following words:
bring, from, wake, dim, soft, weave, change, death, bare, convex, child, fresh.
3. Mother earth *dances about* the sun i.e., it revolves around the sun.
Dances about is a prepositional phrase. Use the following idiomatic phrases in sentences of your own. The meanings of these phrases are given:
to dance attendance upon: to follow or pay great attention to.
to dance to somebody's tune: to obey him in every respect.
under one's wing: under one's protection.
out of the woods: out of danger.
rainy days: difficult time.
to be at sea: to be perplexed, at a loss what to do.
to get wind of: to come to know of.
a bolt from the blue: a disaster that comes suddenly.
to move heaven and earth: to use every means, to make all efforts.
to dance for joy: to feel very happy.
to bring about: to achieve, to cause something to happen.
to bring out: to expose, to bring to light, to publish, to produce from inside something.
to bring home: to produce a vivid impression or deep realization of something.
to bring to book: to call to account.

COMPOSITION

1. Write in not more than 400 words what happens when the rains fail. Use the points given on the next page:

oppressive heat — drought — taps run dry — load-shedding — prices sour — crop loss — widespread rural unemployment — the sufferings of cattle — sharing of the common calamity as a solution.

2. It has rained incessantly for three days. On the fourth day the sky clears and you are able to attend college. Write a dialogue between you and your friend comparing your experiences during the deluge. Use verbless clauses wherever appropriate.

GRAMMAR

See Appendix II, page 177.

Benares

ALDOUS HUXLEY

It was said that the eclipse of the sun would be visible from Benares. But it needed more than smoked glass to see it; the eye of faith was also indispensable. That, alas, we did not possess. Partial to the point of being non-existent, the eclipse remained, for us at least, unseen. Not that we minded. For it was not to look at the moon's silhouette that we had rowed out that morning on the Ganges; it was to look at the Hindus looking at it. The spectacle was vastly more extraordinary.

There were, at the lowest estimate, a million of them on the bathing ghats that morning. A million. All the previous night and day they had been streaming into the town. We had met them on every road, trudging with bare feet through the dust, an endless and silent procession. In bundles balanced on their heads they carried provisions and cooking utensils and dried dung for fuel, with the new clothes which it is incumbent on pious Hindus to put on after their bath in honour of the eclipsed sun. Many had come far. The old men leaned wearily on their bamboo staves. Their children astride of their hips, the burdens on their heads automatically balanced, the women walked in a trance of fatigue. Here and there we would see a little troop that had sat down to rest — casually, as is the way of Indians, in the dust of the road and almost under the wheels of the passing vehicles.

And now the day and the hour had come. The serpent was about to swallow the sun. It was about to swallow him in Sumatra, at any rate. At Benares it would do no more than nibble imperceptibly at the edge of his disk. The serpent, should one say, was going to try to swallow the sun. A million of men and women had come together at Benares to assist the Light of Heaven against his enemy.

The ghats go down in furlong-wide flights of steps to the river, which lies like a long arena at the foot of enormous tiers of seats. The tiers were thronged today. Floating on the Ganges, we looked up at acres upon sloping acres of humanity.

On the smaller and comparatively unsacred ghats the crowd was a little less densely packed than on the holiest steps. It was at one of these less crowded ghats that we witnessed the embarkation on the sacred river of a princess. Canopied and curtained with glittering cloth of gold, a palanquin came staggering down through the crowd on the shoulders of six red-liveried attendants. A great barge, like a Noah's ark, its windows hung with scarlet curtains, floated at the water's edge. The major-domo shouted and shoved and hit out with his rod of office; a way was somehow cleared. Slowly and with frightful lurchings, the palanquin descended. It was set down, and in the twinkling of an eye a little passage-way of canvas had been erected between the litter and the door of the barge. There was a heaving of the cloth of gold, a flapping of the canvas; the lady — the ladies, for there were several of them in the litter — had entered the barge unobserved of any vulgar eye. Which did not prevent them, a few minuts later when the barge had been pushed out into mid-stream, from lifting the scarlet curtains and peering out with naked faces and unabashed curiosity at the passing boats and our inquisitive camera. Poor princesses! They could not bathe with their plebeian and unimprisoned sisters in the open Ganges. Their dip was to be in the barge's bilge-water. The sacred stream is filthy enough under the sky. What must it be like after stagnating in darkness at the bottom of an ancient barge?

We rowed on towards the burning ghats. Stretched out on their neat little oblong pyres, two or three corpses were slowly smouldering. They lay on burning faggots, they were covered by them. Gruesomely and grotesquely, their bare feet projected, like the feet of those who sleep uneasily on a bed too short and under exiguous blankets.

A little further on we saw a row of holy men, sitting like cormorants on a narrow ledge of masonry just above the water. Cross-legged, their hands dropped limply, palm upwards, on the ground beside them, they contemplated the brown and sweating tips of their noses. It was the Lord Krishna himself who, in the *Bhagavad Gita,* prescribed that mystic squint. Lord Krishna, it is evident, knew all that there is to be known about the art of self-hypnotism. His simple method has never been improved on; it puts the mystical *ecstasy a la portee de tous.* The noise of an assembled million filled the air; but no sound could break the meditative sleep of the nose-gazers.

At a given moment the eye of faith must have observed the nibblings of the demoniacal serpent. For suddenly and simultaneously all those on the lowest steps of the ghats threw themselves into the water and began to wash and gargle, to say their prayers and blow their noses, to spit and drink. A numerous band of police abbreviated their devotions and their bath in the interest of the crowds behind. The front of the waiting queue was a thousand yards wide; but a million people were waiting. The bathing must have gone on uninterruptedly the whole day.

Time passed. The serpent went on nibbling imperceptibly at the sun. The Hindus counted their beads and prayed, made ritual gestures, ducked under the sacred slime, drank, and were moved on by the police to make room for another instalment of the patient million. We rowed up and down, taking snapshots. West is West.

In spite of the serpent, the sun was uncommonly hot on our backs. After a couple of hours on the river, we decided that we had had enough, and landed. The narrow lanes that lead from the ghats to the open streets in the centre of the town were lined with beggars, more or less holy. They sat on the ground with their begging bowls before them; the charitable, as they passed, would throw a few grains of rice into each of the bowls. By the end of the day the beggars might, with luck, have accumulated a square meal. We pushed our way slowly through the thronged alleys. From an archway in front of us emerged a sacred bull. The nearest beggar was dozing at his post — those who eat little sleep much. The bull lowered its muzzle to the sleeping man's bowl, made a scouring movement with its black tongue, and a morning's charity had gone. The beggar still dozed. Thoughtfully chewing, the Hindu totem turned back the way it had come and disappeared.

Being stupid and having no imagination, animals often behave far more sensibly than men. Efficiently and by instinct they do the right, appropriate thing at the right moment — eat when they are hungry, look for water when they feel thirst, make love in the mating season, rest or play when they have leisure. Men are intelligent and imaginative; they look backwards and ahead; they invent ingenious explanation for observed phenomena; they devise elaborate and roundabout means for the achievement of remote ends. Their intelligence, which has made them the masters of the world, often causes them to act like imbeciles. No animal, for example, is clever and imaginative enough to suppose that an eclipse is the work of a serpent devouring the sun. That is the sort of explanation that could occur only to the human mind. And only a human being would dream of making ritual gestures in the hope of influencing, for his own benefit, the outside world. While the animal, obedient to its instinct, goes quietly about its business, man, being endowed with reason and imagination, wastes half his time and energy in doing things that are completely idiotic. In time, it is true, experience teaches him that magic formulas and ceremonial gestures do not give him what he wants. But until experience has taught him — and he takes a surprisingly long time to learn — man's behaviour is in many respects far sillier than that of the animal.

So I reflected, as I watched the sacred bull lick up the rice from the dozing beggar's bowl. While a million people undertake long journeys, suffer fatigue, hunger, and discomfort in order to perform, in a certain stretch of very dirty water, certain antics for the benefit of a fixed star ninety million miles away, the bull goes about looking for food and fills its belly with whatever it can find. In this case, it is obvious, the bull's brainlessness causes it to act much more rationally than its masters.

To save the sun (which might, one feels, very safely be left to look after itself) a million of Hindus will assemble on the banks of the Ganges. How many, I wonder, would assemble to save India? An immense energy which, if it could be turned into political channels, might liberate and transform the country, is wasted in the name of imbecile superstitions. Religion is a luxury which India, in its present condition, cannot possibly afford. India will never be free until the Hindus and the Moslems are as tepidly enthusiastic about their religion as we are about the Church of England. If I were an Indian millionaire, I would leave all my money for the endowment of an Atheist Mission.

NOTES

the eye of faith: blind faith, irrational belief
indispensable: absolutely essential
silhouette: picture in solid black showing only the outline
nibble: take tiny bites, eclipse only partially
barge: a large flat-bottomed boat for carrying goods and people on rivers etc.
major domo: head steward in a great household
heaving: to rise and fall regularly, to move up and down
litter: a palanquin; a couch or bed, often with a covering and curtains in which a person may be carried about e.g. on men's shoulders.
plebian: a person of the lower social classes
bilge-water: the water that collects in the almost flat part of a ship's bottom
exiguous: scanty, insufficient
cormorants: large greedy long-necked sea birds
ledge: narrow horizontal shelf coming out from a wall
abbreviated: shortened
sacred slime: holy but dirty and very muddy water of the Ganges
totem: an animal, plant or object regarded by a class or tribe with superstitious respect as an outward symbol of an existing intimate unseen relation
ingenious: clever skilful
antics: absurd and strange movements
tepidly: in a lukewarm manner, not very enthusiastic.

COMPREHENSION

1. What, according to Aldous Huxley, is the Hindu explanation for a solar eclipse?
2. Why did the author go to Benares?
3. What did the author see on one of the burning ghats?
4. What did the people do when it was time for the eclipse?

5. In what way, according to the author, does the behaviour of human beings differ from that of animals?
6. What, according to Huxley, should be our attitude to religion? Is the author secular or is he lukewarm towards religious beliefs?
7. What did the bull do? In what way was the behaviour of the bull different from that of human beings?
8. What does the author propose for the betterment of India? Do you agree with his views? Give reasons for your answer.

LANGUAGE STUDY

1. Add a suitable prefix to each of the following words so as to form words having the opposite meaning:

interrupted	intelligent	abashed
rational	quiet	existent
comfort	imaginative	seen
observed	common	experience
credible	existent	enthusiastic
credulous	sacred	interested
interesting	inquisitive	perceptibly
ordinary	numerous	pious

2. Make adjectives from the following:

part	vision	spectacle
vehicle	serpent	curiosity
charity	rite	benefit
instinct	ceremony	reason
enthusiasm	luxury	peculiarity

COMPOSITION

1. Describe a solar eclipse. What is the scientific explanation for an eclipse?

2. All religions have some superstitions. Do you agree with this view? Would it not be advisable to get rid of all superstitions?
3. Describe some interesting superstitions.
4. Some religious customs are cruel and inhuman. Describe some of these customs and what should be done to abolish them.
5. What is secularism? Does it mean absence of religion or indifference to it, or does it mean something else?
6. What is the solution proposed by the author? Do you agree with this solution? Give reasons for your answer.

GRAMMAR

See Appendix II, page 184.

The Adventure of the Blue Carbuncle

ARTHUR CONAN DOYLE

I had called upon my friend Sherlock Holmes upon the second morning after Christmas, with the intention of wishing him the compliments of the season. He was lounging upon the sofa in a purple dressing-gown, a pipe-rack within his reach upon the right, and a pile of crumpled morning papers, evidently newly studied, near at hand. Beside the couch was a wooden chair, and on the angle of the back hung a very shabby and disreputable hard felt hat, much the worse for wear, and cracked in several places. A lens and a forceps lying upon the seat of the chair suggested that the hat had been suspended in this manner for the purpose of examination.

"You are engaged" said I; "perhaps I interrupt you."

"Not at all. I am glad to have a friend with whom I can discuss my results. The matter is a perfectly trivial one" — he jerked his thumb in the direction of the old hat "— but there are points in connection with it which are not entirely without interest and even instruction."

I seated myself in his armchair and warmed my hands before his crackling fire, for a sharp frost had set in, and the windows were thick with the ice crystals. "I suppose", I remarked, "that, homely as it looks, this thing has some deadly story linked on to it — that it is the clue which will guide you in the solution of some mystery, and the punishment of some crime."

"No, no. No crime," said Sherlock Holmes, laughing. "Only one of those whimsical little incidents which will happen when you have four million human beings all jostling each other within the space of a few square miles. Amid the action and reaction of so dense a swarm of humanity, every possible combination of events may be expected to take place, and many a little problem will be presented which may be striking and strange without being criminal. We have already had experience of such."

"So much so," I remarked, "that of the last six cases which I have added to my notes, three have been entirely free of any legal crime."

"Precisely. You allude to my attempt to recover the Irene Adler papers, to the singular case of Miss. Sutherland, and to the adventure of the man with the twisted lip. Well, I have no doubt that this small matter will fall into the same innocent category. You know Peterson, the commissionaire?"

"Yes."

"It is to him that this trophy belongs."

"It is his hat."

"No, no; he found it. Its owner is unknown. I beg that you will look upon it, not as a battered billycock, but as an intellectual problem. And, first, as to how it came here. It arrived upon Christmas morning in company with a good fat goose, which is, I have no doubt, roasting at this moment in front of Peterson's fire. The facts are these: about four o'clock on Christmas morning, Peterson, who, as you know, is a very honest fellow, was returning from some small jollification and was making his way homeward down Tottenham Court Road. In front of him he saw, in the gaslight, a tallish man, walking with a slight stagger, and carrying a white goose slung over his shoulder. As he reached the corner of Goodge Street, a row broke out between this stranger and a little knot of roughs. One of the latter knocked off the man's hat, on which he raised his stick to defend himself and, swinging it over his head, smashed the shop window behind him. Peterson had rushed forward to protect the stranger from his assailants; but the man, shocked at having broken the window, and seeing an official-looking person in uniform rushing towards him, dropped his goose, took to his heels, and vanished amid the labyrinth of small streets which lie at the back of Tottenham Court Road. The roughs had also fled at the appearance of Peterson, so that he was left in possession of the field of battle, and also of the spoils of victory in the shape of this battered hat and a most unimpeachable Christmas goose."

"Which surely he restored to their owner?"

"My dear fellow, there lies the problem. It is true that "For Mrs Henry Baker" was printed upon a small card which was tied to the bird's left leg, and it is also true that the initials "H.B." are legible upon the lining of this hat; but as there are some thousands of Bakers, and some hundreds of Henry Bakers in this city of ours, it is not easy to restore lost property to any one of them."

"What, then, did Peterson do?"

"He brought round both hat and goose to me on Christmas morning, knowing that even the smallest problems are of interest to me. The goose we retained until this morning, when there were signs that, in spite of the slight frost, it would be well that it should be eaten without unnecessary delay. Its finder has carried it off, therefore, to fulfil the ultimate destiny of a goose, while I continue to retain the hat of the unknown gentleman who lost his Christmas dinner."

"Did he not advertise?"

"No."

"Then, what clue could you have as to his identity?"

"Only as much as we can deduce."

"From his hat?"

"Precisely."

"But you are joking. What can you gather from this old battered felt?"

"Here is my lens. You know my methods. What can you gather yourself as to the individuality of the man who has worn this article?"

I took the tattered object in my hands and turned it over rather ruefully. It was a very ordinary black hat of the usual round shape, hard and much the worse for wear. The lining had been of red silk, but was a good deal discoloured. There was no maker's name; but, as Holmes had remarked, the initials 'H.B.' were scrawled upon one side. It was pierced in the brim for a hat securer, but the elastic was missing. For the rest, it was cracked, exceedingly dusty, and spotted in several places, although there seemed to have been some attempt to hide the discoloured patches by smearing them with ink.

"I can see nothing," said I, handing it back to my friend.

"On the contrary, Watson, you can see everything. You fail,

however, to reason from what you see. You are too timid in drawing your inferences."

"Then, pray tell me what it is that you can infer from this hat."

He picked it up and gazed at it in the peculiar introspective fashion which was characteristic of him. "It is perhaps less suggestive than it might have been," he remarked, "and yet there are a few inferences which are very distinct, and a few others which represent at least a strong balance of probability. That the man was highly intellectual is of course obvious upon the face of it, and also that he was fairly well-to-do within the last three years, although he has now fallen upon evil days. He had foresight, but has less now than formerly, pointing to a moral retrogression, which, when taken with the decline of his fortunes, seems to indicate some evil influence, probably drink, at work upon him. This may account also for the obvious fact that his wife has ceased to love him."

"My dear Holmes!"

"He has, however, retained some degree of self-respect," he continued, disregardig my remonstrance. "He is a man who leads a sedentary life, goes out little, is out of training entirely, is middle-aged, has grizzled hair which he has had cut within the last few days, and which he anoints with lime-cream. These are the more patent facts which are to be deduced from his hat. Also, by the way, that it is extremely improbable that he has gas laid on in his house."

"You are certainly joking, Holmes."

"Not in the least. Is it possible that even now, when I give you these results, you are unable to see how they are attained?"

"I have no doubt that I am very stupid, but I must confess that I am unable to follow you. For example, how did you deduce that this man was intellectual?"

For answer Holmes clapped the hat upon his head. It came right over the forehead and settled upon the bridge of his nose. "It is a question of cubic capacity," said he; "a man with so large a brain must have something in it."

"The decline of his fortunes, then?"

"This hat is three years old. These flat brims curled at the edge came in then. It is a hat of the very best quality. Look at the band of ribbed silk and the excellent lining. If this man could afford to buy so expensive a hat three years ago, and has had no hat since, then he has assuredly gone down in the world."

"Well, that is clear enough, certainly. But how about the foresight and the moral retrogression?"

Sherlock Holmes laughed. "Here is the foresight," said he, putting his finger upon the little disc and loop of the hat-securer. "They are never sold upon hats. If this man ordered one, it is a sign of a certain amount of foresight, since he went out of his way to take this precaution against the wind. But since we see that he has broken the elastic and has not troubled to replace it, it is obvious that he has less foresight now than formerly, which is a distinct proof of a weakening nature. On the other hand, he has endeavoured to conceal some of these stains upon the felt by daubing them with ink, which is a sign that he has not entirely lost his self-respect."

"Your reasoning is certainly plausible."

"The further points, that he is middle-aged, that his hair is grizzled, that it has been recently cut, and that he used lime-cream, are all to be gathered from a close examination of the lower part of the lining. The lens discloses a large number of hair-ends clean cut by the scissors of the barber. They all appear to be adhesive, and there is a distinct odour of lime-cream. This dust, you will observe, is not the gritty, gray dust of the street but the fluffy brown dust of the house, showing that it has been hung up indoors most of the time; while the marks of moisture upon the inside are proof positive that the wearer perspired very freely, and could, therefore, hardly be in the best of training."

"But his wife — you said that she had ceased to love him."

"This hat has not been brushed for weeks. When I see you, my dear Watson, with a week's accumulation of dust upon your hat, and when your wife allows you to go out in such a state, I shall fear that you also have been unfortunate enough to lose your wife's affection."

"But he might be a bachelor."

"Nay, he was bringing home the goose as a peace-offering to his wife. Remember the card upon the bird's leg."

"You have an answer to everything. But how on earth do you deduce that the gas is not laid on in his house?"

"One tallow stain, or even two, might come by chance: but when I see no less than five, I think that there can be little doubt that the individual must be brought into frequent contact with burning tallow — walks upstairs at night probably with his hat in one hand and a guttering candle in the other. Anyhow, he never got tallow stains from a gas jet. Are you satisfied?"

"Well, it is very ingenious," said I, laughing; "but since, as you said just now, there has been no crime committed, and no harm done save the loss of a goose, all this seems to be rather a waste of energy."

Sherlock Holmes had opened his mouth to reply, when the foor flew open, and Peterson the commissionaire rushed into the apartment with flushed cheeks and the face of a man who is dazed with astonishment.

"The goose, Mr Holmes! The goose, sir! he gasped.

"Eh? What of it, then? Has it returned to life and flapped off through the kitchen window?" Holmes twisted himself round upon the sofa to get a fairer view of the man's excited face.

"See here, sir! See what my wife found in its crop!" He held out his hand and displayed upon the centre of the palm a brilliantly scintillating blue stone, rather smaller than a bean in size, but of such purity and radiance that it twinkled like an electric point in the dark hollow of his hand.

Sherlock Holmes sat up with a whistle. "By Jove, Peterson!" said he, "this is a treasure-trove indeed! I suppose you know what you have got?"

"A diamond, sir? A precious stone. It cuts into glass as though it were putty."

"It's more than a precious stone. It is the precious stone."

"Not the Countess of Morcar's blue carbuncle!" I ejaculated.

"Precisely so. I ought to know its size and shape, seeing that I have read the advertisement about it in *The Times* every day lately. It is absolutely unique, and its value can only be conjectured, but the reward offered of £1,000 is certainly not within a twentieth part of the market price."

"A thousand pounds! Great Lord of mercy!" The commissionaire plumped down into a chair and stared from one to the other of us.

"That is the reward, and I have reason to know that there are sentimental considerations in the background which would induce the Countess to part with half her fortune if she could but recover the gem."

"It was lost, if I remember aright, at the Hotel Cosmopolitan," I remarked.

"Precisely so, on 22 December, just five days ago. John Horner, a plumber, was accused of having abstracted it from the lady's jewel-case. The evidence against him was so strong that the case has been referred to the Assizes. I have some account of the matter here, I believe." He rummaged amid his newspapers, glancing over the dates, until at last he smoothed one out, doubled it over, and read the following paragraph:

"Hotel Cosmopolitan Jewel Robbery. John Horner, 26, plumber, was brought up upon the charge of having upon the 22nd inst., abstracted from the jewel-case of the Countess of Morcar the valuable gem known as the blue carbuncle. James Ryder, upper-attendant at the hotel, gave his evidence to the effect that he had shown Horner up to the dressing-room of the Countess of Morcar upon the day of the robbery in order that he might solder the second bar of the grate, which was loose. He had remained with Horner some little time, but had finally been called away. On returning, he found that Horner had disappeared, that the bureau had been forced open, and that the small morocco casket in which, as it aftewards transpired, the Countless was accustomed to keep her jewel, was lying empty upon the dressing-table. Ryder instantly gave the alarm, and Horner was arrested the same evening; but the stone could not be found either upon his person or in his rooms. Catherine Cusack, maid to the Countess, deposed to having heard Ryder's cry of dismay on discovering the robbery, and to having rushed into the room, where she found matters as described by the last witness. Inspector Bradstreet, B Division, gave evidence as to the arrest of Horner, who struggled frantically, and protested his innocence in the strongest terms. Evidence of a previous conviction for robbery having been given against the prisoner, the magistrate refused to deal summarily with the offence, but referred it to the Assizes. Horner who had shown signs of intense emotion during the proceedings, fainted away at the conclusion and was carried out of court."

"Hum! So much for the police-court," said Holmes thoughtfully, tossing aside the paper. "The question for us now to solve is the sequence of events leading from a rifled jewel-case at one end to the crop of a goose in Tottenham Court Road at the other. You see, Watson, our little deductions have suddenly assumed a much more important and less innocent aspect. Here is the stone; the stone came from the goose, and the goose came from Mr Henry Baker, the gentleman with the bad hat and all the other characteristics with which I have bored you. So now we must set ourselves very seriously to finding this gentleman, and ascertaining what part he has played in this little mystery. To do this, we must try the simplest means first, and these lie undoubtedly in an advertisement in all the evening papers. If this fail, I shall have recourse "to other methods."

"What will you say?"

"Give me a pencil and that slip of paper. Now, then:

"Found at the corner of Goodge Street, a goose and a black felt hat. Mr Henry Baker can have the same by applying at 6.30 this evening at 221B, Baker Street."

That is clear and concise."

"Very. But will he see it?"

"Well, he is sure to keep an eye on the papers, since, to a poor man, the loss was heavy one. He was clearly so scared by his mischance in breaking the window and by the approach of Peterson that he thought of nothing but flight, but since then he must have bitterly regretted the impulse which caused him to drop his bird. Then, again, the introduction of his name will cause him to see it, for everyone who knows him will direct his attention to it. Here you are, Peterson, run down to the advertising agency and have this put in the evening papers."

"In which, sir?"

"Oh, in the *Globe, Star, Pall Mall, St James's Gazette, Evening News, Standard, Echo,* and any others that occur to you."

"Very well, sir. And this stone?"

"Ah, yes, I shall keep the stone. Thank you. And, I say, Peterson, just buy a goose on your way back and leave it here with me, for we must have one to give to this gentleman in place of the one which your family is now devouring."

When the commissionaire had gone, Holmes took up the stone and held it against the light. "It's a bonny thing,' said he. "Just see how it glints and sparkles. Of course it is a nucleus and focus of crime. Every good stone is. They are the devil's pet baits. In the larger and older jewels every facet may stand for a bloody deed. This stone is not yet twenty years old. It was found in the banks of the Amoy river in southern China and is remarkable in having every characteristic of the carbuncle, save that it is bluein shade instead of ruby red. In spite of its youth, it has already a sinister history. There have been two murders, a vitriol-thowing, a suicide, and several robberies brought about for the sake of this forty-grain weight of crystallized charcoal. Who would think that so pretty a toy would be a purveyor to the gallows and the prison? I'll lock it up in my strong-box now and drop a line to the Countess to say that we have it."

"Do you think that this man Horner is innocent?"

"I cannot tell."

"Well, then, do you imagine that this other one, Henry Baker, had anything to do with the matter?"

"It is, I think, much more likely that Henry Baker is an absolutely innocent man, who had no idea that the bird which he was carrying was of considerably more value than if it were made of solid gold. That, however, I shall determine by a very simple test if we have an answer to our advertisement."

"And you can do nothing until then?"

"Nothing."

"In that case I shall continue my professional round. But I shall come back in the evening at the hour you have mentioned, for I should like to see the solution of so tangled a business."

"Very glad to see you. I dine at seven. There is a woodcock, I believe. By the way, in view of recent occurrences, perhaps I ought to ask Mrs Hudson to examine its crop."

I had been delayed at a case, and it was a little after half-past six when I found myself in Baker Street once more. As I approached the house, I saw a tall man in a Scotch bonnet with a coat which was buttoned up to his chin, waiting outside in the bright semicircle which was thrown from the fanlight. Just as I arrived the door was opened, and we were shown up together to Holmes's room.

"Mr Henry Baker, I believe," said he, rising from his armchair and greeting his visitor with the easy air of geniality which he could so readily assume. "Pray take this chair by the fire, Mr Baker. It is a cold night, and I observe that your circulation is more adapted for summer than for winter. Ah, Watson, you have just come at the right time. Is that your hat, Mr Baker?"

"Yes sir, that is undoubtedly my hat."

He was a large man with rounded shoulders, a massive head, and a broad, intelligent face, sloping down to a pointed beard of grizzled brown. A touch of red in nose and cheeks, with a slight tremor of his extended hand, recalled Holmes's surmise as to his habits. His rusty black frock-coat was buttoned right up in front, with the collar turned up, and his lank wrists protruded from his sleeves without a sign of cuff or shirt. He spoke in a slow staccato fashion, choosing his words with care, and gave the impression generally of a man of learning and letters who had had ill-usage at the hands of fortune.

"We have retained these things for some days," said Holmes, "because we expected to see an advertisement from you giving your address. I am at a loss to know now why you did not advertise."

Our visitor gave a rather shamefaced laugh. "Shillings have not been so plentiful with me as they once were," he remarked. "I had no doubt that the gang of roughs who assaulted me had carried off both my hat and the bird. I did not care to spend more money in a hopeless attempt at recovering them."

"Very naturally. By the way, about the bird, we were compelled to eat it."

"To eat it!" Our visitor half rose from his chair in his excitement.

"Yes, it would have been of no use to anyone had we not done so. But I presume that this other goose upon the sideboard, which is about the same weight and perfectly fresh, will answer your purpose equally well?"

"Oh, certainly, certainly," answered Mr Baker with a sigh of relief.

"Of course, we still have the feathers, legs, crop, and so on of your own bird, if you so wish—"

The man burst into a hearty laugh. "They might be useful to me as relics of my adventure," said he, "but beyond that I can hardly see what use the *disjecta membra* of my late acquaintance are going to be to me. No, sir, I think that, with your permission, I will confine my attentions to the excellent bird which I perceive upon the sideboard."

Sherlock Holmes glanced sharply across at me with a slight shrug of his shoulders.

"There is your hat, then, and there your bird," said he. "By the way, would it bore you to tell me where you got the other one from? I am somewhat of a fowl fancier, and I have seldom seen a better-grown goose."

"Certainly, sir," said Baker, who had risen and tucked his newly gained property under his arm. "There are a few of us who frequent the Alpha Inn, near the Museum — we are to be found in the Museum itself during the day, you understand. This year our good host, Windigate by name, instituted a goose-club, by which, on consideration of some few pence every week, we were each to receive a bird at Christmas. My pence were duly paid, and the rest is familiar to you. I am much indebted to you, sir, for a Scotch bonnet is fitted neither to my years nor my gravity." With a comical pomposity of manner he bowed solemnly to both of us and strode off upon his way.

"So much for Mr Henry Baker," said Holmes when he had closed the door behind him. "It is quite certain that he knows nothing whatever about the matter. Are you hungry, Watson?"

"Not particularly."

"Then I suggest that we turn our dinner into a supper and follow up this clue while it is still hot."

"By all means."

It was a bitter night, so we drew on our ulsters and wrapped cravats about our throats. Outside, the stars were shining coldly in a cloudless sky, and the breath of the passer-by blew out into smoke like so many pistol shots. Our footfalls rang out crisply and loudly as we swung through the doctors" quarter, Wimpole Street, Harley Street, and so through Wigmore Street into Oxford Street. In a quarter of an hour we were in Bloomsbury at the Alpha Inn, which is a small public-house at the corner of one of the streets which runs down into Holborn. Holmes pushed open the door of the private bar and ordered two glasses of beer from the ruddy-faced, white-aproned landlord.

"Your beer should be excellent if it is as good as your geese," said he.

"My geese!" The man seemed surprised.

"Yes. I was speaking only half an hour ago to Mr Henry Baker, who was a member of your goose-club."

"Ah! yes, I see. But you see, sir, them's not *our* geese."

"Indeed! Whose, then?"

"Well, I got the two dozen from a salesman in Covent Garden."

"Indeed? I know some of them. Which was it?"

"Breckinridge is his name."

"Ah! I don't know him. Well, here's your good health, landlord, and prosperity to your house. Good night."

"Now for Mr Breckinridge," he continued, buttoning up his coat as we came out into the frosty air. "Remember, Watson, that though we have so homely a thing as a goose at one end of this chain, we have at the other a man who will certainly get seven years' penal servitude unless we can establish his innocence. It is possible that our inquiry may but confirm his guilt; but in any case, we have a line of investigation which has been missed by the police, and which a singular chance has placed in our hand. Let us follow it out to the bitter end. Faces to the south, then, and quick march!"

We passed across Holborn, down Endell Street, and so through a zigzag of slums to Covent Garden Market. One of the largest stalls bore the name of Breckinridge upon it, and the proprietor, a horsy-looking man, with a sharp face and trim side-whiskers, was helping a boy to put up the shutters.

"Good evening. It's a cold night," said Holmes.

The salesman nodded and shot a questioning glance at my companion.

"Sold out of geese, I see," continued Holmes, pointing at the bare slabs of marble.

"Let you have five hundred tomorrow morning."

That's no good."

"Well, there are some on the stall with the gas flare."

"Ah, but I was recommended to you."

"Who by?"

"The landlord of the Alpha."

"Oh, yes; I sent him a couple of dozen."

"Fine birds they were, too. Now where did you get them from?"

To my surprise the question provoked a burst of anger from the salesman.

"Now, then, mister," said he, with his head cocked and his arms akimbo, "what are you driving at? Let's have it straight, now."

"It is straight enough. I should like to know who sold you the geese which you supplied to the Alpha."

"Well, then, I shan't tell you. So now!"

"Oh, it is a matter of no importance; but I don't know why you should be so warm over such a trifle."

"Warm! You'd be as warm, may be, if you were as pestered asI am. When I pay good money for a good article there should be an end to the business; but it's "Where are the geese?" and "Who did you sell the geese to?" and "What will you take for the geese?" One would think they were the only geese in the world, to hear the fuss that is made over them."

"Well, I have no connection with any other people who have been making inquiries," said Holmes carelessly. "If you won't tell us the bet is off, that is all. But I'm always ready to back my opinion on a matter of fowls, and I have a fiver on it that the bird I ate is country bred."

"Well, then, you've lost your fiver, for it's town bred," snapped the salesman.

"It's nothing of the kind."

"I say it is"

"I don't believe it."

"D'you think you know more about fowls than I, who have handled them ever since I was a nipper? I tell you, all those birds that went to the Alpha were town bred."

"You'll never persuade me to believe that."

"Will you bet, then?"

"It's merely taking your money, for I know that I am right. But I'll have a sovereign on with you, just to teach you not to be obstinate."

The salesman chuckled grimly. "Bring me the books, Bill," said he.

The small boy brought round a small thin volume and a great greasy-backed one, laying them out together beneath the hanging lamp.

"Now then, Mr Cocksure," said the salesman, "I thought that I was out of geese, but before I finish you'll find that there is still one left in my shop. You see this little book?"

"Well?"

"That's the list of the folk from whom I buy. D'you see? Well, then, here on this page are the country folk, and the numbers after their names are where their accounts are in the big ledger. Now, then! You see this other page in red ink? Well, that is a list of my town suppliers. Now, look at that third name. Just read it out to me."

"Mrs Oakshott, 117 Brixton Road — 249," read Holmes.

"Quite so. Now turn that up in the ledger."

Holmes turned to the page indicated. "Here you are, Mrs Oakshott, 117 Brixton Road, egg and poultry supplier."

"Now, then, what's the last entry?"

"December 22. Twenty-four geese at *7s 6d*."

"Quite so. There you are. And underneath?"

"Sold to Mr Windigate of the Alpha, at *12s*."

"What have you to say now?"

Sherlock Holmes looked deeply chagrined. He drew a sovereign from his pocket and threw it down upon the slab, turning away with the air of a man whose disgust was too deep for words. A few yards off he stopped under a lamp-post and laughed in the hearty, noiseless fashion which was peculiar to him.

"When you see a man with whiskers of that cut and the "Pink 'Un" protruding out of his pocket, you can always draw him by a bet," said he. "I dare say that if I had put a hundred pounds down in front of him, that man would not have given me such complete information as was drawn from him by the idea that he was doing me on a wager. Well, Watson, we are, I fancy, nearing the end of our quest, and the only point which remains to be determined is whether we should go on to this Mrs Oakshott tonight, or whether we should reserve it for tomorrow. It is clear from what that surly fellow said that there are others besides ourselves who are anxious about the matter, and I should—'

His remarks were suddenly cut short by a loud hubbub which broke out from the stall which we had just left. Turning round we saw a little rat-faced fellow standing in the centre of the circle of yellow light which was thrown by the swinging lamp, while Breckinridge, the salesman, framed in the door of his stall, was shaking his fists fiercely at the cringing figure.

"I've had enough of you and your geese," he shouted. "I wish you were all at the devil together. If you come pestering me any more with your silly talk I'll set the dog at you. You bring Mrs Oakshott here and I'll answer her, but what have you to do with it? Did I buy the geese off you?"

"No; but one of them was mine all the same," whined the little man.

"Well, then, ask Mrs Oakshott for it."

"She told me to ask you."

"Well, you can ask the King of Proosia, for all I care, I've had enough of it. Get out of this!" He rushed fiercely forward, and the inquirer fitted away into the darkness.

"Ha! this may save us a visit to Brixton Road," whispered Holmes. "Come with me, and we will see what is to be made of this fellow." Striding through the scattered knots of people who lounged round the flaring stalls, my companion speedily overtook the little man and touched him upon the shoulder. He sprang round, and I could see in the gaslight that every vestige of colour had been driven from his face.

"Who are you, then? What do you want?" he asked in a quavering voice.

"You will excuse me," said Holmes blandly, "but I could not help overhearing the questions which you put to the salesman just now. I think that I could be of assistance to you."

"You? Who are you? How could you know anything of the matter?"

"My name is Sherlock Holmes. It is my business to know what other people don't know."

"But you can know nothing of this?"

"Excuse me, I know everything of it. You are endeavouring to trace some geese which were sold by Mrs Oakshott, of Brixton Road, to a salesman named Breckinridge, by him in turn to Mr Windigate, of the Alpha, and by him to his club, of which Mr Henry Baker is a member."

"Oh, sir, you are the very man whom I have longed to meet," cried the littel fellow with outstretched hands and quivering fingers. "I can hardly explain to you how interested I am in this matter."

Sherlock Holmes hailed a four-wheeler which was passing. "In that case we had better discuss it in a cosy room rather than in this wind-swept market-place," said he. "But pray tell me, before we go farther, who it is that I have the pleasure of assisting."

The man hesitated for an instant. "My name is John Robinson," he answered with a sidelong glance.

"No, no; the real name," said Holmes sweetly. "It is always awkward doing business with an *alias*."

A flush sprang up the white cheeks of the stranger.

"Well, then," said he, "my real name is James Ryder."

"Precisely so. Head attendant at the Hotel Cosmopolitan. Pray step into the cab, and I shall soon be able to tell you everything which you would wish to know."

The little man stood glancing from one to the other of us with half-frightened, half-hopeful eyes, as one who is not sure whether he is on the verge of a windfall or of a catastrophe. Then he stepped into the cab, and in half an hour we were back in the sitting-room at Baker Street. Nothing had been said during our drive, but the high, thin breathing of our new companion, and the claspings and unclaspings of his hands, spoke of the nervous tension within him.

"Here we are!" said Holmes cheerily as we filed into the room. "The fire looks very seasonable in this weather. You look cold, Mr Ryder. Pray take the basket-chair. I will just put on my slippers before we settle this little matter of yours. Now, then! You want to know what became of those geese?"

"Yes, sir."

"Or rather, I fancy, of that goose. It was one bird, I imagine, in which you were interested — white, with a black bar across the tail."

Ryder quivered with emotion. "Oh, sir," he cried, "can you tell me where it went to?"

"It came here."

"Here?"

"Yes, and a most remarkable bird it proved. I don't wonder that you should take an interest in it. It laid an egg after it was dead — the bonniest, brightest, little blue egg that ever was seen. I have it here in my museum."

Our visitor staggered to his feet and clutched the mantelpiece with his right hand. Holmes unlocked his strong-box and held up the blue carbuncle, which shone out like a star with a cold, brilliant, many-pointed radiance. Ryder stood glaring with a drawn face uncertain whether to claim or to disown it.

"The game's up, Ryder," said Holmes quietly. "Hold up, man, or you'll be into the fire! Give him an arm back into his chair, Watson. He's not got blood enough to go in for felony with impunity. Give him a dash of brandy. So! Now he looks a little more human. What a shrimp it is, to be sure!"

For a moment he had straggered and nearly fallen but the brandy brought a tinge of colour into his cheeks, and he sat starting with frightened eyes at his accuser.

"I have almost every link in my hands, and all the proofs whicl could possibly need, so there is little which you need tell me. Still, that little may as well be cleared up to make the case complete. You had heard, Ryder, of this blue stone of the Countess of Morcar's?"

"It was Catherine Cusack who told me of it," said he in a crackling voice.

"I see. Her Ladyship's waiting-maid. Well, the temptation of sudden wealth so easily acquired was too much for you, as it has been for better men before you; but you were not very scrupulous in the means you used. It seems to me, Ryder, that there is the making of a very pretty villain in you. You knew that this man Horner, the plumber, had been concerned in some such matter before, and that suspicion would rest the more readily upon him. What did you do, then? You made some small job in my lady's room — you and your confederate Cusack —and you managed that he should be the man sent for. "Then, when he had left, you rifled the jewel-case, raised the alarm, and had this unfortunate man arrested. You then—"

Ryder threw himself down suddenly upon the rug and clutched at my companion's knees. "for God's sake, have mercy!" he shrieked. "Think of my father! Of my mother! I would break their hearts. I never went wrong before! I never will again. I swear it. I'll swear it on a Bible. Oh, don't bring it into court! For Christ's sake, don't!"

"Get back into your chair!" said Holmes sternly. "It is very well to cringe and crawl now, but you thought little enough of this poor Horner in the dock for a crime of which he knew nothing."

"I will fly, Mr Holmes. I will leave the country, sir. Then the charge against him will break down."

"Hum! We will talk about that. And now let us hear a true account of the next act. How came the stone into the goose, and how came the goose into the open market? Tell us the truth, for there lies your only hope of safety."

Ryder passed his tongue over his parched lips. "I will tell you just as it happened, sir," said he. "When Horner had been arrested, it seemed to me that it would be best for me to get away with the stone at once, for I did not know at what moment the police might not take it into their heads to search me and my room. There was no place about the hotel where it would be safe. I went out, as if on some commission, and I made for my sister's house. She had married a man named Oakshott, and lived in Brixton Road, where she fattened fowls for the market. All the way there every man I met seemed to me to be a policeman or a detective; and, for all that it was a cold night, the sweat was pouring down my face before I came to the Brixton Road. My sister asked me what was the matter, and why I was so pale; but I told her that I had been upset by the jewel robbery at the hotel. Then I went into the backyard and smoked a pipe, and wondered what it would be best to do.

"I had a friend once called Maudsley, who went to the bad, and has just been serving his time in Pentonville. One day he had met me, and fell into talk about the ways of thieves, and how they could get rid of what they stole. I knew that he would be true to me, for I knew one or two things about him; so I made up my mind to go right on to Kilburn, where he lived, and take him into my confidence. He would show me how to turn the stone into money. But how to get to him in safety? I thought of the agonies I had gone through in coming from the hotel. I might at any moment be seized and searched, and there would be the stone in my waistcoat pocket. I was leaning against the wall at the time and looking at the geese which were waddling about round my feet, and suddenly an idea came into my head which showed me how I could beat the best detective that ever lived.

"My sister had told me some weeks before that I might have the pick of her geese for a Christmas present and I knew that she was always as good as her word. I would take my goose now and in it I would carry my stone to Kilburn. There was a little shed in the yard, and behind this I drove one of the birds — a fine big one, white, with a barred tail. I caught it and, prying its bill open, I thrust the stone down its throat as far as my finger could reach. The bird gave a gulp, and I felt the stone pass along its gullet and down into its crop. But the creature flapped and struggled, and out came my sister to know what was the matter. As I turned to speak to her, the brute broke loose and fluttered off among the others.

"Whatever were you doing with that bird, Jem?" says she.

"Well," said I, "you said you'd give me one for Christmas, and I was feeling which was the fattest."

"Oh," says she, "we've set yours aside for you — Jem's bird, we call it. It's the big white one over yonder. There's twenty-six of them, which makes one for you, and one for us, and two dozen for the market."

"Thank you, Maggie," said I; "but if it is all the same to you, I'd rather have that one I was handling just now."

"The other is a good three pound heavier," she said, "and we fattened it expressly for you."

"Never mind. I'll have the other, and I'll take it now," said I.

"Oh, just as you like," said she, a little huffed. "Which is it you want, then?"

"That white one with the barred tail, right in the middle of the flock."

"Oh, very well. Kill it and take it with you."

"Well, I did what she said, Mr Holmes, and I carried the bird all the way to Kilburn. I told my pal what I had done, for he was a man that it was easy to tell a thing like that to. He laughed until he choked, and we got a knife and opened the goose. My heart turned to water, for there was no sign of the stone. I knew that some terrible mistake had occurred. I left the bird, rushed back to my sister's and hurried into the backyard. There was not a bird to be seen there.

"Where are they all, Maggie?" I cried.

"Gone to the dealer's, Jem."

"Which dealer's?"

"Breckinridge, of Covent Garden."

"But was there another with a barred tail?" I asked, "the same as the one I chose?"

"Yes, Jem; there were two barred-tailed ones, and I could never tell them apart."

"Well, then, of course I saw it all, and I ran off as hard as my feet would carry me to this man Breckinridge; but he had sold the lot at once, and not one word would he tell me as to where they had gone. You heard him yourselves tonight. Well, he had always answered me like that. My sister thinks that I am going mad. Sometimes I think that I am myself. And now — and now I am myself a branded thief, without ever having touched the wealth for which I sold my character. God help me! God help me!" He burst into convulsive sobbing, with his face buried in his hands.

There was a long silence, broken only by his heavy breathing, and by the measured tapping of Sherlock Holmes's finger-tips upon the edge of the table. Then my friend rose and threw open the door.

"Get out!" said he.

"What, sir! Oh, Heaven bless you!"

"No more words. Get out!"

And no more words were needed. There was rush, a clatter upon the stairs, the bang of a door, and the crisp rattle of running footfalls from the street.

"After all, Watson," said Holmes, reaching up his hand for his clay pipe, "I am not retained by the police to supply their deficiencies. If Horner were in danger it would be another thing; but this fellow will not appear against him, and the case must collapse. I suppose that I am commuting a felony, but it is just possible that I am saving a soul. This fellow will not go wrong again; he is too terribly frightened. Send him to jail now, and you make him a jail-bird for life. Besides, it is the season of forgiveness. Chance has put in our way a most singular and whimsical problem, and its solution is its own reward. If you will have the goodness to touch the bell, Doctor, we will begin another investigation in which, also, a bird will be the chief feature."

NOTES

carbuncle: a precious stone usually red; any of various types of red jewels especially a garnet; this particular carbuncle was, however, blue

commissionaire: a door-keeper in uniform; a uniformed attendant at the entrance to a cinema theatre, hotel etc

trophy: a token of an enemy's defeat; a prize (usually a cup) awarded in a sports contest

billycock: a round, low-crowned, soft felt hat

labyrinth: a network of narrow twisting passages

unimpeachable: blameless, the quality of which cannot be doubted

retrogression: return to an earlier or worse state

grizzled: greyish

cubic capacity: size, volume

crop: a special pouch—like enlargement of the gullet of many birds in which food is stored and partly digested

the Assizes: a meeting or meetings of a special court held by an important judge, travelling from one country to another

bureau: a large desk or a writing table with a wooden cover which slides over the top to close it; or a writing table with drawers for papers

morocco: a fine, tanned goat-skin leather

sinister: threatening, intending or leading to evil

vitriol: pure sulphuric acid which burns flesh deeply

geniality: quality of being cheerful, kind and good-tempered

staccato: made up of distinct sounds

disjecta membra: disjoined limbs

pomposity: the quality of being foolishly solemn and self-important

ulsters: a long loose heavy overcoat especially one with a belt

cravats: a neckcloth or scarf, a necktie

penal servitude: work imposed as punishment for crime

akimbo: with arms on hips and elbows bent outwards

warm: to become excited, disagreeable or uncomfortable

snapped: to speak or utter sharply as in anger

nipper: (slang) a small child

Mr Cocksure: said derisively of Holmes who claimed to be very sure of himself

cringing: to draw back, bend, crouch etc as when afraid to act, to act in a timid and servile manner

Proosia: Prussia

felony: a serious crime

impunity: freedom from punishment

shrimp: (colloq.) a small or insignificant person

crackling: making repeated small, sharp and sudden sounds

scrupulous: conscientiously honest; a person who pays careful attention to what is right or proper

rifled: search through and stole everything valuable out of a place

has been serving his term in Pentonville: has been undergoing imprisonment in jail

waddling: to walk with short steps

prying: raising, moving, lifting

gullet: throat, food pipe from mouth to stomach

huffed: offended

retained: employed, engaged

commuting: to make a punishment less severe

another investigation.....chief feature: carving and eating the woodcock which Sherlock Holmes' housekeeper Mrs Hudson had cooked for dinner.

LANGUAGE STUDY

1. Fill in the blanks in the following sentences by selecting and using words from the box given below. The box contains two extra words which are not required in these sentences:
   a. The dog ______ up its ears on hearing a noise in the adjacent room
   b. I suddenly yielded to the ______ to miss that flight.
   c. It ______ me deeply to know that the gift I had sent her had been, by mistake, delivered to her mother.
   d. As the ship was sinking a number of thoughts ______ through his mind.
   e. Heavy artillery fire ______ the town for more than an hour.
   f. There is not a ______ of truth in your story.
   g. I invited my friend to tea but he ______ told me that he was engaged in the evening.
   h. I have had a ______ in the form of a rich inheritance from my deceased uncle.
   i. A ______ fear gripped him and he stood shaking all over.
   j. His writings are full of ______ dialogue.

Flitted, blandly, chagrined, vestige, impulse, windfall, convulsive, pestered, battered, scintillating, cocked, trivial

2. Match the words in List A with the meanings indicated in List B. Then use these words in sentences of your own.

List A	ListB
putty	to determine, to decide from general principles to a particular thing or fact
plausible	fanciful, with strange ideas
to abstract	showing that one is sorry about it
whimsical	needing long sitting and only slight activity
ingenious	seeming to be true or reasonable
to deduce	having or showing cleverness in making or inventing things
ruefully	animal fat used for making candles
tallow	soft, easily shaped pale-coloured oily paste
to rummage	to remove by drawing out gently
sedentary	to turn things over and look into all the corners while trying to find something.

COMPOSITION

1. What does Sherlock Holmes mean when he says that most of us can see everything but we fail to reason from what we can see? Do you agree with this statement?
2. Do you agree with the assessment that there is no mystery in this story and that everything is based on cool reasoning and commonplace human psychology?
3. What are the qualities that make Sherlock Holmes such a clever and successful detective?
4. Narrate in your own words a good detective story that you have read.

GRAMMAR

See Appendix II, page 186.

Ultima Thule

J. GALSWORTHY

Ultima Thule! The words come into my head this winter night. That is why I write down the story, as I know it, of a little old friend.

I used to see him first in Kensington Gardens, where he came in the afternoons, accompanied by a very small girl. One would see them silent before a shrub or flower, or with their heads inclined to heaven before a tree, or leaning above water and the ducks, or stretched on their stomachs watching a beetle, or on their backs watching the sky. Often they would stand holding crumbs out to the birds, who would perch about them, and even drop on their arms little white marks of affection and esteem. They were admittedly a noticeable couple. The child, who was fair-haired and elfin-like, with dark eyes and a pointed chin, wore clothes that seemed somewhat hard put to it. And, if the two were not standing still, she went along pulling at his hand, eager to get there; and, since he was a very little, light old man, he seemed always in advance of his own feet. He was garbed if I remember, in a daverdy brown overcoat and broad-brimmed soft grey hat, and his trousers, what was visible of them, were tucked into half length black gaiters which tried to join with very old brown shoes. Indeed, his costume did not indicate any great share of prosperity. But it was his face that reveted attention. Thin, cherry-red, and wind-dried as old wood, it had a special sort of brightness, with its spikes and waves of silvery hair, and blue eyes which seemed to shine. Rather mad, I used to think. Standing by the rails of an enclosure, with his withered lips pursed and his cheeks drawn in till you would think the wind might blow through them, he would emit the most enticing trills and pipings, exactly imitating various birds.

Those who rouse our interest are generally the last people we speak to, for interest seems to set up a kind of special shyness; so it was long before I made his acquaintance. But one day by the Serpentine, I saw him coming along alone, looking sad, but still with that queer brightness about him. He sat down on my bench with his little dried hands on his thin little knees, and began talking to himself in a sort of whisper. Presently I caught the words: "God cannot be like us." And for fear that he might go on uttering such precious remarks that were obviously not intended to be heard, I had either to go away or else address him. So, on an impulse, I said:

"Why?"

He turned without surprise.

"I've lost my landlady's little girl," he said. "Dead! And only seven years old."

"That little thing I used to watch you with?"

"Did you? Did you? I'm glad you saw her."

"I used to see you looking at flowers, and trees and those ducks."

His face brightened wistfully. "Yes; she was a great companion to an old man like me." And he relapsed into his contemplation of the water. He had a curious, precise way of speaking, that matched his pipchinesque little old face. At last he again turned to me those blue youthful eyes which seemed to shine out of a perfect little nest of crow's feet.

"We were great friends! But I couldn't expect it. Things don't last, do they?" I was glad to notice that his voice was getting cheerful. "When I was in the orchestra at the Harmony Theatre, it never used to occur to me that some day I shouldn't play there any more. One felt like a bird. That's the beauty of music, sir. You lose yourself; like that blackbird there." He imitated the note of a blackbird so perfectly that I could have sworn the bird started.

"Birds and flowers! Wonderful things; wonderful! Why, even a buttercup—!" He pointed at one of those little golden flowers with his toe. "Did you ever see such a marvellous thing?" And he turned his face up at me. "And yet, somebody told me once that they don't agree with cows. How can that be? I'm not a countryman — though I was born at Kingston."

"The cows do well enough on them," I said, "in my part of the world. In fact, the farmers say they like to see buttercups."

"I'm glad to hear you say that. I was always sorry to think they disagreed."

When I got up to go, he rose, too.

"I take it as very kind of you," he said, "to have spoken to me."

"The pleasure was mine. I am generally to be found hereabouts in the afternoons any time you like a talk."

"Delighted," he said; "delighted. I make friends of the creatures and flowers as much as possible, but they can't always make us understand." And after we had taken off our respective hats, he reseated himself, with his hands on his knees.

Next time I came across him standing by the rails of an enclosure, and, in his arms, and old and really wretched-looking cat.

"I don't like boys," he said, without preliminary of any sort. "What do you think they were doing to this poor old cat? Dragging it along by a string to drown it; see where it's cut into the fur! I think boys despise the old and weak!" He held it out to me. At the ends of those little sticks of arms the beast looked more dead than alive: I had never seen a more miserable creature.

"I think a cat," he said, "is one of the most marvellous things in the world. Such a depth of life in it."

And, as he spoke, the cat opened its mouth as if protesting at that assertion. It was the sorriest-looking beast.

"What are you going to do with it?"

"Take it home; it looks to me as if it might die."

"You don't think that might be more merciful?"

"It depends; it depends. I shall see. I fancy a little kindness might do a great deal for it. It's got plenty of spirit. I can see from its eye."

"May I come along with you a bit?"

"Oh!" he said; "delighted."

We walked on side by side, exciting the derision of nearly everyone we passed — his face looked so like a mother's when she is feeding her baby!

"You'll find this'll be quite a different cat tomorrow," he said. "I shall have to get in, though, without my landlady seeing, a funny woman! I have two or three strays already."

"Can I help in any way?"

"Thank you," he said. "I shall ring the are a bell, and as she comes out below I shall go in above. She'll think it's boys. They are like that."

"But doesn't she do your rooms, or anything?"

A smile puckered his face. "I've only one; I do it myself. Oh, it'd never do to have her about, even if I could afford it. But, " he added, "if you're so kind as to come with me to the door, you might engage her by asking where Mr. Thompson lives. That's me. In the musical world my name was Moronelli; not that I have Italian blood in me, of course."

"And shall I come up?"

"Honoured; but I live very quietly."

We passed out of the gardens at Lancaster Gate, where all the house-fronts seem so successful, and out of it into a little street that was extremely like grubby child trying to hide under its mother's skirts. Here he took a newspaper from his pocket and wrapped it round the cat.

"She's a funny woman," he repeated; "Scotch descent, you know." Suddenly he pulled an area bell and scuttled up the steps.

When he had opened the door, however, I saw before him in the hall a short, thin woman dressed in black, with a sharp and bumpy face. Her voice sounded brisk and resolute.

"What have you got there, Mr. Thompson?"

"Newspaper, Mrs. March."

"Oh, indeed! Now you're not going to take that cat upstairs!"

The little old fellow's voice acquired a sudden shrill determination. "Stand aside, please. If you stop me, I'll give you notice. The cat is going up. It's ill, and it is going up."

It was then I said:

"Does Mr. Thompson live here?"

In that second he shot past her, and ascended.

"That's him," she said; "and I wish it wasn't, with his dirty cats. Do you want him?"

"I do."

"He lives at the top." Then, with a grudging apology: "I can't help it; he tries me — he's very trying."

"I am sure he is."

She looked at me. The longing to talk that comes over those who answer bells all day, and the peculiar Scottish desire to justify oneself, rose together in that face which seemed all promontories dried by an east wind.

"Ah" she said; "he is. I don't deny his heart; but he's got no sense of anything. Goodness knows what he hasn't got up there. I wonder I keep him. An old man like that ought to know better; half-starving himself to feed them." She paused, and her eyes, which had a cold and honest glitter, searched me closely.

"If you're going up," she said, "I hope you'll give him good advice. He never lets me in. I wonder I keep him."

There were three flights of stairs, narrow, clean and smelling of oilcloth. Selecting one of two doors at random, I knocked. His silvery head and bright, pinched face were cautiously poked out.

"Ah!" he said; "I thought it might be her!"

The room, which was fairly large, had a bare floor with little on it save a camp-bed and chest of drawers with jug and basin. A large bird-cage on the wall hung wide open. The place smelt of soap and a little of beasts and birds. Into the walls, whitewashed over a green wall paper which stared through in places, were driven nails with their heads knocked off, on to which bits of wood had been spiked, so that they stood out as bird-perches high above the ground. Over the open window a piece of wire-netting had been fixed. A little spirit-stove and an old dressing-gown hanging on a peg completed the accoutrements of a room which one entered with a certain diffidence. He had not exaggerated. Besides the new cat, there were three other cats and four birds, — all save one, a bullfinch — invalids. The cats kept close to the walls avoiding me, but wherever my little old friend went they followed him with their eyes. The birds were in the cage, except the bullfinch, which had perched on his shoulder.

"How on earth," I said, "do you manage to keep cats and birds in one room?"

"There is danger," he answered, "but I have not had a disaster yet. Till their legs or wings are mended, they hardly come out of the cage; and after that they keep up on my perches. But they don't stay long, you know, when they're once well. That wire is only put over the window while they're mending; it'll be off tomorrow for this lot."

"And then they'll go?"

"Yes. The sparrow first, and then the two thrushes."

"And this fellow?"

"Ask him," he said. "Would you go, bully?" But the bull finch did not design to answer.

"And were all those cats, too, in trouble?"

"Yes," he said. "They wouldn't want me if they weren't."

Thereupon he began to warm some blue-looking milk, contemplating the new cat, which he had placed in a round basket close to the little stove, while the bullfinch sat on his head. It seemed time to go.

"Delighted to see you, sir," he said, "any day." And, pointing up at the bullfinch on his head, he added: "Did you ever see anything so wonderful as that bird? The size of its heart! Really marvellours."

To the rapt sound of that word marvellous, and full of the memory of his mysterious brightness while he stood pointing upward to the bird perched on his thick, silvery hair, I went.

The landlady was still at the bottom of the stairs, and began at once: "So you found him! I don't know why I keep him. Of course, he was kind to my little girl." I saw tears gather in her eyes.

"With his cats and his birds, I wonder I keep him! But where would he go? He's no relations, and no friend — not a friend in the world, I think! He's a character. Lives on air — feeding them cats! I've no patience with them, eating him up. He never lets me in. Cats and birds! I wonder I keep him. Losing himself for those rubbishy things! It's my belief he was always like that; and that's why he never got on. He's no sense of anything."

And she gave me a shrewd look, wondering, no doubt, what the deuce I had come about.

I did not come across him again in the gardens for some time, and went at last to pay him a call. At the entrance to a mews just round the corner of his grubby, side street, I found a lot of people collected round one of those bears that are sometimes led through the less conspicuous streets of our huge towns. The yellowish beast was sitting up in deference to its master's rod, uttering little grunts, and moving its uplifted snout from side to side, in the way bears have. But it seemed to be extracting more amusement than money from its audience.

"Let your bear down off its hind legs and I'll give you a penny." And suddenly I saw my little old friend under his flopping grey hat, amongst the spectators, all taller than himself.

But the bear's master only grinned and prodded the animal in the chest. He evidently knew a good thing when he saw it.

"I'll give you two pence to let him down."

Again the bear-man grinned. "More!" he said, and again prodded the bear's chest. The spectators were laughing now.

"Three pence! And if you don't let him down for that, I'll hit you in the eye."

The bear-man held out his hand. "All-a-right," he said, "three pence: I let him down."

I saw the coins pass and the beast dropping on his fore-feet; but just then a policeman coming in sight, the man led his bear off, and I was left alone with my little old friend.

"I wish I had that poor bear," he said; "I could teach him to be happy. But, even if I could buy him, what could I do with him up there? She's such a funny woman."

He looked quite dim, but brightened as we went along.

"A bear," he said, "is really an extraordinary animal. What wise little eyes he had! I do think he's a marvellous creation! My cats will have to go without their dinner, though. I was going to buy it with that threepence."

I begged to be allowed the privilege.

"Willingly!" he said. "Shall we go in here? They like cod's head best."

While we stood waiting to be served I saw the usual derisive smile pass over the fishmonger's face. But my little old friend by no means noticed it; he was too busy looking at the fish. "A fish is a marvellous thing, when you come to think of it," he murmured. "Look at its scales. Did you ever see such mechanism?"

We bought five cod's heads, and I left him carrying them in a bag, evidently lost in the anticipation of five cats eating them.

After that I saw him often, going with him sometimes to buy food for his cats, which seemed ever to increase in numbers. His talk was always of his strays, and the marvels of creation, and that time of his life when he played the flute at the Harmony Theatre. He had been out of a job, it seemed, for more than ten years; and when questioned, only sighed and answered "Don't talk about it, please?"

His bumpy landlady never failed to favour me with a little conversation. She was one of those women who have terrific consciences, and terrible grudges against them.

"I never get out," she would say.

"Why not?"

"Couldn't leave the house."

"It won't run away!"

But she would look at me as if she thought it might, and repeat:

"Oh! I never get out."

An extremely Scottish temperament.

Considering her descent, however, she was curiously devoid of success, struggling on apparently from week to week, cleaning, and answering the bell, and never getting out, and wondering why she kept my little old friend; just as he struggled on from week to week, getting out and collecting strays, and discovering the marvels of creation, and finding her a funny woman. Their hands were joined, one must suppose, by that dead child.

One July afternoon, however, I found her very much upset. He had been taken dangerously ill three days before.

"There he is," she said; "can't touch a thing. It's my belief he's done for himself, giving his food away all these years to those cats of his. I shooed 'em out to-day, the nasty creatures; they won't get in again."

"Oh!" I said "you shouldn't have done that. It'll only make him miserable."

She flounced her head up. "Hoh!" she said; "I wonder I've kept him all this time, with his birds and his cats dirtying my house. And there he lies, taling gibberish about them. He made me write to a Mr. Jackson, of some theatre or other — I've no patience with him. And that little bullfinch all the time perching on his pillow, the dirty little thing! I'd have turned it out, too, only it wouldn't let me catch it."

"What does the doctor say?"

"Double pneumonia — caught it getting his feet wet, after some stray, I'll be bound. I'm nursing him. There has to be someone with him all the time."

He was lying very still when I went up, with the sunlight falling across the foot of his bed, and sure enough, the bullfinch perching on his pillow. In that high fever he looked brighter than ever. He was not exactly delirious, yet not exactly master of his thoughts.

"Mr. Jackson! He'll be here soon. Mr. Jackson! He'll do it for me. I can ask him, if I die. A funny woman. I don't want to eat;

I'm not a great eater — I want my breath, that's all."

At the sound of his voice the bullfinch fluttered off the pillow and flew round and round the room, as if alarmed at something new in the tones that were coming from its master.

Then he seemed to recognize me. "I think I'm going to die," he said; "I'm very weak. It's lucky there's nobody to mind. If only he'd come soon. I wish" — and he raised himself with feeble excitement — "I wish you'd take that wire off the window; I want my cats. She turned them out. I want him to promise me to take them, and bully-boy, and feed them with my money, when I'm dead."

Seeing that excitement was certainly worse for him than cats, I took the wire off. He fell back, quiet at once; and presently, first one and then another cat came stealing in, till there were four or five seated against the walls. The moment he ceased to speak the bullfinch, too came back to his pillow. His eyes looked most supernaturally bright, staring out of his little, withered-up old face at the sunlight playing on his bed; he said just audibly: "Did you ever see anything more wonderful than that sunlight? It's really marvellous!" After that he fell into a sort of doze or stupor. And I continued to sit there in the window, relieved, but rather humiliated, that he had not asked me to take care of his cats and bullfinch.

Presently there came the sound of motor-car in the little street below. And almost at once the landlady appeared. For such an abrupt woman, she entered very softly.

"Here he is," he whispered.

I went out and found a gentleman, perhaps sixty years of age, in a black coat, buff waistcoat, gold watch chain, light trousers, patent-leather boots, and a wonderfully shining hat. His face was plump and red, with a glossy grey moustache; indeed, he seemed to shine everywhere, save in the eyes, which were of a dull and somewhat liverish hue.

"Mr. Jackson?"

"The same. How is the little old chap?"

Opening the door of the next room, which I knew was always empty, I beckoned Mr. Jackson in.

"He's really very ill; I'd better tell you what he wants to see you about."

He looked at me with that air of "You can't get at me

—whoever you may be," which belongs to the very successful.

"Right-o!" he said. "Well?"

I described the situation. "He seems to think," I ended, "that you'll be kind enough to charge yourself with his strays, in case he should die."

Mr. Jackson prodded the unpainted wash stand with his gold-headed cane.

"Is he really going to kick it?"

"I'm afraid so; he's nothing but skin, bone, and spirit, as it is."

"H'm Stray cats, you say, and a bird. Well, there's no accounting. He was always a cracky little chap. So that's it! When I got the letter I wondered what the deuce! We pay him his five quid a quarter regular to this day. To tell truth, he deserved it. Thirty years he was at our shop; never missed a night. First-rate flute he was. He ought never to have given it up, though I always thought it showed a bit of heart in him. If a man don't look after number one, he's as good as gone; that's what I've always found. Why, I was no more than he was when I started. Shouldn't have been worth a plum if I'd gone on his plan, that's certain." And he gave that profound chuckle which comes from the very stomach of success. "We were having a rocky time at the Harmony; had to cut down everything we could — music, well, that came about first. Little old Moronelli, as we used to call him—old Italian days before English names came in, you know — he was far the best of the flutes; so I went to him and said: "Look here, Moronelli, which of these other boys had better go?" "Oh" he said — I remember his funny little old mug now —"has one of them to go, Mr. Jackson? Timminsa" — that was the elder — "he's a wife and family; and Smetoni" — Smith, you know —"he's only a boy. Times are bad for flutes." "I know it's a bit hard," I said, "but this theatre's goin' to be run much cheaper, one of 'em's got to get." "Oh!" he said, "dear me!" he said. What a funny little old chap it was! Well — what do you think? Next day I had his resignation. Give you my word I did my best to turn him. Why, he was sixty then if he was a day — at sixty a man don't get jobs in a hurry. But, not a bit of it ! All he'd say was: "I shall get a place all right!" But that's it, you know — he never did. Too long in one shop. I heard by accident he was on the rocks; that's how I make him that allowance. But that's the sort of hopeless little old chap he is

— no idea of himself. Cats! Why not! I'll take his old cats on; don't you let him worry about that. I'll see to his bird, too. If I can't give 'em a better time than ever they have here, it'll be funny!" And, looking round the little empty room, he again uttered that profound chuckle: "Why, he was with us at the Harmony thirty years — that's time, you know; I made my fortune in it."

"I am sure," I said, "it'll be a great relief to him."

"Oh! Ah! that's all right. You come down to my place" — he handed me a card: "Mr. Cyril Porteous Jackson, Ultima Thule, Wimbledon" — "and see how I fix 'em up. But if he's really going to kick it, I'd like to have a look at the little old chap, just for old times' sake."

We went, as quietly as Mr. Jackson's bright boots would permit, into his room, where the landlady was sitting gazing angrily at the cats. She went out without noise, flouncing her head as much as to say: "Well, now you can see what I have to go through, sitting up here. I never get out."

Our little old friend was still in that curious stupor. He seemed unconscious, but his blue eyes were not closed, staring brightly out before them at things we did not see. With his silvery hair and his flushed frailty, he had an unearthly look. After standing perhaps three minutes at the foot of the bed, Mr. Jackson whispered:

"Well, he does look queer. Poor little old chap! You tell him from me I'll look after his cats and bird: he needn't worry. And now, I think I won't keep the car. Makes me feel a bit throaty, you know. Don't move; he might come to."

And, leaning all the weight of his substantial form on those bright and creaking toes, he made his way to the door, flashed at me a diamond ring, whispered hoarsely: "So long! That'll be all right!" and vanished. And soon I heard the whirring of his car and just saw the top of his shiny hat travelling down the little street.

Sometimes I sat on there, wanting to deliver that message. An uncanny vigil in the failing light, with those five cats — yes, five at least — lying or sitting, against the walls, staring like sphinxes at their motionless protector. I could not make out whether it was he in his stupor with his bright eyes that fascinated them, or the bullfinch perched on his pillow, who they knew perhaps might soon be in their power. I was glad when the landlady came up and I could leave the message with her.

When she opened the door to me next day at six o'clock I knew that he was gone. There was about her that sorrowful, unmistakable importance, that peculiar mournful excitement, which hovers over houses where death has entered.

"Yes," she said, "he went this morning. Never came round after you left. Would you like to see him?"

We went up.

He lay, covered with a sheet, in the darkened room. The landlady pulled the window-curtains apart. His face, as white now almost as his silvery head, had in the sunlight a radiance like that of small, bright angel gone to sleep. No growth of hair, such as comes on most dead faces, showed on those frail cheeks that were now smooth and lineless as porcelain. And on the sheet above his chest the bullfinch sat, looking into his face.

The landlady let the curtains fall, and we went out.

"I've got the cats in here" — she pointed to the room where Mr. Jackson and I had talked — "all ready for that gentleman when he sends. But that little bird, I don't know what to do; he won't let me catch him, and there he sits. It makes me feel all funny."

It had made me feel all funny, too.

"He hasn't left the money for his funeral. Dreadful, the way he never thought about himself. I'm glad I kept him, though." And, not to my astonishment, she suddenly began to cry.

A wire was sent to Mr. Jackson, and on the day of the funeral I went down to "Ultima Thule", Wimbledon, to see if he had carried out his promise.

He had. In the grounds, past the vinery, an out-house had been cleaned and sanded, with cushions placed at intervals against the wall, and a little trough of milk. Nothing could have been more suitable or luxurious.

"How's that", he said. "I've done it thoroughly." But I noticed that he looked a little glum.

"The only thing," he said, "is the cats. First night they seemed all right; and the second, there were three of 'em left. But to-day the gardener tells me there's not the ghost of one anywhere. It's not for want of feeding. They've had tripe, and liver, and milk — as much as ever they liked. And cod's heads, you know

—they're very fond of them. I must say it's a bit of a disappointment to me."

As he spoke, a sandy cat, which I perfectly remembered, for it had only half its left ear, appeared in the doorway, and stood, crouching, with its green eyes turned on us; then, hearing Mr. Jackson murmur, "Puss, puss!" it ran for its life slinking almost into the ground, and vanished among some shrubs.

Mr. Jackson sighed. "Perversity of the brutes!" he said. He led me back to the house through a conservatory full of choice orchids. A gilt bird cage was hanging there, one of the largest I had ever seen, replete with every luxury the heart of bird could want.

"Is that for the bullfinch?" I asked him.

"Oh!" he said; "didn't you know? The little beggar wouldn't himself be caught, and the second morning when they went up, there he lay on the old chap's body, dead. I thought it was very touchin''. But I kept the cage hung up for you to see that I should have given him a good time here. Oh, yes, "Ultima Thule" would have done him well!"

And from a bright leather case Mr. Jackson offered me a cigar.

The question I had long been wishing to ask him slipped out of me then:

"Do you mind telling me why you called your house 'Ultima Thule'?"

"Why?" he said. "Found it on the gate. Think it's rather distingue; don't you?" and he uttered his profound chuckle.

"First-rate. The whole place is the last word in comfort."

"Very good of you to say so," he said. "I've laid out a goodish bit on it. A man must have a warm corner to end his days in. 'Ultima Thule', as you say — it isn't bad. There's success about it, somehow."

And with that word in my ears, and in my eyes a vision of the little old fellow in his "Ultima Thule", with the bullfinch lying dead on a heart that had never known success, I travelled back to town.

NOTES

little white marks: bird droppings
garbed: dressed

daverdy: faded

gaiters: cloth or leather covering for the leg from knee to ankles

trills: shaky or vibrating sound made by the voice or as in a bird song

pipchinseque: From Mrs. Pipchin a boarding-house keeper at Brighton; a character in Dickens' novel *Dombey And Son*

buttercup: a wild plant with yellow flowers

puckered: to draw or come together into small folds or wrinkles

grubby: dirty, unwashed

scuttled: hurried flight or departure, cowardly avoidance of or running away from difficulties or dangers

promontory: headland, high point of land standing out from the coastline

pinched face: a face with sunken cheeks

accoutrements: outfit, equipment etc. for military service

bullfinch: a small song bird with rounded beak and brightly coloured feathers

mending: to regain health, to heal

thrushes: songbirds

deign: be kind or gracious enough to

mews: stables or carriage houses converted into dwellings, grouped around a court or oblong street

flopping: to move or fall clumsily or helplessly

gibberish: meaningless sounds, unintelligible talk

flounced: jerked impatiently

delirium: suffering from violent mental disturbance often accompanied by wild talk especially during feverish illness

stupor: almost unconscious condition

kick it: to die. The idiom is "to kick the bucket"

quid: pound

plum: a sum of £100,000

on the rocks: (of a person) very short of money

throaty: uttered deep in the throat, husky, hoarse

to come to: to recover consciousness

substantial: largely or strongly built

uncanny: unnatural, mysterious

Sphinx: A stone statue in Egypt, with a lion's body and a woman's head; a person who keeps his thoughts and intentions secret

the vinery: greenhouse for growing grapes

tripe: part of the wall of the stomach of an ox or cow used as food

sandy: (of hair) yellowish-red

slinking: to go or move away in a secret or guilty manner

perversity: (of behaviour) contrary to reason

conservatory: building with glass walls and roof in which plants are protected from cold

distingue: distinguished, having an air of distinction.

COMPREHENSION

1. What was noticeable about the old man and his companion? Who was the old man's companion?
2. Why did the old man, a few days later, come alone along the Serpentine?
3. Why didn't the old man like boys? What were the boys doing?
4. What did the old man do to the injured cat? Why didn't he let it die?
5. How did people react on seeing the old man with an injured cat in his arms?
6. How did the old man manage to take the injured cat to his room upstairs?
7. What did the author see in the old man's room?
8. What did the old man do to the creatures after they had fully recovered?
9. Why did the old man demand that the bear be let down off its hind legs?
10. Why did the fishmonger smile when the old man and the author went to his shop to buy cod's heads?
11. Why did the old man resign his job in the orchestra at the Harmony Theatre?
12. What is the meaning of "Ultima Thule"? Why was Jackson's house called "Ultima Thule"?
13. Did the old man's pet strays live happily at "Ultima Thule" after the old man's death? What happened to them?
14. The landlady didn't like the old man's habits and yet she

said after his death, "I am glad I kept him though." How do you account for this contradictory attitude of hers?

15. Do the events in the story justify the name "Ultima Thule" given to Mr. Jackson's house? Which was the real "Ultima Thule"?

LANGUAGE STUDY

1. Find words in the story which have the following meanings. Choose the words from the box given below:

   to hate, to hurry up, determined, to climb up, to fall back into the old state, to attract, surprise, full of ridicule, an earnest desire, clever, full of, lack of confidence, an an animal lost from its home, wonderful.

detest, diffidence, strays, astonishment, marvellous, fascinate, derision, shrewd, longing, scuttle, relapse, resolute, despise, ascend, replete with.

2. Use the following words in sentences of your own both as verbs and as nouns:

   back, watch, perch, search, thought, look, touch, master, want, stomach, time.

3. Add a suitable prefix to each of the following words to make words having the opposite meaning:

inclined	accompanied	enclosed
precise	expected	perfect
pleasure	engage	successful
resolute	determination	justified
conspicuous	harmony	carry

COMPOSITION

1. What type of a person was this old man? What do you think of him?
2. What is real happiness? Can money alone bring it?

3. What was the old man's philosophy of life. Do you agree with his philosophy? Give reasons for your answer.
4. If you had the authority, what steps would you like to take to make people happy?
5. To what extent has science added to human happiness?
6. Do you agree with view that it is very often the poor who sincerely try to help the needy and very often it is the unhappy who try to give happiness to others. Give reasons for your answer.
7. Are you in favour of discovering new drugs that could make men forget their worries and make them happy? Give a reasoned answer.

GRAMMAR

See Appendix II, page 189.

Grief

ANTON CHEKOV

"To whom shall I tell my grief?"

It is twilight. A thick wet snow is slowly twirling around the newly lighted street-lamps, and lying in soft thin layers on the roofs, the horses' backs, people's shoulders and hats. The cab-driver, Iona Potapov, is quite white, and looks like a phantom; he is bent double as far as a human body can bend double; he is seated on his box, and never makes a move. If a whole snowdrift fell on him, it seems as if he would not find it necessary to shake it off. His little horse is also quite white and remains motionless; its immobility, its angularity, and its straight wooden-looking legs, even close by give it the appearance of a ginger-bread horse worth a kopech. It is, no doubt, plunged in deep thought. If you were snatched from the plough, from your usual grey surroundings, and were thrown into this slough full of monstrous lights, unceasing noise and hurrying people, you too would find it difficult not to think.

Iona and his little horse have not moved from their place for a long while. They left their yard before dinner, and up to now, not a 'fare'. The evening mist is descending over the town, the white lights of the lamps are replacing brighter rays, and the hubbub of the street is getting louder. "Cabby, for Viborg way!" suddenly hears Iona. 'Cabby!'

Iona jumps, and through his snow-covered eyelashes, sees an officer in a greatcoat, with his hood over his head.

"Viborg way!" the officer repeats. "Are you asleep, eh? Viborg way!"

With a nod of assent Iona picks up the reins, in consequence of which layers of snow slip off the horse's back and neck. The officer seats himself in the sleigh, the cab-driver smacks his lips to encourage his horse, stretches out his neck, like a swan, sits up, and, more from habit than necessity, brandishes his whip. The little horse also stretches his neck, bends his wooden-looking legs, and makes a move undecidedly.

"What are you doing, were-wolf!" is the exclamation Iona hears, from the dark mass moving to and fro as soon as they start. "Where the devil are you going? To the r-r-right!"

"You do not know how to drive. Keep to the right!" calls the officer angrily.

A coachman from a private carriage swears at him; a passer-by, who has run across the road and rubbed his shoulder against the horse's nose, looks at him furiously as he sweeps the snow from his sleeve. Iona shifts about on his seat as if he were on needles, moves his elbows as if he were trying to keep his equilibrium, and gapes about like someone suffocating, who does not understand why and wherefore he is there.

"What scoundrels they all are!" jokes the officer; "one would think they had all entered into an agreement to jostle you or fall under your horse."

Iona looks round at the officer and moves his lips. He evidently wants to say something, but the only sound that issues is a snuffle.

"What?" asks the officer.

Iona twists his mouth into a smile, and with an effort says hoarsely:

"My son, Barin, died this week."

"Hm! What did he die of?

Iona turns with his whole body towards his fare, and says: "And who knows! They say high fever. He was three days in hospital and then died... God's will be done."

"Turn round! The devil!" sounded from the darkness. "Have you popped off, old doggie, eh? Use your eyes!"

"Go on, go on," said the officer, "otherwise we shall not get there by tomorrow. Hurry a bit!"

The cab-driver again stretches his neck, sits up, and with a bad grace, brandishes his whip. Several times again he turns to look at his fare, but the latter has closed his eyes, and apparently is not disposed to listen. Having deposited the officer in the Viborg, he stops by the tavern, doubles himself up on his seat, and again remains motionless, while the snow once more begins to cover him and his horse. An hour, and another... Then, along the footpath, with a squeak of goloshes, and quarrelling, come three young men, two of them tall and lanky, the third one short and hump-backed.

"Cabby, to the Police Bridge!" in a cracked voice calls the hump-back. "The three of us for two grivenicks!"

Iona picks up his reins, and smacks his lips. Two grivenicks is not a fair price, but he does not mind if it is a ruble or five kopecks — to him it is all the same now, so long as they are wayfarers. The young men, jostling each other and using bad language, approach the sleigh, and all three at once try to get on to the seat; then begins a discussion which two shall sit and who shall be the one to stand. After wrangling, abusing each other, and much petulance, it is at last decided that the hump-back should stand, as he is the smallest.

"Now then, hurry up!" says the hump-back in a twanging voice, as he takes his place, and breathes in Iona's neck. "Old Furry. Here, mate, what a cab you have got, there is not a worse one to be found in all Petersburg!..."

"Hi-hi-hi-hi," giggles Iona. "Such a..."

"Now you, 'sucha', hurry up, are you going the whole way at this place? Are you?... Do you want it in the neck?"

"My head feels like bursting," says one of the lanky ones. "Last night at the Donkmasovs, Vaska and I drank the whole of four bottles of cognac."

"I don't understand what you lie for," says the other lanky one angrily; "you lie like a brute."

"God strike me, it's the truth!"

"It's as much a truth as that a louse coughs!"

"Hi, hi," grins Iona, "what gay young gentlemen!"

"Pshaw, go to the devil!" indignantly says the hump-back. "Are you going to get on or not, you old pest? Is that the way to drive? Use the whip a bit. Go on, devil, go on, give it him well!"

Iona feels at his back the little man wriggling, and the tremble in his voice. He listens to the insults hurled at him, sees the people, and little by little the feeling of loneliness leaves him. The hump-back goes on swearing until he gets mixed up in some elaborate six-foot oath, or chokes with coughing. The lankies begin to talk about a certain Nadejda Petrovna. Iona looks round at them several times; he waits for a temporary silence, then turning round again, he murmurs:

"My son — died this week."

"We must all die," sighs the hump-back, wiping his lips after an attack of coughing. "Now, hurry up, hurry up! Gentlemen, I really cannot go any farther like this! When will he get us there?"

"Well, just you stimulate him a little in the neck!"

"You old pest, do you hear, I'll bone your neck for you! If one treated the like of you with ceremony one would have to go on foot! Do you hear, old serpent Gorinytch! Or do you not care a spit?"

Iona hears rather than feels the blows they deal him.

"Hi, hi," he laughs. "They are gay young gentlemen, God bless 'em!"

"Cabby, are you married?" asks a lanky one.

"I? Hi, hi, gay young gentlemen! Now I have only a wife: the moist ground... Hi, ho, ho... that is to say, the gráve! My son has died, and I am alive... A wonderful thing, death mistook the door... instead of coming to me, it went to my son..."

Iona turns round to tell them how his son died, but at this moment the hump-back, giving a little sigh, announces, Thank God, they have at last reached their destination, and Iona watches them disappear through the dark entrance. Once more he is alone, and again surrounded by silence...

His grief, which had abated for a short while, returns and rends his heart with greater force. With an anxious and a hurried look, he searches among the crowds passing on either side of the street to find if there is one person who will listen to him. But the crowds hurry by without noticing him or his trouble. Yet it is such an immense, illimitable grief. Should his heart break and the grief pour out, it would flow over the whole earth it seems, and yet, no one sees it. It has managed to conceal itself in such an insignificant shell that no one can see it even by day and with a light.

Iona sees a hall-porter with some sacking and decides to talk to him.

"Friend, what sort of time is it?" he asks.

"Past nine. What are you standing here for? Move on."

Iona moves on a few steps, doubles himself up, and abandons himself to his grief. He sees it is useless to turn to people for help. In less than five minutes he straightens himself, holds up his head as if he felt some sharp pain, and gives a tug at the reins: he can bear it no longer.

"The stables," he thinks and the little horse, as if he understood, starts off at a trot.

About an hour and a half later Iona is seated by a large dirty stove. Around the stove, on the floor, on the benches people are snoring; the air is thick and suffocatingly hot. Iona looks at the sleepers, scratches himself, and regrets having returned so early.

"I have not even earned my fodder," he thinks. "That's what's my trouble. A man who knows his job, who has had enough to eat, and his horse too, can always sleep peacefully."

A young cab-driver in one of the corners half gets up, grunts sleepily, and stretches towards a bucket of water.

"Do you want a drink?" Iona asks him.

"Don't I want a drink!"

"That's so? Your good health! But listen, mate — you know, my son is dead... Did you hear? This week, in hospital... It's a long story."

Iona looks to see what effect his words have, but sees none — the young man has hidden his face, and is fast asleep again. The old man sighs, and scratches his head. Just as much as the young one wanted to drink, the old man wanted to talk. It will soon be a week since his son died, and he has not been able to speak about it properly to anyone. One must tell it slowly and carefully; how his son fell ill, how he suffered, what he said before he died, how he died. One must describe every detail of the funeral, and the journey to the hospital to fetch the defunct's clothes. His daughter Anissia remained in the village — one must talk about her too. Was it nothing he had to tell? Surely the listener would gasp and sigh, and sympathize with him? It is better, too, to talk to women; although they are stupid, two words are enough to make them sob.

"I'll go and look at my horse," thinks Iona; "there's always time to sleep. No fear of that!"

He puts on his coat, and goes to the stables to his horse; he thinks of the corn, the hay, the weather. When he is alone, he dare not think of his son; he could speak about him to anyone, but to think of him, and picture him to himself, is unbearably painful.

"Are you tucking in?" Iona asks his horse, looks at his bright eyes; "go on, tuck in though we've not earned our corn, we can eat hay. Yes! I am too old to drive — my son could have, not I. He was a first-rate cab-driver. If only he had lived!"

Iona is silent for a moment, then continues:

"That's how it is, my old horse. There's no more Kuzma Ionitch. He has left us to live, and he went off pop. Now let's say, you had a foal, you were that foal's mother, and suddenly, let's say, that foal went and left you to live after him. It would be sad, wouldn't it?"

The little horse munches, listens, and breathes over his master's hand....

Iona's feelings are too much for him and he tells the little horse the whole story.

NOTES

phantom: ghost, a shadowy likeness of a dead person that seems to appear on earth.

snowdrift: a deep bank or mass of snow formed by the wind.

ginger-bread horse: fancy carving on furniture, gables etc; cheap and showy.

kopeck: a monetary unit equal to one-hundredth of a Russian ruble.

slough: a swamp, bog or marsh, a place full of soft deep mud

a fare: a passenger who hires a cab.

cab: a horse-drawn carriage especially for public hire.

sleigh: a light vehicle on runners, usually horse-drawn for carrying persons over snow and ice.

werewolf: a person capable of assuming the form of a wolf.

snuffle: the sound of somebody breathing audibly.

hoarse: sounding rough and husky.

galoshes: heavy shoes, over-shoes.

hump-backed: a person having a hunch-back.

grivenick: equal to ten kopecks.

petulance: showing childish bad temper over unimportant things.

cognac: French brandy distilled from wine in the area of Cognac, France.

gay: joyous and lively, light-hearted.

the defunct: a person no longer living or existing. Here Brian Kuzma Ionitch, the dead son of Iona Potapov.

COMPREHENSION

1. Why does the cab driver "make a move undecidedly" when he is told to drive to Viborg?
2. What does the officer think of cab-drivers in general?
3. What was the officer's response to Iona's remark?
4. Why did the three young men quarrel?
5. How did Iona react to the insults of the young men?
6. Make a list of the people with whom Iona tried to share his grief. Did he ultimately manage to find a listener?
7. Explain the following phrases from the text:

    a. If you were snatched from the plough.... and thrown into this slough of monstrous lights...... you too would find it difficult not to think.
    b. I haven't even earned my fodder.
    c. The bright lights of the lamp are replacing brighter rays.
    d. We have not earned our corn, we can eat hay.
    e. Now I have only a wife, the moist ground.
    f. Death mistook the door.
    g. The cab driver more from habit than necessity brandishes his whip.
    h. Iona hears rather than feels the blows they deal him.
    i. Should his heart break and the grief pour out, it would flow over the whole earth it seems, and yet, no one sees it.
    j. Iona gapes about like someone suffocating, who does not understand why and wherefore he is there.

8. Choose the correct answer:

   Iona Potapov drives a cab because:

   a. He enjoys driving a cab.
   b. He has nothing else to do.
   c. He earns his livelihood by driving a cab.
   d. He loves to meet people and to talk to them.

   Iona wants to talk to somebody:

   a. To tell his life story.
   b. To share his intense sorrow.
   c. To entertain his customers.
   d. To while away time while driving his cab.

   Iona finds himself all alone because:

   a. He did not get a passenger for a long time.
   b. It was rather late in the evening and the roads were deserted.
   c. He was not a good talker and didn't know how to engage others in a friendly conversation.
   d. People in general are indifferent to the sufferings of others.

   Iona considers women to be stupid because:

   a. They are slow to understand things.
   b. They are physically weak and timid.
   c. Women are much more sensitive than men.

LANGUAGE STUDY

Read the following sentences. In each group, the same word has been used but the meaning is not the same.

Descend

He descended the stairs.

The evening mist descended over the town.

He claims to have descended from a very rich family.

Reins

Iona picked up the reins of the horse.

The reins of administration are in very competent hands.

He gave free rein to his imagination.

Whip

The cab driver brandished his whip.
The ruling party has issued a whip to its members to support the new bill.
Mohammed Ali whipped Frazer.

Stretch

The cab driver stretched his neck.
The stretch of road ahead is very treacherous.
You can stretch the law to make an exception in this case.

1. Use the following words with at least two different meanings:
   Move, yard, smack, rub, shift, crack, fair, mind, stand.
2. Make a list of the expressions from the text which indicate that snow is falling.
3. Make a list of the expressions from the text which describe the lean and thin appearance of Iona Potapov.

COMPOSITION

1. All the passengers who hire Iona's cab treat him like a cab-driver and not like a fellow-being. Comment.
2. Describe how having failed to find a sympathetic listener Iona turns to his horse, a co-sufferer and finds consolation there.
3. How does Chekov describe the loneliness of Iona Potapov?
4. Describe those poignant moments in your life when you felt very lonely.
5. Describe a chance meeting with a fellow-traveller in a train and the experiences he shared with you.

GRAMMAR

See Appendix II, page 192 .

Bachcha Lieutenant

MANOHAR MALGONKAR

The dog barked, alarmed and frightened, the yelping, whining, trailing-off-into-a-howl sort of bark of a piedog, and Jamadar Tukaram Shindey froze in his tracks, fighting the impulse to fling himself on the ground. He could hear his own quick gasping breathing and feel his heart pounding violently against his chest, and in his head surged all the thoughts, confused and fragmentary, that come to one in the face of imminent death – when one expects an instantaneous hail of enemy bullets.

But with equal suddenness, he realised that he was being foolish, nervous like a new *rangroot*, and not the veteran soldier he was on his second campaign in Burma. There was no danger of death. The night was pitch dark; you couldn't see your hand in front of your face. So long as you kept your head, so long as you did not make any noise that would give away your position, you were all right.

Someone gave an order. The dog stopped barking, abruptly, and the Arakan jungle resumed its heavy silence. Cautiously, inch by inch, Jamadar Tukaram Shindey lowered himself down, and lay prone on the warm earth. His clothes were wet with sweat.

He unbuckled his belt, and took out from the haversack a thick roll of dry *chapatis* and two large onions. He peeled off two onions and began to munch his dinner, biting off the *chapatis* and the onions alternately.

Two hundred yards away, where the cart track dipped into the dry bed of the Chaung, the dog scratched his ear, and curled up and lay shivering in spite of the stuffy, oppressive heat. He was a stringy, mustard and white mongrel, and he was kept permanently hungry so that he should always remain wide awake. Three days ago, he had been taken from his village near

Buthidaung, and now he was tied to a post near the bend of the road with strong coir rope. He felt angry and vicious and ready to snap at all times. He was an unwilling and bewildered participant in the war, but he made an alert sentry.

To Jamadar Tukaram, the dog barking like that in the middle of the jungle at least a mile away from the nearest hamlet could only mean one thing; there was a Japanese position near the bend of the road.

Tukaram looked longingly at the two remaining *chapatis*. Then, folding them carefully so that they shouldn't break into pieces, he put them back in the mess tin. After that he unslung his water bottle and put it to his mouth.

The night was warm, the forest giving out a steamy heat, and there wasn't a breath of air. Tukaram took a tiny sip to wet his tongue and the water was cloying and tepid, as though the heat had made it thicker, and it tasted foully of chlorine. He was thirsty and wanted to go on drinking, allowing the water to run extravagantly gurgling down his throat. But after three unsatisfying gulps he stopped. This self-discipline too had become a matter of habit. While on patrol, however close you were to camp, three mouthfuls was all that you allowed yourself with a meal.

Actually, Jamadar Tukaram could have gone back to the company position and had as much water to drink as he wanted. And perhaps the Intelligence Officer, Lieutenant Wilson, would have even offered him some tea. The I.O. always seemed to be drinking tea.

Yes, Tukaram could have gone back to his unit, for his mission had been accomplished. He and another scout had been sent out to find how far down the Taungdaw road the first enemy position was, and as usual, Jamadar Tukaram had left the other scout behind.

He always preferred to go on a patrol of this sort alone. He was a jungle man, born and brought up in the jungles of North Kanara, and he used to be a big-game tracker before he joined the army. To him, there was nothing strange about the Burmese jungles. He could move in them as silently as any animal of the jungle itself, and as long as he was sent out on his own, he could get all the information they wanted. But taking someone else along was always dangerous. It certainly complicated matters.

That had been the cause of his first clash with Lieutenant Wilson. The new I.O., Wilson, a bespectacled, fair-haired, thin young man with a large Adam's apple, had joined the 4th Satpuras barely two months ago. He was nineteen years old, and he had not seen any action so far. He read poetry, and he didn't drink or smoke or use swearwords, and he was serious at all times. As such, he was unlike any officer the 4th Satpuras had had so far, and God knows they had had a goodly number of queer ones since the war started. Everyone called him the *Bachcha* Lieutenant.

But Wilson had done an Intelligence Course at the School in Karachi, and had managed to get a D grading at the course, and he was convinced that he knew all about how patrols should be carried out.

"No use going out on your own, Jamadar saab," he had said, pronouncing the "saab" as though it rhymed with 'nab'. "Two can observe much better than one."

"Two people moving about in the jungle make much more noise than one, sir," Tukaram had pointed out.

"Well, supposing you went on patrol by yourself, Jamadar saab, and you were shot down or captured. Who would bring back the information?"

"There is much more likelihood of both of us being killed or captured, sir, if two of us were to go, than there is of my being killed or captured if I went by myself," Tukaram had said.

But it had been no use. The Bachcha Lieutenant had ordered that his intelligence personnel must never go out on patrol except in batches of at least two. Actually, he himself preferred a patrol of four, particularly at night. But in view of the shortage of men, he could not always insist on patrols of four.

So, soon after sunset, Jamadar Tukaram Shindey and Havaldar Ranga had set out along the Taungdaw cart track, but after they had gone about a mile, Tukaram had left the other scout behind, telling him to wait until he returned. And now he was all alone, lying on his back, trying to fight a desperate longing for a cigarette, and hardly a couple of hundred yards away from an enemy position.

For a whole hour, Tukaram had waited in the hope of being able to find out something more about the enemy. If they only talked or coughed or made some noise, he would have a rough idea of how many there were. But there had been no telltale sounds. After the barking of the dog, and the sharp word of command, everything had been silent.

Tukaram Shindey shook his head and cursed silently. Then he put on his equipment and without making the slightest noise, slid away from his position and made his way back to the track junction where he had left the other scout.

Two low whistles repeated at two-second intervals brought Havaldar Ranga out of the shadows. The first thing that Tukaram said to him was, "Do you think you can find your way back to camp?"

"Why aren't you coming back?"

"I have discovered a Jap position, but unless I watch them in daylight I can't find out anything more about them. I propose to go back and take a position near them and see what they are up to, find out how many there are, what weapons they possess, and things like that."

"Of course, I can find my way back; it is hardly a mile away to camp. But Bachcha saab is not going to like your going on your own like this."

"I'm sure he won't. But that can't be helped."

"He is bound to blow me up. What shall I tell him?"

"Tell him I ordered you to go back."

"Yes, sir," said Havaldar Ranga.

Then Tukaram gave the other all the information he had obtained. It wasn't much. There was an enemy position approximately one and a half miles down the Taungdaw track. Strength not known, weapons not known. He gave a four-figure map reference. He told Ranga to say that Jamadar Tukaram was going to try and keep the enemy under observation during the next day, to be able to make a fuller report in the evening.

"Is that all?" asked Ranga.

"That's all. I say, you haven't got any haversack rations you can spare, have you? I will have to carry on the whole of tomorrow on two dry *chapatis* and my last onion."

"No, I have finished all mine," said Ranga. "I always feel very hungry when I am on patrol."

"Oh, never mind."

"You are sure you can make your way back?"

"Of course, I can find my way back," the other had said, sounding hurt, and within twenty minutes after that was hopelessly lost. He never returned to the battalion. Early the next morning as he was still wandering in a daze along a footpath in the forest, he had been neatly picked out by a Japanese sniper.

As soon as Jamadar Tukaram Shindey was back at the spot where he had eaten his dinner, he put his head on his haversack and fell asleep. He woke up before dawn, and for a long time lay straining to locate any sounds coming from the direction of the track. Just before first light, he drank another three mouthfuls of water and ate one of the *chapatis*. After that, he began to crawl forward towards where he had heard the dog bark the previous night.

He moved through the undergrowth silently, crouching and crawling on his stomach and every now and then raising his head to see how far he was from the track.

A large uprooted tree lay between him and the open track, and if he could only get behind the tree, he could keep a longish stretch of the road under observation. The only snag in getting behind the fallen tree would be that it would then be impossible to get away from there without being seen. In the grey-green darkness of the jungle dawn it was easy enough to approach the tree unseen, but once there it was almost certain that he would have to wait until evening to get away.

But it was equally apparent that if he wanted to keep the track under observation, the tree was the best place, and cautiously, his stomach feeling empty with nervousness, he made his way through the open ground to the tree.

He could now observe the Taungdaw cart track for a stretch of nearly 200 yards, with the bend of the track directly below him, hardly fifty yards away.

He was just in time. As soon as the first light of the summer sun touched the tops of the trees, the Japanese soldiers began to come out one by one, and soon, there were almost twenty of them on the road. Jamadar Tukaram's unshaven face contorted itself into a fearsome grin. With a Bren, he could have picked them all out; at times they were bunched up beautifully, making an ideal target. One burst, and half of them would lie dead. But there was no point in thinking about a Bren — he didn't have a Bren with him. All he had was a Sten, with three spare magazines, and six 63 grenades fitted with four-second fuses.

But it was much more important to observe these men and take back the information to the I.O. than to kill a few of them. Because once you had observed them well, you could come with the necessary number of men and finish them off in one go.

The Japanese soldiers were digging shallow trenches right in the middle of the track. Tukaram wondered what they were up to. Surely, they were not digging slit trenches in the middle of the open track.

But their purpose was soon apparent. They were obviously putting down AP mines and laying boobytrap wires along the track. Fascinated, Tukaram watched the little khaki figures working with the jerky movements of mechanical toys. In no time at all, they had put in half a dozen brass AP mines and laid several strands of trip wire across the track. Then they had put back the earth and the leaves on the road to make the surface look undisturbed.

They finished off soon after nine and then posting a sentry on either side of the bend they began to dig their foxholes on the opposite slope of the hill. Methodically, putting their heads close to the ground, they cleared the intervening undergrowth to give their guns an unrestricted field of fire. Their purpose was clear. They would sit in their foxholes, guarding the track, and ambush any enemy troops that happened to be walking along the track.

Jamadar Tukaram congratulated himself on having come back for a second look. If he had waited until daylight, he would never have been able to approach so close to their position.

The craving for a cigarette had come back, stronger than ever, and in an effort to drag his mind away, Tukaram began to think about his impending interrogation by the I.O. He was quite looking forward to it although he knew that Bachcha Lieutenant would be peeved with him for disregarding his orders, and that he would try to be aloof and frosty and take down the vital information brought back by Tukararn as though he were writing up the log for a 'blank' patrol.

Tukaram pictured himself telling the I.O. all the details: nearest enemy position — one and a half miles along the Taungdaw track, a map reference, this, this, this, this, this, this; strength —approximately thirty. And then he could almost hear Wilson asking in that squeaky voice of his: "How approximately, saab?" Wilson always suspected approximate figures. "Well, not more than thirty-two and not less than twenty-eight, sir," he would say. "They are dug in about thirty yards up the slope of the hill to the north of the track and they are armed with rifles, two LMGs and a Japanese type mortar, and of course, the dog.... the damned dog..."

It was nearly midday and all of a sudden, the dog who had been lying quietly in the sun tied up to a stake buried in the middle of the track, began to yelp, and Tukaram saw a thickset Japanese soldier clumsily swiping at the dog with a heavy spade. He missed twice, and for that time, the dog continued his furious yelping and then, as the next blow hit him squarely on the skull, fell limply on the ground and lay silently twitching for some seconds before he became absolutely still.

There was a clammy, choking feeling in Tukaram's throat. "You dog-killing...," he said to himself, "you s.... ."

The Japanese soldier had dragged away the dog's body and was shovelling earth on the road in order to obliterate the bloodstains and Tukaram had a wild desire to let him have a burst from his Sten. Instead, he decided to have a drink of water.

It took a long time for him to unbuckle the water bottle and then he brought it slowly to his mouth and with deliberate recklessness drained all its contents, knowing that he had nothing to wash down his last *chapati* and onion which he had been saving up. The sight of the dog, the faithful sentry of the previous night, being finished off in that brutal manner was somehow more horrifying than many things he had seen in this war.

But as a soldier, he could see the reason why the dog had been killed. He was a two-edged weapon. He could act as a sentry, of course, but he could just as easily give your own position away by barking, and if you wanted to lie waiting for an ambush, it was no use having a dog around. Soon, all was quiet again, and the thin red meandering line of the cart track looked desolate and deserted. Even the sentries had been withdrawn.

Jamadar Tukaram grinned, and smacked his lips. At least he knew exactly where they had dug their position. Tomorrow he would himself lead a party and finish them off neatly, as they sat in their trenches with their LMGs trained on the bend of the road, "The dog-killing swines!"

But as far as Jamadar Tukaram was concerned, tomorrow never came. Angrily, biting his nails nervously, Lieutenant Wilson had waited from early morning for the return of his two scouts. As the day wore on, he had become more and more fidgety and irritable. He had not heard any firing during the night and refused to believe that both his scouts had been killed. It was imperative to find out exactly how far the nearest enemy position was, and that cocky Jamadar of his had let him down. Both he and the other scout sent out the previous evening had failed to return.

At midday, Wilson sent for his Subedar. "I want two jawans," he told him. "They are to take haversack rations, torches, Stens with three spare magazines, and six grenades each. Rubbersoled shoes." Lieutenant Wilson was nothing if not thorough. "I am going on a patrol myself down the Taungdaw road. You will have to act for me," he added.

Tapping his rubbersoled shoes with his fingers to keep his feet from going to sleep, Jamadar Tukaram Shindey squirmed behind the fallen tree. Despite the cramp and his hunger, he was pleased with himself, and waited patiently for the release from his position that darkness would bring.

But he did not have to wait for darkness. Late in the afternoon he saw from his vantage point three men in olive green uniforms walking along the cart tracks from the direction of the Satpura position. He watched them in disbelief, coming nearer and nearer to the death-trap in the bend of the track, walking carefully, watching both sides of the track and keeping dispersed. He could see Lieutenant Wilson's thin, ungainly figure in the lead followed by two other men who were still too far away to be identified. "Blast that Bachcha of a Lieutenant Wilson," he said to himself. "Blast him." And then he acted.

"Stop, sahib! Halt!" he shouted at the top of his voice. "Ambush, ambush, stop," and then he charged at the trenches of the enemy, firing his Sten gun and yelling hoarsely at the same time.

Close to where the dog had been killed was an anthill beside the road, and Tukaram flung himself behind it and began to hurl his grenades: one, two, three; they went off with resounding booms amidst the din and whine of enemy bullets. As he was about to pull out the pin from another grenade he felt a white-hot pain in his shoulder and fell down with an oath, the grenade dropping from his suddenly powerless hands.

Lieutenant Wilson and his two guides had flung themselves face downwards on the road and the bullets spattered the ground in front of them on the bend. From there, they watched Jamadar Tukaram's single-handed attack against the Japanese position. They saw him fall down and then rise, shouting at them, "Get back, you fools, get back, you fool Bachcha Lieutenant! There are thirty Japs dug in there!" They saw his shirt redden with the blood squirting from his shoulder and saw him pull out the pin from the grenade with his teeth and fling it at the enemy trenches with his left hand, shouting, "Take that, you dog-killing..." and then fall down again.

And then the Bachcha Lieutenant had risen to his feet uttering an unaccustomed oath and running madly into the dust rising from the bullets which kicked the road near the anthill. With open mouths, his two scouts watched him run through the screen of dust and reach the anthill unharmed. They saw him pick up Jamadar Tukaram Shindey, and they were even more aghast when they heard the Jamadar shouting at the sahib in a voice that could be heard distinctly above the storm of bullets, "Get back, sahib, get back, you fool Bachcha, run into the jungle!" They saw the Bachcha Lieutenant pick up the Jamadar and sling him across his shoulder and run and stumble and fall, and rise heavily and run again. And they saw him stumble and fall again and lie in a heap in the bend of the cart track in the bed of the Chaung. And they saw more and more bullets riddling the two prone bodies making their limbs twitch with each hit.

The rest of Lieutenant Wilson's patrol got back to the battalion. Neither Jamadar Tukaram Shindey nor the Bachcha Lieutenant ever knew just how much they had contributed to each other's death.

NOTES

surge: to move forward, to roll on like waves.

fragmentary: separate or incomplete part.

veteran: a person who has had much or long experience.

campaign: a group of military operations with a set purpose usually in one area; series of planned activities to gain a special object.

hamlet: a group of houses in the country or in a small village.

haversack: a canvas bag (especially one used by soldiers, hikers and others).

the Chaung: a river in Burma.

vicious: given or done with evil intent.

longingly: having or showing an earnest desire.

tepid: lukewarm

patrol: (v) to go around (a camp, town, the streets, roads etc.) to look out (for wrong doers, persons in need of help, the enemy): (n) those who do so.

mission: sending out a number of persons entrusted with special work.

scout: a person,(not a spy) ship or small aircraft sent out to get information of the enemy's movements, strength etc.

big-game catcher: a hunter of the larger animals like elephants, lions, tigers etc.

Adam's apple: part that projects in the front of the throat especially in males and moves up and down when one speaks.

tell-tale: circumstances that reveal a person's thoughts activities etc.

contorted: forced or twisted out of the usual shape or appearance.

Bren: a light-weight, semi-automatic machine-gun.

slit trenches: a long, narrow cut, tear or an opening. Slit trench is a narrow trench made for one soldier or a group of soldiers.

A.P. mines: anti-personnel mines, mines that blow up when a human-being treads upon them.

booby trap: an apparently harmless object that will kill or injure somebody when picked up or interfered with.

trip wire: a wire stretched along the ground, working a trap when a human-being or an animal trips against it; to trip means to catch one's foot etc. in an obstacle and to stumble.

fox-holes: a hole in the ground used as a shelter against enemy fire and as firing point.

undergrowth: shrubs, bushes, low trees growing among taller trees.

ambush: the placing of troops etc. lying in wait for a surprise attack.

blank patrol: a patrol that failed to collect useful information.

sniper: a person who fires shots from a hiding place.

snag: hidden, unknown or unexpected difficulty or obstacle.

swiping: (colloq.) hit hard.

limply: lacking strength.

twitching: sudden, quick, uncontrollable movement of a muscle, jerk, sudden quick-pull.

clammy: damp, moist.

obliterate: to rub or blot out, to remove all signs of, to destroy.

burst: (n) a short spurt of gun fire, a few shots fired in quick succession.

a two-edged weapon: a weapon with two cutting edges which may operate for or against.

smack: to part the lips with a sound to show pleasure at food or drink or in anticipation of other sensual pleasures.

trained: (gun) pointed aimed.

imperative: urgent, essential, needing immediate attention.

squirmed: twisted the body, wriggled (from discomfort, shame or embarrassment).

vantage-point: place from where one has a good view of something.

ungainly: clumsy, awkward, ungraceful, rough and harsh.

resounding: echoing and re-echoing.

whine: a long drawn complaining cry or high-pitched sound (as made by a miserable dog, a siren, a motor, or a shell in flight).

spatter: splash, scatter.

riddling: making holes in something by firing bullets.

squirting: forced out in a thin stream or jet.

COMPREHENSION

1. Where was the dog? Why was it barking?
2. From where had the dog been brought? Why was it kept permanently hungry?
3. What conclusion did Jamadar Tukaram draw on hearing the dog bark?
4. What equipment did Jamadar Tukaram carry with him on patrol duty?
5. Why did Jamadar Tukaram prefer to take only three

mouthfuls of water while on patrol duty?

6. Why did Jamadar Tukaram prefer to go alone on patrol duty?
7. What were the views of the Intelligence Officer about the size of the patrol party?
8. To what extent was Jamadar Tukaram familiar with life in the jungle?
9. Why did Jamadar Tukaram clash with his Intelligence Officer for the first time?
10. Describe the appearance of the Intelligence Officer, Lt. Wilson. How old was he? For how long had he been in the army? Why had he been appointed Intelligence Officer?
11. Why was Lt. Wilson called Bachcha Lieutenant?
12. What was the mission of Jamadar Tukaram and Havaldar Ranga?
13. What did Jamadar Tukaram do to call Havaldar Ranga out of his hiding place?
14. Why did Jamadar Tukaram decide to send back Havaldar Ranga? Why didn't the two together return to their base?
15. Did Havaldar Ranga reach his base? If he did, at what time? If he didn't, why?
16. What were Tukaram's thoughts when he saw the Japanese soldiers early in the morning? Why didn't he kill all of them?
17. Who killed the dog? Why did he do so?
18. What were the Japanese soldiers planning? What did they do to execute their plan?
19. What did Lt. Wilson do when his patrol did not return by morning?
20. Who were the three men in olive green uniform walking along the cart track?
21. What would have happened if Jamadar Tukaram had not shouted to them to stop?
22. What is a booby trap? Describe the trap that the Japanese had laid. Where had they laid the trap?
23. What was the first physical injury that Jamadar Tukaram sustained? What did he do after that?
24. What did Lt. Wilson do on hearing Jamadar Tukaram shout? What did he do to Jamadar Tukaram?
25. What happened to Jamadar Tukaram and Lt. Wilson at the end of the episode?

LANGUAGE STUDY

1. Find out from the text words and expressions meaning the following. The words in the box below will help you.
   a. to kill, to destroy somebody.
   b. to scold severely.
   c. to reveal intentionally or unintentionally.
   d. to disappoint, to fail to help.
   e. alone, without anybody's help.
   f. complete in every way, not forgetting or overlooking anything.
   g. Intentional rashness, knowing disregard or consequences.
   h. a land or country unlived in, barren and unfit to live in.
   i. to begin a journey.
   j. to interfere so as to prevent something or to change the result.

to give away, to let down, by onesself, to blow somebody up, to set out, to finish off, to give away, to intervene, deliberate recklessness, thorough, desolute.

2. Replace the italicised expressions with words from the box on the next page. Restructure the sentences wherever necessary:
   a. He *smiled broadly, showing his teeth.*
   b. A general strike is *like a weapon with two cutting edges.*
   c. Repeated wars *destroyed* the Trojan civilization.
   d. The policeman noticed stains of blood on the fugitive's hands. The blood-stains *revealed* what the fugitive had done.
   e. Girls stood *in a group* in a corner of the park.
   f. *Isolated bits* of knowledge of any subject are not very useful.
   g. The expression on his face revealed *an earnest desire* to return home immediately.
   h. He felt a *very strong desire* for a cup of tea.
   i. Since I could not keep the appointment he was *annoyed with* me.
   j. It was not very late in the evening. Yet the road was *lonely and no one could be seen* there.

a craving for, a desperate longing for, desolate, deserted, be peeved with, buched up, fragmentary, a double-edged weapon, grinned, tell-tale, obliterate

3. How well do you know your prefixes and suffixes?
   a. *Disbelief* means lack of belief, refusal to believe. Make a list of ten more words with the prefix *dis-*.
   b. The prefix *re-* means again as in 'resume'. Make a list of five more words with the prefix *re-*.
   c. To *unbuckle* means to undo the buckle. Make a list of ten more words with the prefix *un-*.
   d. *Fearsome* means frightening in appearance. Draw up a list of five other words with the suffix *some*.

4. With the help of the word *local* we can make other words such as 'locate', 'locality', 'location', 'localise' etc. The word *local* in this example is the 'stem' or 'root' and other words in this example are 'derivations' from the 'stem' or 'root'.

   Make as many words as you can from each of the roots given below.
   frag, extra, div, mili, amb, amp, el.

5. Fill in the blanks in the following sentences with appropriate prepositions:
   a. Jamadar Tukaram froze ______ his tracks.
   b. He felt his heart pounding violently ______ his chest.
   c. His clothes were wet ______ sweat.
   d. He peeled ______ two onions and began to munch his dinner biting ______ the chapatis and the onions alternately.
   e. He was at least a mile ______ from the nearest hamlet.
   f. Self-discipline is always a matter ______ habit.
   g. He always wanted to go ______ a patrol ______ this sort alone.
   h. There is much more likelihood ______ us being killed.
   i. Intelligence personnel must never go out ______ patrol except ______ batches, particularly ______ night.
   j. But in view ______ the shortage ______ men he would not always insist ______ patrols ______ four.

k. He put ______ his equipment and proceeded cautiously ______ the enemy position.
l. I always feel hungry when I am ______patrol duty.
m. His views ______ patrols were the cause ______ his first clash ______ his lieutenant.
n. And now he was all alone lying ______ his back.
o. I propose to go back and take a position near them and see what they are ______ ______.
p. He moved ______ the undergrowth silently.
q. Tukaram's face contorted itself ______ a fearsome grin.
r. They were all bunched ______ beautifully, making an ideal target.
s. The Japanese were digging shallow trenches ______ the middle ______ the track.
t. Jamadar Tukaram congratulated himself ______ having come back ______ a second look.
u. The craving ______ a cigarette had come back.
v. He knew that the Bachcha Lieutenant would be peeved ______ him ______ disregarding his orders
w. He was looking forward ______ his meeting ______ the Intelligence Officer.
x. The Lieutenant said, "You will have to act ______ me."
y. He shouted ______ the top of his voice.

COMPOSITION

1. If the Satpura Regiment had not discovered the presence of the Japanese picket what would have been its fate?
2. How did the Japanese plan to entrap the enemy?
3. What would you have done if you had been the Intelligence Officer in place of Lt. Wilson?
4. Describe an imaginary infantry attack at night.

GRAMMAR

See Appendix II, page 209.

A Ballad of Heaven

JOHN DAVIDSON

He wrought at one great work for years;
    The world passed by with lofty look;
Sometimes his eyes were dashed with tears;
    Sometimes his lips with laughter shook.

His wife and child went clothed in rags,
    And in a windy garret starved;
He trod his measure on the flags,
    And high on heaven his music carved.

Wistful he grew but never feared;
    For always on the midnight skies
His rich orchestral score appeared
    In stars and zones and galaxies.

He thought to copy down his score;
    The moonlight was his lamp; he said,
'Listen my love,' but on the floor
    His wife and child were lying dead.

NOTES

wrought: worked (only literary use)
one great work: a work of art, a masterpiece
lofty: haughty, proud, consciously superior

garret: a room (often small and dark) on the top floor of a house

measure: verse rhythm, metre, time of a piece of music.

on the flags: flat, square or oblong piece of stone for a floor, path or pavement.

music carved: inscribed by cutting on a surface. The poet imagined that he saw musical notation in the sky.

wistful: sad, moved by a rather unsatisfied and often vague desire.

orchestral score: copy of music showing what each instrument is to play or each voice to sing.

galaxies: large-scale clusters of stars in outer space.

COMPREHENSION

1. Why was the poet sometimes happy and sometimes sad?
2. Was the poet really worried about the condition of his wife and child or was he indifferent to their suffering?
3. What engaged the poet? What did he really want to achieve?
4. Could the poet's wife and child rejoice in his achievement? Where were they at that time?
5. Describe in your own words the poignant struggle of the poet.

LANGUAGE STUDY

1. Make a list of words/expressions which describe the poverty of the poet.
2. Despite his difficulties the poet was not entirely sad or without hope. Pick out words/expressions which describe moments of joy and hope in the life of the poet.
3. Which line in the poem describes the contemptuous attitude of the general public.
4. Make a list of words connected with rhythm and music.
5. Pick out expressions which describe the sufferings of the poet.
6. Give the antonyms of the following words/expressions: lofty look, wistful, feared, windy, laughter, heaven, high.

COMPOSITION

1. Do you like poetry? Give reasons for your answer.
2. "Our sweetest songs are those that tell of saddest thought" (Shelley). Do you think what Shelley said about poetry is true of this poem as well?
3. What impression do you get about poets after reading this poem?
4. Poems have beautiful images and expressions. Does this poem appeal to your sense of beauty? Describe some of these beautiful images in your own words.
5. Describe how the poet struggled to create one masterpiece and what the result was.

GRAMMAR

See Appendix II, page 211.

Bankers are Just Like Anybody Else, Except Richer

OGDEN NASH

This is a song to celebrate banks,
Because they are full of money and you go into them and all you hear is clinks and clanks,
Or may be a sound like the wind in the trees on the hills,
Which is the rustling of the thousand dollar bills.
Most bankers dwell in marble halls,
Which they get to dwell in because they encourage deposits and discourage withdrawals,
And particularly because they all observe one rule which woe betide the banker who fails to heed it,
Which is you must never lend any money to anybody unless they don't need it.
I know you, you cautious conservative banks!
If people are worried about their rent it is your duty to deny them the loan of one nickel, yes, even one copper engraving of the martyred son of the late Nancy Hanks;
Yes, if they request fifty dollars to pay for a baby you must look at them like Tarzan looking at an uppity ape in the jungle,
And tell them what do they think a bank is, anyhow, they had better go get the money from their wife's aunt or ungle.
But suppose people come in and they have a million and they want another to pile on top of it,
Why, you brim with the milk of human kindness and you urge them to accept every drop of it,
And you lend them the million so then they have two million and this gives them the idea that they would be better off with four,
So they already have two million as security so you have no

hesitation in lending them two more,
And all the vice-presidents nod their heads in rhythm,
And the only question asked is do the borrowers want the
money sent or do they want to take it withm.
But please do not think that I am not fond of banks,
Because I think they deserve our appreciation and thanks,
Because they perform a valuable public service in eliminating
the jackasses who go around saying that health and happiness
are everything and money isn't essential,
Because as soon as they have to borrow some unimportant
money to maintain their health and happiness they starve
to death so they can't go around any more sneering at good
old money, which is nothing short of providential.

NOTES

celebrate: to praise and honour.

conservative: cautious, moderate, opposed to great or sudden change.

uppity: (colloq) uppish, conceited, self-assertive.

ungle: humorous for 'uncle'.

the jackasses: foolish persons.

providential: through Providence i.e. God's care for human-beings and all He has created.

COMPREHENSION

1. List the sounds you are likely to hear in a bank. Which words in the poem describe the sounds of coins and how does the poet describe the sound of the counting of currency notes?
2. How do bankers become rich? Which expressions in the poem describe their richness?
3. What is the golden rule that banks follow while lending money?

4. Is it easy to get a loan from a bank? Will a bank grant a loan for paying one's rent or for meeting the expenses of the birth of a child in the family?
5. Who are the people who manage to get loans from banks and how do they manage this?
6. What do the banks suggest when they refuse a loan?
7. What is the only question that banks ask when they sanction loans to their rich customers?
8. The poet says "He likes banks." Does he really like banks or is his remark sarcastic?
9. Does the poem really celebrate banks? Give reasons for your answer.
10. Complete the following sentences:
    a. The poet praises banks because _____.
    b. All bankers observe a golden rule. The rule is that _____.
    c. Those who fail to get loans from banks can get money from _____.
    d. Those who have a million, easily get a loan of a million or even more because _____.
    e. Banks deserve our appreciation and thanks for _____.

LANGUAGE STUDY

1. The following words have more than one meaning. Look up the following words in a dictionary and find out their meaning/s in the following sentences:

celebrate

He *celebrated* his twentieth birthday last week.
He is a *celebrated* scientist.
The marriage *celebration* was on a grand scale.
This is a song to *celebrate* banks.

dwell

Most bankers *dwell* in marble halls.
He *dwelt* on the population problem for quite some time.
That was a modest *dwelling*.
He was a man who *dwelt* apart.

suppose

Let us *suppose* that nobody deposits money in a bank.
He is *supposed* to be a lawyer.
Your *supposition* may not be correct.
The *supposed* deal in fact never took place.
You are always *supposing* things.

worry

Don't *worry* too much.
They *worried* the poor cat.
Worries cause a lot of suffering.
He is a *worrying* sort of person.
He looks *worried*.

2. Make a list of expressions in the poem which describe the counting of money.
3. Make a list of expressions used in the poem which show that bankers are very practical and successful people.
4. Enlist expressions which show that those who don't care for money are fools.
5. Which expressions in the poem show that the entire banking system is hypocritical.
6. Make a list of expressions which contain an element of sarcasm in the poem.

COMPOSITION

1. Describe in about 300 words the role that banks play in modern society?
2. It is generally felt that with the nationalisation of banks the quality of service rendered by the banks has deteriorated.
   Write a letter to the editor of a newspaper suggesting what steps should be taken to improve the quality of service in banks.
3. Suppose that you gave your bank a cheque for collection but the bank has taken an inordinately long time to collect it. Write a complaint to the Manager of the bank protesting against the undue delay in the collection of your cheque.

4. Banks favour the rich and rob the poor. Do you agree with this statement? Give reasons for your answer.
5. After graduation you want to set up a factory. Write an application to the Manager of a nationalised bank asking for a loan. Give details of the proposed venture.
6. Only fools and simpletons deposit money in banks, the wise obtain loans. Do you agree that this is really a wise policy? Write a reasoned answer in about 300 words.
7. Draw up a proposal for setting up a bank for financing scientific research.

GRAMMAR

See Appendix II, page 213.

The Discovery

HERMAN OULD

CHARACTERS

CHRISTOPHER COLUMBUS
PEDRO GUTIERREZ, an officer
PEPE, a page-boy
JUAN PATINO
DIEGO GARCIA — other seamen.
FRANCISCO
GUILLERMO IRES

SCENE — On board the "Santa Maria."
TIME — October 11, 1492.

(The ship is seen from an angle, which brings the poop somewhat to the left, the quarter-deck taking up the greater part of the stage. If it is visible, the midmast should bear a crucifix, in passing which everybody mechanically crosses himself. A large lantern, containing a lighted candle, is fixed at the extreme top of the poop. The night is still, and there is little movement in the sails.

Two seamen are visible, both well by the right. JUAN *is on his knees, adjusting rigging:* DIEGO *is helping. The actions of both of them are indeterminate, clearly designed to conceal their real purpose. They speak in loud whispers.)*

DIEGO: Within the next half an hour he will go to the poop-head as sure as God's alive. He can't keep away from it. His eyes are glued on the sky as if he expected his precious New World to burst out of it like thunderbolt! (*He laughs derisively*)

JUAN: Poor wretch!

DIEGO: Now, then Juan — quaking again!

JUAN: That's a lie! Why should I quake? What is there to fear? (*after a brief pause*) But I am sorry for him.

DIEGO: Why waste your pity? Shall it be one madman, his head stocked with visions, or forty honest seamen pining for their homes?

JUAN: *Santisma Maria* but he's a *gracious* madman...

DIEGO: (*impatiently*) Gracious when all goes to his pleasure, but as irritable as a teething child when crossed!

(The song of seamen is heard; it is a scarcely distinguishable murmur.

"Here's a keg o'rum
To Kingdom Come!
The Devil laughs
But God is dumb!"

JUAN: (*sharply*). They ought to stop that. The captain is always furious when he hears it.

DIEGO: Shan't we even sing to keep up our spirits? Sh!

(They attend with assumed assiduity to the rigging. PEDRO GUTIERREZ *comes in; he is somewhat surprised when he sees the others.)*

PEDRO: Who's that?

DIEGO: (*rising*). Diego Garcia and Juan Patino, sir.

PEDRO: (*inclined to be communicative*). It's dark. I would welcome the moon.................

DIEGO: Aye, aye, Don Pedro. Some of us would welcome the coast of Spain still more.

PEDRO: (*pumping*). Impatient, Diego?

DIEGO: (*surlily*). There are limits to patience, sir.

PEDRO: (*humouring him*). And you've reached them, eh?

DIEGO: We're like bats trying to fly by day. It's time he gave way. Why should one man have the lives of fifty in his hands?

PEDRO: (*with authority*). I hope we are not entertaining mutinous thoughts, Diego.

DIEGO: Mutiny is an ugly word, sir.

PEDRO: And an uglier deed.

(JUAN, *finishing his job at the rigging, rises, and with a salute goes off.* COLUMBUS *comes on. He is a tall, well-built man of forty-six. Hair prematurely white, complexion fair, almost ruddy. A man of quick temper and irritability which he controls only with an effort. His face, in repose, is melancholy. Seeing* DON PEDRO *in conversation with* DIEGO, *he looks a trifle suspicious. He turns quickly to* DIEGO.)

COLUMBUS: That candle on the foremost is guttering; see that it is put right.

DIEGO: (*sullenly*). Aye, aye, sir. (*He goes*).

COLUMBUS: (*recalling him*). And Diego!

DIEGO: (*coming back*) Yes, sir.

COLUMBUS: This is the quarter-deck.

DIEGO: Yes, sir.

COLUMBUS: A good sailor knows his place.

DIEGO: (*with repressed fury*) Yes, Sir.

(COLUMBUS *points off;* DIEGO *scarcely concealing a scowl, goes off.*)

COLUMBUS: (*to* PEDRO). A surly dog!

PEDRO: And a dangerous one. He does more than his share to inspire discontent.

COLUMBUS: I have remarked it.

(COLUMBUS) *is thoughtful for a moment and remains stationary. Presently he goes on to the poop and looks on to sea.* PEDRO *follows him. Simultaneously,* PEPE, *the page-boy, emerges from the hatchway, against which he stands, out of sight of the others. When they began to talk he listens eagerly.*)

COLUMBUS: Easterly, ever easterly. God is in the wind, Don Pedro.

PEDRO: (*with a short laugh*). The crew would say that is the Devil, rather Captain. All day, and every day, the wind blows easterly, blowing them away from their homes and their country, their wives and children, their friends and sweethearts.

COLUMBUS: (*hastily*), You too, Don Pedro? Do you, too doubt?

PEDRO: Have I said so, Captain? Am I not have by your side, prepared?

COLUMBUS: Forgive me, friend, You are one of the few with faith, and it is not easy to hold fast to faith when nothing seems to warrant faith. Listen to that.

SEAMEN: (*off singing*):—

"Here's a keg o 'rum
To Kingdom Come!
The Devil laughs
But God is dumb!"

(COLUMBUS *and* PEDRO *descend to the quarter-deck.*)

COLUMBUS: Madre de Dios, they drink too much.

PEDRO: They are simple men and must have their relaxation.

(*The next words break from him almost involuntarily.*) We have not all your vision, Captain.
COLUMBUS: You *are* beginning to doubt, Don Pedro. Give me the content of your mind. I am an impatient man and prone to be unjust; but (*whimsically*) I mean well, Don Pedro. I mean well. Speak without fear.
PEDRO: (*at first with diffidence, but rapidly gaining confidence*). Today is the 11th of October — more than two months since we saw the shores of Spain receding. You held a glittering hope of discovery before us and we had faith. Day followed day, and soon we found ourselves in unchartered seas, but still we had faith... I, at least, had faith. (*with dignity*) I am a man of some little learning, not easily led to wonder at natural phenomena as the unlettered might be. But I confess that I knew some uneasiness when the needle of the compass, instead of pointing to the constant North, jumped as if the Devil had laid hand on it, and pointed to the North-west. I am not a child, nor a simpleton, nor a superstitious seaman; but there is such a thing as being too clever, prying into mysteries which were not meant for our eyes. In all humility, Captain, I ask if it is God's will that we should pursue this voyage in the face of every portent of ill-luck?
COLUMBUS: (*impatiently*) It is my will. Is that not enough?
PEDRO: (*bowing his head*) I am answered.
COLUMBUS: (*hastily*) Forgive me, Don Pedro. A curb for my tongue — oh, a curb for my unbridled tongue, my worst enemy! (*More quietly*) *My* will, friend, because God's will. Shall that suffice?
PEDRO: (*not appeased*) I do not claim your confidence, sir.
COLUMBUS: (*thundering again*) But I claim yours. (*The sound of the seamen's song is again heard.*) A blight upon their singing! Bid them stop. (PEDRO *goes off, with an air of discontent. When he is alone,* COLUMBUS *looks out at sea. Muttering.*) Mystery? Would God implant the desire to solve mysteries and not provide the solution? (*Suddenly PEPE runs up the steps to the poop.* COLUMBUS *is startled* Paneta! Who is that?
PEPE: Me, Captain—Pepe!
COLUMBUS: (*frowning on him*). Have you been there all the time?
PEPE: Please, sir, I am off duty.

COLUMBUS: Then why aren't you down below?
PEPE: (*whimsically, knowing that he is privileged*). I prefer your company to theirs. (*He points below.*) Am I in the way here, sir?
COLUMBUS: (*humouring him*). What a boy! And what do they say of the preference?
PEPE: I don't speak to them. I hate them.
COLUMBUS: 'Sh, Pepe! And get you gone! (PEPE *turns reluctantly*). Quick! (*They boy goes more quickly*). Here! You heard what Don Pedro said?
PEPE: Yes, captain. And he is the best..........
COLUMBUS: (*bitterly*). Everybody.............
PEPE: (*eagerly*). Except me, captain, except me.
(*He goes to him impetuously.*)
COLUMBUS: (*laying a hand on the boy's head*). You are young enough to have faith. Thank you, boy.
(*The seamen's song is heard again.*)
PEPE: They are horrible when they drink too much. They say it makes them forget.
COLUMBUS: Poor fellows!
PEPE: (*approaching nearer*). Captain, be careful! Sometimes they are desperate.
(*The song surges up like a growl*).
COLUMBUS: That is ugly. I bade Don Pedro stop them. So you think they might become dangerous?
(DON PEDRO *returns*). Go boy. (PEPE *moves away, but does not go out.*) Well, Don Pedro? Their singing changes to a roar. The deepening of their discontent is ominous.
(*The noise grows louder.*)
PEDRO: Captain, they ignore my order.
COLUMBUS (*furious*). I'll make an example of one of them (*Suddenly*). Hallo, there! What sneaking mischief-maker is that crawling about the deck? Show yourself?!
(FRANCISCO *appears from the right.*)
COLUMBUS: Ho, Francisco—you, it it?
FRANCISCO: Yes, sir. And I'm no sneaking mischief-maker.
COLUMBUS: Then why behave as one? Why are you here? Did I send for you? Is discipline obsolete in the Ocean Sea? Is Jack as good as his master now-a-days?
FRANCISCO: (*humbly*). Your words sting, sir!
COLUMBUS: And are meant to. I am tired of the mumbling

and grumbling of the crew. I have been patient too long.
FRANCISCO: I came to warn you, sir. The temper of the crew is dangerous.
COLUMBUS: Danger is the breath of my life. I should doubt I lived if I lived outside danger.
FRANCISCO: (*the words springing from him spasmodically*). Our power of endurance has go on. We refuse to gon, I warn you. I respect your person and do not wish to see violence used; but it is more than mortal can bear, this endless sailing into unknown seas.
COLUMBUS: (*to* PEDRO). Don Pedro, the ship is in your hands. I will talk to our friend, as man to man. (PEDRO *goes on to the poop.* COLUMBUS, *his voice gentler, almost ingratiating, turns to* FRANCISCO, *who shifts from foot to foot, nervous by reason of the unaccustomed propinquity*). Francisco, let me plead with you There are men whom God has chosen for the working of His will. I am such a man. There is no more merit in me than in this ship; we are both instruments of God. Sometimes He chooses oddly; a stronger man than I might have served His purpose better. But since God chose me, who shall withstand me? The four corners of the earth are to be linked up in the knowledge of their Saviour. I have lifted the veils which obscured the prophecies of Holy Writ, and I have learned that it was ordained that I, chosen among all men, should discover that great world beyond the ocean which I know exists as surely as I know that Heaven exists.
FRANCISCO: Must simple men suffer because of *your* knowledge?
COLUMBUS: (*quickly*). Simple men shall do their duty.
FRANCISCO: There are limits to duty. Men will give up many things for duty and for gain, but you ask too much. Country, family, friends, perhaps even life itself — all these things you ask us to give up for *your* glory. We are not chosen of God to open up new ways: we are simple, humble men, sick for our homes and hungry for our wives.
COLUMBUS: My Heaven, Francisco, you try me.....
FRANCISCO: (*gaining courage*). Not more than you try us, sir. I come to you as a friend, sir. The men are at the end of their patience and spoiling for a fight. The stoutest rope breaks at last.(*The song swells up again. Spoken words mingle with the song,*

and the voice of GUILLERMO IRES *is heard above the rest*) Did you hear that sir!

COLUMBUS: I heard the snarling of angry beasts.

FRANCISCO: You heard the just complaints of angry men, sir. (*Again* GUILLERMO'S *voice pierces the din.* COLUMBUS *stands rigid, endeavouring to catch the words.*) Did you hear *that*, sir?

PEPE: (*who has been unobserved*). They shan't! They shan't!

COLUMBUS: Boy, come here. What were the words?

PEPE: (*almost weeping*). He said: "The *Santa Maria* will be the lighter for his carcass."

COLUMBUS: (*bitterly*). He said that, did he? (*He blinks —is moved more than he will show.*)

FRANCISCO: I am sorry, sir... I knew how high feeling had run.

COLUMBUS: (*authoritatively*). Send Guillermo Ires to me!

FRANCISCO: (*not without diffidence*). Sorry sir, but...

COLUMBUS: Discipline knows no buts.

FRANCISCO: (*angrily*). Discipline is a thing of the past, sir. It's you or us.

COLUMBUS: (*to* DON PEDRO) Don Pedro, let Guillermo Ires be sent to me. He shall know what it is like in irons.

(PEDRO *is half-way down the stairs to the quarter-deck when* GUILLERMO IRES *and other seamen rush in an agry mass towards* COLUMBUS, *growing like infuriated animals.*)

COLUMBUS: (*in a thunderous*) Stop! What is the meaning of this wild uproar? (*The men stand transfixed*). The first man to move shall spend the rest of the night in irons!

(*There is a perceptible pause, during which nobody moves. Then with a wild cry,* GUILLERMO IRES *breaks away from the others and advances towards COLUMBUS.*)

GUILLERMO: And who's to put him in irons? We are thirty to one.

COLUMBUS: (*calmly*). If nobody else is available for the office, I will perform it myself. Get below! Let me hear no more of this.

GUILLERMO: (*in high excitement*). We 've stood too much. We've been duped day in and day out. We're men with the common feelings of men. We want our homes and our women. I say the *Santa Maria* shall turn her helm towards Spain at once, or we are not men but sheep.

COLUMBUS: (*still calm*). And who shall navigate her?

GUILLERMO: There's plenty here who can do that. The Devil's

with *you,* we all know that, riding the easterly wind; but we are not men unused to the sea. Once clear of this Devil's track to nowhere, we'll blow our way back to home.

(*Signs of assent from the rest of the crew.* COLUMBUS *raises his hand, appealing for silence. He is paler than his want, but very calm.*)

COLUMBUS: Don Guillermo, you are an excellent sailor, a man of abundant resourcefulness. Some day, if your tongue does not run away with your discretion, you will achieve prosperty in your calling. Today you are an able-bodied seaman, and no more: I am your captain. Your duty is to obey me as mine is to obey the Royal Sovereigns of Spain who sent me. Let that be clearly understood between us and we shall not fall out. Now return to your duties.

(*Again a perceptible pause.* COLUMBUS'S *authoriative manner holds them. Presently* DIEGO *breaks out.*)

DIEGO: Words for children! Froth and scum! We are men: reason with us!

COLUMBUS: Silence!

(*The tone of authority calms the men, who remain, however, in a huddled crowd, murmuring discontentedly.* COLUMBUS *turns and goes up the stairs to the poop, where he stands and looks down upon the men.*)

DIEGO: (*snarling*). I suppose you think you're on holy ground now?

(*He bounds towards the stairs*)

VOICES: (*tumultuously*). Have him down! Pitch him overboard! Put *him* in irons! Devel's tool! Italian renegade!

(*They are about to stampede up the poop gangway, when* PEPE *runs to the foot of the stairs and stnads with his arms spread out.*)

PEPE: Cowards! Cowards! You will have to kill *me* first!

VOICES: Out of the way! Devil's help! Lick-spittle!

COLUMBUS: What! Does that child stand between me and death? (*silence follows the commencement of his speech*). Pepe! Come here!

PEPE: (*going to him quickly*). My captain!

(*The men are somewhat sheepish*)

COLUMBUS: Pepe! This is a voyage of discovery. (*The men growl.*) I set out to discover a new world, a radiant land beyond unknown seas; to find new wealth and dominion for our Sovereign King and Queen, new souls for the sacrifice of our

Saviour to redeem. So far I have discovered but one thing. (*He pauses and continues with slow deliberation*). I have discovered that when a man is given a vision he must follow it along. Loyalty passes like seaweed on an outgoing tide. Friendship breaks as a mast hollowed by worms breaks. Discipline, duty, and honourable obedience are bubbles that burst at the first contact. There remains but oneself. That is my only discovery so far, Pepe.

PEPE: (*his eyes gleaming with excitement*). Captain I am loyal, I am still obedient, still your devoted servant...

COLUMBUS: (*with some emotion*). I am not ungrateful.

PEDRO: (*scraping his throat with dignity*). I hope my loyalty has never been in question sir? (*He salutes.*)

COLUMBUS: (*returning the salute*). You have sometimes been silent, Don Pedro, when speech would have made your loyalty clear. But I thank you...

(COLUMBUS *turns and looks out at sea; for a moment his attention is fixed. He peers more earnestly into the darkness. There is a movement among men. He turns.*)

JUAN: We are simple men, sir...

COLUMBUS: (*hastily*). Shall simple men judge their betters?

GUILLERMO: (*surlily*). We may as well wait till tomorrow, at any rate.

COLUMBUS: Dark deeds are better done in the dark.

(GUILLERMO, *scowling but sheepish, slinks off, followed by one or two of the seamen.*)

FRANCISCO: Desperate men do not always act up to the best that is in them, sir.

COLUMBUS: (*with quiet irony*). I thank you for reminding me, Francisco. Your best cannot be bettered. Goodnight!

(FRANCISCO *half-turns to speak again, but thinks better of it and goes, shame faced. Several others go, too, sheepish. A brief silence.* COLUMBUS *does not move; he is struggling with overwrought emotion. When he speaks his voice is not steady.*)

COLUMBUS: Go, boy!

(PEPE *seizes his hand, kisses it, and hastily descends to the quarter-deck and goes out.*)

COLUMBUS: (*turning to* PEDRO). Two minutes ago, Don Pedro, I saw... I thought I saw... (*He peers into the darkness*). It was... It is...

PEDRO: (*in excitement*). What, sir?

COLUMBUS: A light, faintly flickering, rising up and down. Look!
(*He points.*)
PEDRO: It is, sir! Glory be to God!
(*At this moment there is wild shout, off.*)
VOICE: (*off*). A light! A light! Land! Land!
(*A sailor comes running on, delirious with joy and excitement.*)
SAILOR: Did you see it, sir A light! Blessed Mother of God! A light!
COLUMBUS: (*with quiet authority*). Give the order to heave to.

NOTES

Santa Maria : The name of the ship in which Columbus and his men sailed on their voyage of discovery of the New World beyond the seas.

poop: a raised deck at the stern of a ship.

rigging: all the ropes, sails etc. with whcih a ship is rigged.

derisively: laughing at or making fun of.

quaking: shaking, trembling.

Santisma Maria: Most Holy Mary (an oath).

crossed: opposed in his plans or wishes.

keg: a small barrel.

the Captain: Columbus.

assiduity: careful continual attention.

foremost: the most nearest the bow of a ship.

page-boy: a boy servant usually uniformed. (*Now rare:* a boy in service to a person of high rank)

hatchway: an opening in deck for lowering cargo.

Madre de Dios: The Mother of God (an oath).

unchartered seas: where no chartered ship has ever sailed, unexplored, seas.

When the needle of the compass... pointed to the North-West: refers to the discover of the deviation of the geographical pole from the magnetic pole. The deviation between the magnetic pole and the geographical pole is not the same in different parts of the earth.

portent: omen, sign or warning especially of something strange or undesirable.

appeased: made calm or satisfied.

impetuously: showing swift action but lack of thought.

obsolete: no longer used; out of date.

spasmodically: of or like a spasm, (a sudden violent effort, feeling or action)

ingratiating: showing that one wishes to gain favour.

propinquity: nearness.

carcass: dead body.

perceptible: that which can be perceived, noticeable.

wont: a person's habit or custom.

froth and scum: idle talk.

renegade: a traitor, a person who deserts the country or belief to join another.

stampede up: to take part in a sudden mad rush or mass movement.

scraping: clearing.

to heave to: to throw anchor (to bring the ship to a halt).

COMPREHENSION

1. Explain what the following sentences mean:
   a. We are like bats trying to fly by day.
   b. It is not easy to hold fast to faith when nothing seems to warrant faith.
   c. There is such a thing as being too clever — prying into mysteries which were not meant for our eyes.
   d. Would God implant the desire to solve mysteries and not provide the solution?
   e. Is Jack as good as his master nowadays.
   f. The stoutest rope breaks at last.
   g. The Santa Maria will be lighter for his carcass.
   h. Some day, if your tongue does not run away with your discretion you will achieve prosperity in your calling.
   i. I have discovered that when a man is given a vision he must follow it alone.

j. Men will give up many things for duty and for gain but you ask too much.

2. Why does the crew say that the Devil and not God is in the easterly wind?
3. Why is the crew of Santa Maria unhappy with Columbus?
4. What is the significance of the song that the crew sing?
5. Columbus believes in discipline. Find out at least two examples from the play that show this.
6. How does Columbus deal with the mutiny in this ship?
7. Columbus made two discoveries — one during the voyage and the other at the end of it. What were these discoveries?
8. What did the crew want to do to Columbus? Why did they not succeed in their plan?

LANGUAGE STUDY

1. Please note that:
   Descend is the opposite of *ascend*.
   Decelerate is the opposite of *accelerate*.
   Make a list of seven words with the prefix *de-* and write against each the word having the opposite meaning.
2. You know that:
   Impatient is the opposite of *patient*.
   Improper is the opposite of *proper*.
   Make a list of seven words which have the prefix *im-* and write against each the word having the opposite meaning.
3. The prefix *pre-* means before e.g. prewar; and in advance of e.g. prearrange.
   Similarly the prefix *post-* means later than, after e.g. postwar, post-mortem etc.
   Make a list of five words with the prefix *pre* and five words with the prefix *post-*
4. A number of verbs take the suffix *-ate* e.g. calculate, rehabilitate, indicate etc.
   Make a list of seven verbs which have the suffix *-ate* and mention against each the corresponding noun, e.g.
   calculate : calculation.

rehabilitate : rehabilitation.
indicate : indication.

5. Use the following words as verbs:
rig, warrant, temper, spoil for, stand (tolerate), design (in the passives, characterise.

COMPOSITION

1. Who do you sympathise with more — the crew of Santa Maria or Columbus? Give reasons for your answer.
2. Describe the qualities that made Columbus a great sailor and explorer. What do you think were his weaknesses?
3. How many sympathisers does Columbus have among his crew. To what extent do they sympathise with and understand him?
4. How would you as the manager of an industrial undertaking deal with a workers'strike? Write an imaginary dialogue between the management and the representative of the workers concerning the workers' demands.

Appendices

Appendix I: Developing Writing Skills

Appendix II: Grammar

Appendix I

Description of Objects/Materials/Articles in Science and Technology

Much of our learning about science takes place through definitions. It often becomes necessary to define as well as describe things in science.

A complete description of an article/object deals with much more than its appearance. A description includes:

1. a. definition (if possible)
   b. accuracy
   c. the need for brevity.

2. a. the appearance
   b. function or use
   c. mechanism (if any).

EXAMPLES:

1. Siphon

Look at the following explanation and illustration of a siphon:

A basic siphon essentially consists of an inverted U-shaped tube that pulls liquid up from one level without the aid of gravity to transport it to another (lower) level. The siphon is used particularly when the liquid has to be transported over physical barriers without the help of a pump or motor. As gravity pulls down the liquid into B, a vacuum is created at the highest point of the tube, which is filled by the liquid from A. Liquid from beaker A will pass to B as long as both ends of the tube are below the liquid level.

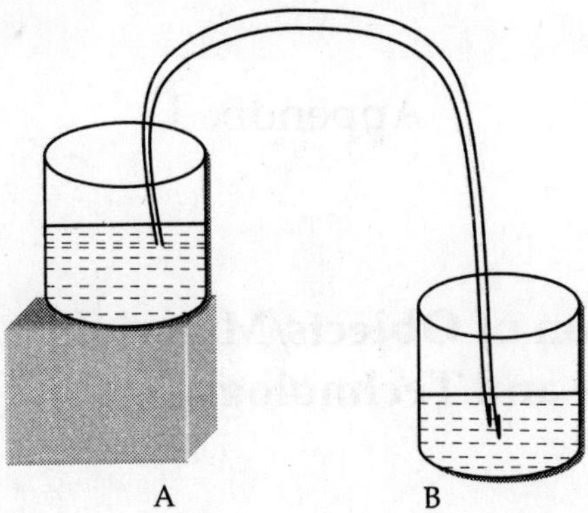

2. The Vernier calipers:

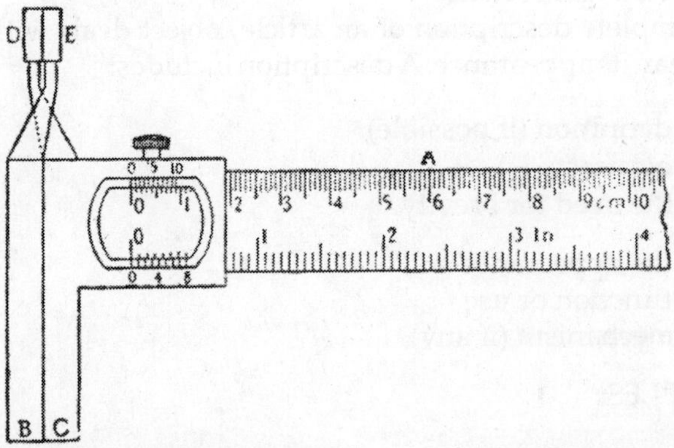

The Vernier calipers are used to measure small lengths accurately. They consist of a flat, polished steel bar about 10 to 15 cms. in length. The main scale is marked on the bar in centimeters and inches. The calipers are provided with a fixed jaw having a plain face on the inner side. Sliding over the main bar is a Vernier bit with the Vernier scale marked on it on both edges. The bit has a screw by which it can be fixed to the bar point.

1. Define and describe the following:

A refrigerator, the Borda pendulum, a barometer, a calorimeter, convex lens, a sonometer, resonance apparatus, a fountain pen, an electric bulb, a balance, a screw gauge,

a lathe, a conical flask, a bunsen burner, a thermometer, a typewriter, fibreglass, a camera, a computer, the gas cylinder, a bicycle pump.

EXAMPLES:

First, define a planetarium and then read the following description

How is the night sky 'film' made and projected on to the planetarium dome? What is the secret life of planetarium stars? These are questions that visitors to the planetarium keep asking.

Actually, there is neither a 'film' nor a single projector like the one used in a cinema. The large dumb-bell-shaped instrument, sitting under the dome like a giant robot, is a composite of nearly a hundred different projectors. The sphere of either end of this instrument carries 32 projectors which have a common lamp (1500 W tungsten with a specially designed filament). But each projector has a separate lens fixed on the sphere.

Each projector projects a template, showing a part of the sky; the 32 images from one sphere enmesh perfectly to produce a full picture. The templates are specially made copper plates with multiple holes which correspond to a required star configuration. But the holes are very precisely made according to the apparent brightness of the stars. Thus brighter stars would require larger holes.

Besides these star projectors, there are other projectors for the Sun, the Moon and the planets, for the constellations, for very bright stars, comets, and the Milky Way, and for an assortment of astronomical coordinates like the equator, the ecliptic (the path traversed by the Sun through the sky), etc. and other markers and pointers.

The projectors for the Sun, the Moon and the five planets that can be seen with the naked eye (Mercury, Venus, Mars, Jupiter and Saturn) are in the cage-like truss across the spheres. Unlike the star projectors, these are not fixed; they have a complex gearing system that makes these planets move at different relative speeds exactly as they do in the sky. Saturn, for instance, moves very slowly compared to Venus or Mercury. The Moon projector even shows the phases of the Moon as it passes through the constellations once a month.

The constellation projectors outline the constellation figures (the hunter for Orion, the bull for Taurus, etc) over the stars of that particular constellation. What is remarkable here is that often one constellation figure is projected in parts by more than one projector. But they are so perfectly matched that it is impossible to make out where one ends and another starts.

Riding piggy-back on the main projector are 10 to 20 other projectors. These project very bright stars, variable stars, comets, the Milky Way, astronomical coordinates, and markers.

The projector has three basic motions: the diurnal motion, simulating the motion of stars through one day; the annual motion, simulating the motion of the Sun, the Moon and the planets over a year or longer periods (with this one can go into the future or revert to the past); and the polar motion which helps change the perspective and observe the sky as seen from any place or latitude on the Earth.

Motors, with gears, manipulate these motions on command from the operator's console. All three motions have servo-indicators on the operator's console and the operator knows exactly what the sky looks like without looking up. The operator takes the cue from the audio record of the script and operates the projector.

For instance, the polar motion motor, when activated, alters the altitude of the Pole Star above the horizon, thus giving the illusion of an increase or decrease in latitude.

Besides the main projector system, movie and slide projectors are separately used to show astronomical objects and events. Like, for example, rotating galaxies, surface features of planets, the launching of a spacecraft or the sequence of processes involved in the birth of a star, or in the death of a star.

NEIL SADWELKAR, *Science Today*

EXERCISES

1. Write a letter to your foreign friend about planetariums in India or the Jantar Mantar in Delhi.
2. A major component of your refrigerator goes out of order during the "guarantee period". Write a letter to your dealer demanding replacement. Be specific about the defect.

3. Place an order with a firm for the supply of important materials for your science laboratory.
4. Describe the shortcomings of your computer lab.
5. Prepare a project for your Principal for the sanction of a trip to a hill-station to enable you to enrich the botanical garden of the college.
6. Prepare a list of things you wnat for your Industrial Chemistry Lab or your Zoology Museum.
7. Write an account of an important experiment you have done in your laboratory for your science teacher.

Precis Writing

In your examination you will be required to write a precis of a given passage. The word 'Precis' means a restatement in a shortened form of the chief ideas of the original passage. A precis is not an outline of a passage, it is a restatement. You must write your precis in your own words. Do not copy expressions or sentences from the original passage. A precis is is not a mere selection of a few important sentences from the passage. You must express in your own words the main points of the passage and these points must be expressed clearly and in as few words as possible and the finished product must be a well-connected piece, not a collection of unconnected facts and statements.

A precis should be about one-third the length of the original passage and it should normally be contained in one paragraph. Precis-writing is an exacting exercise and it demands considerable effort and practice. Writing a precis is more difficult than writing a piece of composition because a precis must be both clear and brief. You must, therefore on your own, attempt the precis of a few passages. It will be much better if, in the examination, you attempt the precis when you have sufficient time at your disposal. Do not make the precis question the last question to be attempted. You may then not have sufficient time for it. Precis-writing demands concentration, skill, time and practice. It is not an exercise you can rush through.

The precis of a speech or a dialogue must be written in the third person, in the indirect form of narration and in the past tense. All these changes are necessary because while you are making a precis of that speech or dialogue you are reporting or describing what somebody else has said at an earlier time.

The passage set for precis-writing will, in all likelihood, be unfamiliar to you. You must read it slowly and carefully. It is quite possible that on the first reading you will not understand the passage or some parts of it. Don't be upset. Read the passage again. You will find that your second reading is more rewarding than the first one. Now read the passage yet again i.e., for the third time. Your third reading should give you reasonably good understanding of the passage. If you have not understood a few expressions in the passage, do not worry.

Having read the passage at least three times you should now start noting down the main points in the passage. This can be done by reading the passage once again, this time sentence by sentence and noting down after every sentence the main idea it expresses. Read the first sentence of the passage and note down the main point it contains. Then read the next sentence. If the second sentence only repeats what had already been said in the first sentence, leave it, and pass on to the next sentence. If it contains a new point, note it down. If it partly repeats what has been said earlier and also adds something new, note down only that which is new. In this way read the rest of the sentences and note down the main points as these occur in the original passage. After you have finished noting down the main points, you have with you a rough outline. Have another look at the original passage to ensure that you have not left out any important point. Also make sure that there is no repetition and that you have not included in the rough outline any unimportant points.

If the original passage contains any stories or examples or similes, these must not be included in the precis. Similarly no ornamental expressions or comparisons should find a place in a precis.

With the help of this rough outline which is for the time being nothing more than a catalogue of points, you can prepare a rough draft of your precis using *words other than those in the original.* Of course this does not mean you are prohibited from using pronouns, articles, conjunctions, prepositions, etc. used in the original. This will require a proper ordering and linking of the points so that it now reads like a well-connected passage. By and large the main points should, as far as possible, be stated in the same order in which these figure in the original passage. You may, however, change their order if you think it will make your precis more readable and more logical.

What you have with you is only the rough draft of your precis. It is not the finished precis. Now count the words both in the given original passage and those in your precis to make sure that your precis is neither too long nor too short. Make necessary changes in the rough draft of your precis to make it one-third of the original passage. You can save words by joining two or more sentences into one, or by splitting a lengthy sentence into two or more sentences. You can also save words by using single words or expressions for lengthy expressions e.g. "He did not know how to read or write," could be react into "He was illiterate." To take another example, the sentence "He delivered a speech without having made any prior preparation for it" can be shortened into "He spoke extempore." You can come across these useful words in exercises described as "One word substitution." All good books of grammar and composition have such an exercise.

It is very important to remember that a precis is not a group of small jerky sentences expressing ideas and arranged in the shape of a paragraph. The sentences in your precis must have a logical order and must be well-connected. The movement from one sentence to the next should be a smooth one and should not create an impression either of repetition or of gaps. Each sentence of your precis should naturally lead to the next one. To connect your sentences you can make use of connectors such as 'and', 'but', 'therefore', 'because', 'further', etc. After you have made all the necessary changes and you feel convinced that your precis is of the required length and you can improve it no further, make a fresh, legible copy of the precis and score out the rough work done so that the examiner may not, by mistake, evaluate your rough precis.

A precis must have a title. It is incomplete without a title. Many students have the wrong impression that a precis can have only one title and that you are lucky if you can discover it somehow. In fact a precis can have a number of suitable titles, though you should give your precis only one title, the best you can think of. Write the title at the top of the precis. Do not write it at the end with an introductory sentence like "The title of the precis is..." All important words in the title should begin with a capital letter. It is always better to give the precis a short title but if a longer title is more appropriate, you may prefer the longer one.

To select a title for the precis ask yourself the quesion "What is the original passage about?" or "What is the most important idea in the passage?" You may, though not always, find an answer to this question in the first or the last sentence of the original passage.

Let us remind you again that you must write your precis in your own words; your precis must be about one-third the length of the original passage; it should be well-knit; and it must have an appropriate title. Revise the final draft of the precis to make sure that there are no spelling mistakes and no chance omissions.

SOLVED EXAMPLES OF PRECIS-WRITING

The Passage

The man who is perpetually hesitating as to which of the two things he will do first, will do neither. The man who resolves, but suffers his resolution to be changed by the first counter suggestion of a friend — who fluctuates from opinion to opinion, and from plan to plan can never accomplish anything great or useful. Instead of being progressive in anything he will be at best stationary, and more probably retrograde in all he does. It is only the man who first consults wisely, then resolves firmly, and then carries out his purpose with inflexible perseverance, undismayed by those petty difficulties which frighten a weaker spirit, who can advance to any eminence in any line. (117 words)

Points

1. A man who is ever wavering can achieve nothing great.
2. Frequent changes in decisions, opinions and plans defeat his aims.
3. For success it is necessary to consult wisely, resolve firmly and work steadily with determination. (35 words)

Rough Draft

A man who is ever wavering can achieve nothing great. If he changes his opinions, decisions and plans constantly he will reach nowhere and may in fact slide back. Success needs careful planning after proper consultation,/the decision to work steadily and with determination. (44 words)

Final Draft

Determination leads to Success: A constantly wavering man cannot succeed. Frequent changes in opinions, decisions and plans defeat him. To succeed one should consult wisely, decide firmly and execute the decisions steadily and with hope and courage. (33 words)

The Passage

The characteristic of genuine heroism is its persistency. All men have wandering impulses, fits and starts of generosity. But when you have resolved to be great, abide by yourself, and do not weakly try to reconcile yourself with the world. The heroic cannot be the common, nor the common the heroic. Yet we have the weakness to expect the sympathy of people in those actions whose excellence is that they outrun sympathy, and appeal to a tardy justice. If you would serve your brother, because it is fit for you to serve him, do not take back your words when you find that prudent people do not commend you. Be true to your own act, and congratulate yourself if you have done something strange and extravagant, and broken the monotony of a decorous age. It was high counsel that I once heard given to a young person, —"Always do what you are afraid to do." (157 words)

EMERSON

Points

1. True heroism requires persistency.
2. Unwillingness to make compromises, come what may, is necessary for achieving greatness.
3. Loneliness, lack of sympathy, slowness of justice do not discourage the great.
4. Worldly wisdom does not change their resolve.
5. Greatness is never common.

6. The great are just and generous despite opposition and lack of praise. They love to live dangerously. (56 words)

Rough Draft

True heroism requires persistence. The truly heroic do not make compromises. They stick to their resolve. They are not deterred by loneliness, lack of sympathy and slowness of justice. Worldly counsels do not change their decisions. True greatness is not common. The great remain just and generous even in the face of opposition, and lack of appreciation. They love to live dangerously. (62 words)

Final Draft

True Heroism: True heroism requires persistence. The truly heroic do not compromise. They remain firm, undeterred by loneliness, lack of sympathy and slow justice. Worldly counsels do not change their decisions. True greatness is not common. The great remain just and generous despite opposition and lack of sympathy. They love to live dangerously. (51 words)

PASSAGES FOR PRECIS-WRITING

1. The behaviour of young boys is the subject of comment the world over. Particularly distressing is the manifestation of insulting conduct towards school and college-going girls in University towns. While no condemnation can be too severe for such ungentlemanly conduct wherever it may take place, a general enquiry is called for into the causes that have led to this kind of behaviour. Lack of reverence for women is only an offshoot from a larger evil. The real tragedy is surely the complete lack of self-discipline evident in the behaviour of these youngsters. This lack of control needs to be dealt with broadly before we can hope to see improvements in its narrower aspects. We all know that the best way to teach a child anything is by example. But cases of young children

who misbehave prove that many parents and teachers undoubtedly fail calamitously in their duty. Both at home and at school far too many children are brought up to do what they like, to do a job badly, to leave it unfinished, to have anything they want at the expense of other people's convenience.

Parents say they cannot manage their children; it grows more and more difficult to find a teacher who can manage a class. And then the behaviour of parents and teachers is not always calculated to inspire respect. But perhaps the greatest harm is done by the perpetual rousing of senses by posters, films, magazines, advertisements, etc. Society will have to make a much more determined effort to mould the character of the children if this normal deterioration is to be halted. (267 words)

2. Broken friendship, like china may be repaired, but the break will alwyas show. Friendship is a precious thing — too precious a treasure to be carelessly broken or thrown away. The world handles the word 'friend' lightly; its real, true deeper meaning is forgotten, and the acquaintance of an hour or the chance-comer is designated by the term which in itself bears a wealth of meaning. Your friend is the one who appreciates you —your faults as well as your virtues, —who understands and sympathises with your defeats and victories, your aims and ideals, your joys and temptations, your hopes and disappointments, as no one else does or can. It is your friend to whom you turn for counsel, for comfort, for praise; he may not be as learned as some or as wise as others, but it suffices that he understands you, and even his quiet listening gives strength and renewed courage.

Blessed is the man or woman into whose life has come the beauty and power of such a friendship. Prize it well. Do all in your power to keep such a friendship unbroken. Avoid the break, for when it comes it cannot be mended and the jarring note mars the harmony. It is not just the forgiveness, but rather the hurt in the heart that will not readily heal and the confidence that will not fully return. (239 words)

Writing Reports

Writing reports has become a part of professional activity in a number of spheres. Committees and Commissions are appointed by the government to investigate a happening, or to study and deal with a problem and to submit their findings and recommendations. Sometimes expert opinion is obtained by private individuals who want to be advised on one subject or the other. In all such situations reports have to be prepared and submitted.

There is a wide variety of subjects on which reports can and may have to be written. Reports on technical subjects will naturally require technical knowledge and the use of technical expressions.

Understandably reports are prepared by those who have expertise in the subject or by those who have studied the problem so much in depth that they know much more about it than do the others. They are, therefore, in a position to arrive at certain findings and to make certain well-considered recommendations.

A report is meant to be a communication between an expert, a specialist or one who has come to acquire special knowledge or experience of a subject and others who are much less informed. Those to whom the report has to be submitted may or may not be experts. Very often a report is meant for members of the general public.

The purpose of every report is to give information to a person or a body of persons who are not aware of the full facts, or who are not in possession of complete information on the subject, or who for lack of the required expertise are not in a position to arrive at proper conclusions and hence cannot take appropriate decisions.

It naturally follows that the writer of the report must be in full possession of facts, should be thoroughly familiar with the matter and should have adequate knowledge of the subject. He may or may not be an expert. But if a non-expert, he must have devoted sufficient time and energy to understand the problem and must have formulated his opinion on the subject.

Reports can be submitted by an expert to his client, either being an individual or a body of individuals; by an employee to his employer, or by a Committee or Commission to the government.

Very often report take the form of a letter, particularly when the author of the report is an individual. In such a case the report is written in the first person and it has the shape and form of a business letter.

The report of a Committee or a Sub-Committee or a Commission constitutes a different class. This class also includes a report submitted jointly by a group of authors. Such a report, it is assumed, contains the considered opinion of a number of individuals. It is a formal document and is, therefore, written impersonally in formal and carefully chosen phraseology. It must be signed by the Chairman, the Chairman and the Secretary, or by the members of the Committee or Commission etc.

Such a report must begin with a preliminary paragraph stating how and when the Committee or the Commission was appointed, who set it up and with what authority, what were its terms of reference, what was the time given to it for submitting its report, what powers were given to the Committee or Commission for discharging the duties entrusted to it, what witnesses were examined, what evidence was available to the Committee or the Commission, who were the experts who deposed before it and what their views were etc. The report must also contain a brief report of the proceedings and discussions of the Committee or Commission, what the views of its members were, whether the report is unanimous or there was a difference of opinion among the members and finally what its proposals and recommendations are.

A well-written report must indicate the issue it deals with, and it must have a logical arrangement of facts. The reasoning must be convincing and appropriately expressed. The arguments must be arranged properly and it must have definite and clear recommendations. A haphazard arrangement will make the report less intelligible and reduce its force.

Since it may not be possible for an average student to know

much about the technical aspects of a problem or matter he may find it considerably difficult to write a report on a subject of a fairly technical nature. Students should, therefore, try to add to their general knowledge so that they can draw upon it in writing reports. Proper attention must, however, always be paid to the structure and form of the report.

The report must be correct in form and general arrangement and should be logical and readable even if it does not show evidence of detailed technical knowledge and information.

An outline of a report on the subject of setting up a new mining company

1. The names and addresses of the promoters of the proposed venture, their past and present association with other business activities highlighting their association with mining activities.
2. Where the new mines will be and why those sites have been selected.
3. How are other mining companies doing at present, the state of the market, where the output will be sold, and what are the expected returns?
4. How much capital will be required? How is the company going to collect so much capital? What part of the capital will be in the form of shares, debentures and loans.
5. Who will be the directors of the company?
6. Does the necessary infrastructure for mining operations exist near the proposed site of the mines?
7. What is the report of the geological experts about the profitability of the venture and what will be the quality of the ore produced?
8. Where will be the head office of the company?
9. Has the proposed company arranged foreign collaboration? From where will the required machinery be imported?
10. Is the government going to give any help to the company?

Outline of a report on the basis of a market survey about the possibility of marketing a new medicine to prevent enteric infection

1. Causes of enteric infection; areas prone to such diseases and the time of the year when such cases rise steeply.
2. Medicines available at present for fighting enteric infection,

their deficiencies and side-effects; the price structure of such medicines.

3. To what extent these medicines have succeeded in eradicating diseases caused by enteric infection.
4. In what way does the formulation of the proposed medicine differ from that of other medicines available to the public at present.
5. Does the new drug have less side-effects, take less time to control the infection, is more acceptable to a wider variety of patients with different manifestations of the disease and is it less expensive than other similar drugs etc.?
6. Have research journals commented upon the new formulation? What has been their reaction?
7. Has the medicine been tried out anywhere, if so with what results?
8. What is the reaction of medical practitioners? Are they taking interest in this new formulation and will they be willing to prescribe it?
9. What incentives is the manufacturer prepared to give to whole-sale and retail dealers?
10. What is the shelf-life of the new formulation? Can it be preserved for a period longer than the one application to other similar formulations?
11. How is the packaging of the new medicine? Is it attractive?

Following a newspaper report that fourteen persons lost their eye sight by consuming spurious liquor, the Lt. Governor of Delhi appointed the District Sessions Judge, Delhi, to investigate the case and submit a report to the Government: Prepare a Draft Report.

1. On...(date) it was reported that fourteen people living in Seelampur lost their eye sight by consuming spurious liquor.
2. Following the above incident the Lt. Governor of Delhi appointed a Judicial Inquiry Commission to report to the government about the details of this case and to recommend steps to check such incidents in the future.
3. The District and Sessions Judge who constituted the one man Judicial Inquiry Committee visited Seelampur on four different days and talked to the people of this area and recorded the evidence of witnesses whose names appear in Annexure A.

4. The Commission also recorded the statement of Doctor X who treated the patients at Seelampur before they were shifted to different hospitals in the city.
5. Illicit distillation of liquor is common since the locality is inhabited by poor people who cannot afford quality liquor.
6. Most of the inhabitants of this area are wage earners and they do manual work. They live in very small houses, in dirty surroundings and are very poor. This lacality is also crime-prone. A number of petty criminals live here.
7. Drug-trafficking is also not uncommon.
8. There were disturbing reports of police complicity in such activities but no conclusive evidence to prove this was produced before the Commission.
9. The man who supplied spurious liquor happens to be one 'Z'. He has a crime record as a bootlegger. He has a well-knit establishment of distillers, suppliers and carriers.
10. The network of his activities includes the cities of Ghaziabad, Hapur and surrounding industrial areas.
11. The names of other such manufacturers of illicit liquor have also been mentioned by the witnesses, five out of these have been arrested while the others are absconding. Mr. Z was arrested at Meerut five days after the tragedy.
12. A report of chemical analysis of the spurious liquor supplied is still awaited.
13. The government must take steps to watch over anti-social elements who manufacture and sell spurious liquor.
14. The S.H.O. should be transferred immediately. A departmental inquiry is called for against police officials whose names are listed in Appendix B.
15. New legislation is needed to check effectively such crimes and to provide deterrent punishment to such offenders. The existing penal laws do not have sufficient teeth.
16. More important than all of these punitive measures is the need for the government to open a liquor shop in the area thus providing an outlet for the sale of certified liquor.
17. Equally important is the need for All India Radio and Doordarshan to issue warnings against the consumption of spurious liquor.

EXERCISES

1. Prepare the report of a committee set up to study why public sector undertakings have been incurring losses year after year and what should be done to bring them out of the red.
2. A committee has been appointed by the government to study the working of the D.T.C. and to recommend steps to improve its working. Prepare a report on behalf of the committee.
3. Prepare a report highlighting the plight of those who are cheated by those who undertake to send persons to foreign countries for employment there, and what should be done to stop such practices and to help those who have got stranded in foreign countries.
4. Your friend has just manufactured a new domestic machine that can be very useful in the kitchen. He wants to apply for a bank loan to expand his business. Draft a report with regard to the prospects of his venture so that the bank may advance him the loan applied for. It is presumed that you have the necessary expertise for submitting such a report.
5. Supposing you are a Police Inspector and the Inspector General of Police has aksed you to submit a report about the smuggling of drugs from across the border. Draft a report outlining the state of smuggling activities and what can be done to check these.
6. Presuming that you are a member of the committee appointed by the Vice-Chancellor to suggest ways and means for improving the system of examination in the University of Delhi, draft a report for submission to the Academic Council of the University of Delhi.
7. You are the director of a private detective agency. You have been employed by a client to find out who has been threatening him on the phone. Prepare a report of your investigation and findings and advise him what he should do.

Appendix II

Clauses

Finite Clause: A (finite) clause is a group of words that has a subject and a predicate i.e., a tense-carrying (finite) verb but forms a part of a sentnece.

A (finite) clause is not an independent sentence. (Finite) clauses other than the Principal Clauses (Superordinate Clauses) are referred to as Subordinate Clauses. e.g.

He is a very helpful person.

This sentence is a complete sentence, but

That he is a very helpful person.....

is not a complete sentence. This group of words has the subject 'he' and the finite verb ('be' realised as 'is') but it needs something more to complete the sentence.

That he is a very helpful person is widely acknowledged. The above sentence is a complete sentence and the group of words 'That he is a very helpful person' is a part of this sentence.

Thus by adding 'that' to the sentence 'He is a very helpful person' we have reduced a full-fledged sentence to the position of a (finite) clause.

The process by which a sentence is reduced to the position of a (finite) clause is called 'subordination'.

Note: A phrase (a non-finite clause), on the other hand is a group of words that does not have a finite (tense-carrying) verb. A noun phrase performs the function of a noun, an adjective phrase that of an adjective and an adverb phrase that of an adverb).

Examples:

Phrase 1. I heard *of his arrival.*

Clause 1. I heard *that he had arrived.1.*

Phrase 2. The girl *living next door* is my class fellow.

Clause 2. The girl *who lives next door* is my class fellow.

Phrase 3. He has not met any one *since his return from the U.S.A.*

Clause 3. He has not met anyone *since he returned from the U.S.A.*

Subordinate clauses are of three types:

- Noun Clauses
- Adjective Clauses
- Adverb Clauses.

Noun Clauses

Since a subordinate noun clause performs the function of a noun it can occupy the position of:

1. The subject of a transitive verb, e.g.
   That he should act in this manner is really shocking.
2. The object of a transitive verb, e.g.
   I fear *that he may not be selected.*
3. The complement of a verb of incomplete predication, e.g.
   The farmers' fear is *that the standing crop may wither away.*
4. The object of a preposition, e.g.
   There is a lot of sense in *what you say.*
5. A noun clause may also be in apposition to a noun or pronoun, e.g.
   The news *that the Prime Minister had resigned* proved to be correct.

Adjective Clauses (Relative Clauses)

An adjective clause performs the function of an adjective. It qualifies a noun or pronoun in the main clause.

1. A *Restrictive (Defining)* relative clause restricts the meaning of the noun or pronoun it qualifies. Such a clause is not placed within commas, e.g.
   My friend who lives in Bombay is a diver in the Indian Navy.
   This sentence means that I have a number of friends but I am referring to the one who lives in Bombay.
2. A*Non-Restrictive (Non-Defining)* relative clause is placed within commas and it provides additional information about the noun or pronoun it qualifies.
   My friend, *who lives in Bombay,* is a diver in the Indian Navy.
   This sentence means that my friend is a diver in the Indian Navy and he lives in Bombay.

3. An adjective clause may be introduced by a relative pronoun *who, whose, whom, that, which,* etc. or by relative adverb: *when, where, why, how,* etc., e.g.

The man *who came to see me* is an actor.
The film *(that) we saw last night* was a comedy.
The table *(which) I bought last month* has broken.
Shashi, *who is waiting outside,* has come to meet you.

Adverb Clauses

An adverb clause is a subordinate clause that performs the function of an adverb, e.g.

I didn't go to office today *because it was raining.*
Though he was very honest he didn't make much progress in his profession.
It rained so heavily *that all ponds and lakes over-flowed.*

Adverb clauses may be broadly classified under the following heads:

1. Adverb clauses of time:
   As soon as you reach there please deliver this message.
   I shall go *when I like.*
2. Adverb clauses of place:
   Wherever he went he was warmly greeted.
   Put it *where you can find it.*
3. Adverbial clauses of purpose:
   They sacrificed their lives *so that their countrymen might live.*
   He wrote it down *lest he should forget it.*
4. Adverbial clauses of reason:
   I bought this house *because my wife like it.*
   Since you say so I shall accept it.
5. Adverbial clauses of condition:
   If you deceive me once I shall not trust you agan.
   He will feel encouraged *if you reward him for his talent and efficiency.*
6. Adverbial clauses of consequence or result:
   So well did they treat him *that he recovered soon.*
   It rained so heavily *that vast areas were submerged.*
7. Adverbial clauses of comparison:
   Things are not as bad *as we thought.*
   He is not as tough *as he pretends to be.*

8. Adverbial clauses of manner:

As you sow so shall you reap.

Treat others *as you wish to be treated.*

9. Adverbial clauses of concession:

Though the child was crying no one came forward to help him.

Even if you beg of him he will not help you.

Verbless Clauses

Since a (finite) clause must have a tense-carrying (finite) verb, a verbless clause appears to be a self-contradictory concept. How can it be a clause if it is verbless?

The explanation is that the finite (tense-carrying) verb is very much there in a verbless clause but it has been ellipted (omitted). It can, however, be recovered from the context, e.g.

1. *Too sad to enjoy the birthday party* he stayed at home. (Verbless clause)

   Feeling too sad to enjoy the birthday party he stayed at home; (Participle phrase restructured.)

   Since he was too sad to enjoy the birthday party he stayed at home. (Adverb clause)

2. *Though poor,* he did well in life. (Verbless clause)

   In spite of poverty he did well in life. (Adverb phrase)

   Though he was poor he did well in life. (Adverb clause)

Notice the use of verbless clauses in the following sentences

I bring fresh showers for the thirsting flowers.
I bear light shade for the leaves when laid.
When rocked to rest on their mother's breast.
I wield the flail of the lashing hail.

In a verbless clause we can infer ellipsis of the verb (i.e. the verb is dropped); the subject when omitted, is recoverable from the context.

Scores of people were injured; some of them women and children. (some of them being women and children.)

Whether good or bad, I am going to buy it. (whether it is good or bad)

Verbless clauses can also be reductions of non-finite clauses.

Too shocked to speak, he stood dumb. (Being too shocked...)

As with participle clauses, the subject is often introduced by 'with'.

With the work now finished, we were free to go.

The following are variations of the structure of verbless clauses:

He ran up the slope, the gun in his hand.

When tired, take glucose.

She looked around, upset.

The child looked with interest at the cat, asleep now in his sister's lap.

Disgraced, he left the room.

If the subject is not actually expressed in a non-finite or verbless clause, it is assumed to be identical with the subject of the superordinate clause.

When ripe, mangoes fall to the ground. (When the mangoes are ripe, mangoes fall...)

They donated liberally, touched by the sufferings of the people. (They were touched...)

But a sentence like the following which violates this rule is not acceptable:

Reading the evening newspaper, a dog started barking.

(Explain why this sentence is incorrect.) This rule does not, however, apply to adjuncts e.g.

Speaking frankly, I do not like him. (I am speaking frankly...)

There are instances of verbless clauses with subject but with ellipsis of infinitival 'be', e.g.

I hate him (to be) driving my car.

We found all the seats (to be) occupied.

Complementation by verbless clauses:

I consider that he is a good friend. (that clause as complement)

I consider him to be a good friend (non-finite clause as complement)

I consider him a good friend. (verbless clause as complement)

Some examples of verbless adjective clauses are:

Beautiful and majestic, the flag fluttered in the breeze.

Eager to reach home in time, he asked for a lift.

An adjective (alone or as head of an adjective phrase) can function as a verbless clause:

(By then) suspicious, the man closed the door.

The man (by then) suspicious, closed the door.

The man closed the door, (by then) suspicious.

The implied subject is usually the subject of the sentence. In the above example "the man was suspicious and he closed the door." The implied subject of the adjective clause can be the whole of the superordinate clause:

Unusual, it was he who lodged the complaint.

This sentence is equivalent to:

That it was he who lodged the complaint is unusual.

An adverb may sometimes take the place of an adjective functioning as a verbless clause.

Listless/Listlessly, he flopped into the chair.

If the subject of the subordinate clause is coreferential with that of the superordinate clause and it is followed by an appropriate form of the verb 'be' both the subject and the verb 'be' can be ellipted:

Although (he was) told to go, he kept sitting.
If (they are) discouraged, they may not do their duty properly.
While (you are) in Rome, do as the Romans do.

EXERCISES

1. Complete the following sentences by using verbless clauses.
   a. When ______, ring me up.
   b. While ______, learn skiing.
   c. Unless ______, you may go whenever you like.
   d. If not ______, don't borrow money.
   e. Although ______, he didn't stop.
   f. If ______, you will have to surrender your driving licence.
   g. (By then) ______, he decided not to continue his work.
   h. Speaking ______, he is not very honest.
   i. We found him______.
   j. I consider him______.
   k. ______, it was he who informed the police.
   l. ______, that he fell ill on the eve of his examination.
   m. ______, he collapsed.
   n. ______, he sang exceedingly well.
   o. ______, I cannot trust him.

2. Complete the following sentences:
   a. If dissatisfied ______.

b. When angry ______.
c. Though mortal ______.
d. Surprising, ______.
e. Speaking honestly ______.
f. If elected ______.
g. Practical considerations apart ______.
h. Listless ______.
i. The police, by then informed ______.
j. Although nervous ______.
k. Deeply hurt ______.
l. Everything considered ______.
m. Properly expressed ______.
n. Hit by a bullet ______.
o. If convicted ______.

Present Participles and Prepositions

Notice that:

bathing ghats mean ghats meant for bathing,
begging bowls mean bowls used for begging,
the sleeping man means the man who is sleeping,
mating season means the season for mating.

In all the above expressions, words with the *-ing* form like *bathing, begging, sleeping* and *mating* perform the function of an adjective. These words are called present participles. You know that the present participle form of a verb is its root form + ing e.g:

He is bathing.
Beggars are begging for alms.
The man was sleeping.

Present participles are, therefore, words which have the structure of a verb but perform the function of an adjective. When these words are used as verbs they follow the auxiliary *be,* but not when they are used as adjectives.

1. Fill in the blanks in the following sentences with appropriate participles. The first one has been done for you.
   a. War correspondents came under heavy artillery fire at the front. It was a ______experience for them. (harrowing)
   b. A ______ partner in business is one who has invested money but who does not actually work.
   c. He was wearing a ______ costume and was going to jump into the river.
   d. He participated in a ______ venture and made a lot of money.
   e. We had to walk the major part of the distance. It was a ______ journey.
   f. I am hard-pressed for money. These are ______ times for me.
   g. The ace sprinter Milkha Singh was described as the ______ Sikh.

h. A ______ elephant was the mascot of Asiad, 1982.
i. The ______ spectators stood up and clapped their hands.
j. The ______ army destroyed all its ammunition dumps and blew up the bridges after crossing them.
k. The ______ procession moved slowly towards the cemetry.
l. The ______ prices are creating problems for all sections of society.

2. Fill in the blanks in the following sentences with appropriate prepositions:
   a. He was here a short while ago and must be ______ the Hall now.
   b. He jumped ______ the river and swam to the other bank.
   c. Millions took a dip ______ the holy water of the Ganges.
   d. As we make our bed so must we lie ______ it.
   e. It is incumbent ______ pious Hindus to wear new clothes after the eclipse.
   f. It is ______ our own interest to pay all taxes honestly.
   g. The streets were lined ______ beggars.
   h. The policeman stood ______ his post.
   i. Animals ______ instinct do the right thing.
   j. What is the scientific explanation ______ a solar eclipse?
   k. Man who is endowed ______ reason is not obedient his own instinct.

3. In the two columns below, the phrases on the left are in the active voice; those on the right in the passive voice.

People say that ______	It is said that ______
People believe that ______	It is believed that ______
People know that ______	It is known that ______

   Put the following sentences into the passive voice:
   a. People assume that bad deeds never prosper.
   b. People wrongly believe that the tortoise always wins the race.
   c. Everybody knows that he has sold all his property in Delhi.
   d. Nobody knows why he resigned his job.
   e. Many assume that money always brings happiness.
   f. People say that he is prospering in Canada.

Tenses in the Past and Reported Speech

Read the following sentences and notice the use of the Past Perfect tense.

(The structure of past perfect tense is Had + Verb 3rd form e.g. had gone, had slept, had spoken, had hit, had won, etc.)

1. There was no maker's name but as Holmes *had remarked*, the initials 'H.B.' were scrawled upon one side.
2. James Ryder, upper attendant at the hotel, gave his evidence to the effect that he *had shown* Horner up to the dressing room of the Countess of Morcar.
3. Horner who *had shown* signs of intense emotion during the proceedings, fainted away at the conclusion.
4. On returning he found that Horner *had disappeared*, that the bureau *had been forced* open..........

Notice that the past perfect tense is used in combination with (mentioned or implied) the past indefinite tense. The past perfect tense is used when the time referred to by a verb preceded a point of time or a point or reference in the past.

Time referred to by the verb in past perfect tense	Point of reference in the past
the present moment	future

I spoke to him on the phone after I had received his message. (The time when the phone call was made is already in the past. The message was received prior to the telephone call.)

In sentence no. 1 Dr. Watson, the narrator of the story had been informed by Sherlock Holmes before the former started examining the hat that the initials 'H.B.' were scrawled upon one side of the hat. It was before that point of time that he (Dr Watson) had been told about the initials.

In sentence no. 2 the point of time with reference to which events are viewed is the time when James Ryder testified.He claimed that he had earlier shown Horner into the dressing room of the Countess of Morcar.

In sentence no. 3 the event being described is the conclusion of the trial at which Horner fainted. Before that during the trial Horner had shown intense emotion.

In sentence no. 4 the point of time with reference to which other events are viewed is when James Ryder returned to the dressing room of the Countess of Morcar. Before his return Horner, the plumber, had left and he (Ryder) found that the bureau had been forced open. Both these actions had taken place before Ryder's return to the dressing room.

In converting direct speech into indirect speech there is always a shift in time if the reporting verb happens to be in the past tense. This is so because what is now being reported was stated by another speaker earlier. When the reporting verb is in the past tense, the verb in the reported speech is changed as follows:

Direct Speech	*Indirect Speech*
Present indefinite/Present continuous	Past indefinite/Past continuous
Past indefinite	Past perfect
Present perfect	Past perfect

Note: If the reporting verb is in the present tense or in the future tense, there is no change in the tense of the verbs in the speech being reported. There is no tense change from Present Indefinite tense if the reported speech describes a universal truth even though the reporting verb happens to be in the past tense.

EXERCISES

1. Complete the following sentences with a proper combination of past indefinte and past perfect tenses.
   a. ______after the rain had stopped.
   b. He told me that ______.
   c. I wrote to him after _____.
   d. I bought a railway ticket after ______.
   e. She discovered that ______.
   f. ______ why I had come so early.
   g. We heard that ______.
   h. We all wondered why ______.

i. ______ before help could reach the victims.
j. We heard on the T.V. that ______.
k. By the time the doctor arrived ______.
l. The accused denied that ______.
m. ______ what places he had been to.
n. ______ what books she had read.
o. He was asked ______.

2. Put the following into reported speech. In some cases the past indefinite tense of the verbs in reported speech need not be changed to past perfect tense.
a. My servant said to me, "Last night I went to the movies. I enjoyed the film very much."
b. I said to my sister, "Have you finished your home work?"
c. My friend said to me, "You don't have to wait. I have finished writing letters."
d. The news-reporter said, "I have visited the site of the accident. I have seen everything."
e. The inquiry clerk said to me, "Sir, you are late. The train has left."
f. The greengrocer said to the customer, "I have already sold out what I had. There is nothing left for you."
g. The teacher said to the parents of his student, "Your son didn't do his home work last week. This week he was late on two days."
h. My friend said to me, "Why didn't you ask me for help?"
i. The scientist exclaimed to himself, "Why did I leave everything like this?"
j. The stranger said to his host's neighbour, "Where have the inmates of this house gone?"
k. I said to the magician, "Have you ever seen a ghost or are you bluffing?"
l. The M.P. said to the members of his constituency, "I did what I thought fit. I don't care what people think of me."
m. The Police Inspector said to me, "It is not very strange. Such incidents have taken place earlier also."

'Used to', Reported Speech and Prepositions

1. Fill in the blanks in the following sentences with appropriate prepositions:
   a. He sat with his head inclined ______ one side.
   b. All of a sudden the thought that I should take a firearm with me came ______ my head.
   c. He was dressed ______ a grey suit.
   d. He is the one man I have never tried to speak ______.
   e. I spoke to him ______ an impulse.
   f. Books are good companies ______ all.
   g. It was very kind ______ you to respond ______ my invitation.
   h. The next time I saw him, he was standing ______ the boundary wall of a house.
   i. A glass ______ milk will do a great deal ______ a patient.
   j. Many persons have no sense ______ cleanliness.

Look at the following sentences from the story you have just read and notice the use of *used to* in these sentences:

I *used to see* him first in Kenington Gardens.

I *used to see* you looking at flowers and trees, and those ducks.

When I was in the orchestra at the Harmony Theatre, it never *used to occur* to me that some day I shouldn't play there any more.

That little thing I *used to watch* you with, who was she?

Habitual activity in the past can be expressed with the help of the simple past tense e.g.

He always wrote with a special pen.

But in such sentences a suitable adverb has to be used to convey such a meaning. *Used to* (or less commonly) *would* can be used to convey this sense e.g.

He used to go out for a walk in the morning. (it was customary)

He would forget his books. (it was characteristic of him)

2. Complete the following sentences:
   a. He spoiled his health because he ______.
   b. He didn't do well in the examination because ______.
   c. He ______ but now he has grown more punctual.
   d. I could never meet him at 2.00 p.m. because he ______.

e. Most of those who became scientists trusted first hand experience and they ______.

f. When he was a boy Thomas Hardy ______ human faces and exclaimed that there was a story in every human face.

g. You have become too miserly. You never ______.

h. He ______ and then finally one day he was caught red-handed.

i. The sailors believed that since rats had deserted their ship ______.

j. The bootlegger told the judge that if he had a bottle of whisky ______.

k. My mother ______ but now I sleep till eight in the morning.

l. You never ______. Now you are seldom in time.

m. She ______. Now she wears only white sarees.

n. The old man ______. Now we seldom see him out of doors.

o. I didn't ask him for money because I knew that he ______.

Used to can express (i) a discontinued habit or (ii) a past routine, not necessarily discontinued e.g.

When it was very hot people used to go to the river bank for a dip. (They did so when we were there and probably they do so even now.)

Would cannot replace *used to* when it expresses a discontinued habit e.g.

I used to like chess but I don't like it any more.

He used to be clean-shaven but now he sports a beard.

Used to is different from the ordinary verb *use* e.g.

I am used to the noise.

One can get used to anything.

3. Change the following passage to reported speech:

"I never get out", the landlady would say.

"Why not?"

"Couldn't leave the house."

"It won't run away."

But she looked at me as if she thought it might, and repeated:

"Oh! I never get out."

One July afternoon I found her very much upset. He had been taken dangerously ill three days before.

"There he is" she said; "can't touch a thing. It's my belief he's done for himself, giving his food away all these years to these cats of his. I shooed 'em out to-day, the nasty creatures; they won't get in again."

"Oh! "I said," you shouldn't have done that. It'll only make him miserable. What does the doctor say?"

"Double pneumonia — caught in getting his feet wet after some stray, I'll be bound. I'm nursing him. There has to be someone with him all the time."

Infinitives, Present Tenses, Conditionals and If-clauses

Read the following sentences. In all these sentences the *infinitive* has been used:

The use of the infinitive with 'to'

The cab-driver smacks his lips *to encourage* his horse.
Several times again he turns *to look* at his fare.
The snow once more begins *to cover* him and his horse.
All three at once try *to get on* tc the seat.
What a cab you have got, there is not a worse one *to be found* in all Petersburg. (Passive Infinitive)

The use of the infinitive without 'to' (Bare Infinitive)

Thank God, they have at least reached their destination, and Iona watches them *disappear* through the dark entrance.
It is better too to talk to women; although they are stupid, two words are enough to make them *sob*.
When he is alone he dare not *think* of his son.

Bare Infinitive

The following verbs and expressions are followed by the infinitive without *to*

a. *will, shall, can do, must, may, let.*

b. *would rather, would sooner, rather than, sooner than,* and *had better*. e.g.

   You *had better tell* him that you have failed in your attempt.
   I *would rather wait* a bit longer.
   Rather than see it stolen I gave it away to a friend.

c. *need* and *dare* except when they are conjugated with *do* or *will/would*. e.g.

   You *need not wait* for her.
   but you won't *need to go* to a doctor.
   You don't *need to wait* for her.
   I *dare not ask* him for moeny.
   but I didn't *dare to ask* him for money.

d. Verbs of sensation *see, feel, hear, notice, observe, smell, watch* etc; *make* and *bid* (except in the passive) and *watch*. e.g.

I *watched him jump* over the fence.

I *saw him throw* the book out of the window.

He *made me run* faster.

I *heard him say* that he would leave for England shortly.

Note: In the passive voice the bare infinitive is replaced by 'to infinitive' e.g.

He made them run. *but*

They were made to run.

He bade me deliver his message. *but*

I was bidden to deliver his message.

I saw him post the letter. *but*

He was seen to post the letter.

e. *help* may be followed by an infinitive with or without *to*. e.g.

He helped me (to) pull a bucketful of water out of the well.

f. The prepositions *but* and *except* are followed by the infinitive without *to* e.g.

There was nothing to do but hear.

He will do nothing except write a letter of recommendation.

Use of the Infinitive

a. The infinitive is used to express purpose e.g.

I am going to the market to buy a book.

I am writing this letter to invite him to Delhi.

Note: After the verbs *go* and *come* in the imperative, the infinitive of purpose is replaced by another imperative joining the two by *and*, e.g.

Go and call him.

Go to call him.

Come and clean up this mess.

Come to clean up this mess.

but both the sentences — Come and see me; and Come to see me — are acceptable.

b. The infinitive is used after *only* to express disappointment over what followed:

He hurried to the library only to find that it was closed.

But the infinitive can be used without *only* without any idea of disappointment or an untoward happening.

He returned from America to find that his daughter had got married to a doctor.

c. The infinitive can be used after *the first, the second* etc. and *the last, the only* and sometimes after superlatives to replace a relative clause: e.g.

She is very regular. She is the first to arrive and the last to depart. (the first who arrives and the last who departs)

d. The infinitive can be placed after nouns/pronouns to show
- how they can be used or
- what is to be done with them, e.g.

We have many letters to write.
I want to find a house to live in.
There is no bus to travel by.
They want something to eat.
I must find someone to talk to.

e. The infinitive can be used after an adjective + noun/pronoun.

It was very kind of you to lend me your book.
It was very brave of the young man to rescue a drowning child.
It was nice of you to drop in.

f. The infinitive can be used after adjectives:

She was very delighted to see me.
My father will be angry to see how I have fared.
I am sorry to tell you that I have misplaced your book.
It was lovely to see the road stretch for miles and miles.

g. An infinitive is often placed after the adjectives, *easy, hard, difficult, awkward, impossible* etc., e.g.

This work is easy to do.
He is a hard nut to crack.
His actions are difficult to explain.
It was impossible to finish the work in time.

h. The infinitive is used after *too/enough* and *so...as*, e.g.

You are old enough to understand.
It is never too late to mend.

a. Verbs followed by the infinitive

The following verbs are followed by the infinitive:

Learn, remember, forget, promise, swear, consent, agree, neglect, refuse, propose, regret, try, endeavour, attempt, fail, refuse, propose, regret, try, endeavour, attempt, fail, care, hope, hesitate, prepare, decide, determine, undertake, manage, arrange, cease, seem:

Verbs when followed by *how to* : discover, wonder, find out, understand, know and explain:

Note: *Remember, propose, regret, attempt* and *try* can also be followed by a gerund.

Auxiliaries like *be, have, will, shall, can, ought, need, dare, do, used*

Note: Of these *will, shall, can, do* and *must* are followed by the infinitive without *to*.

b. Verbs followed by the infinitive or by an object followed by the infinitive:

Want, wish, love, hate, like, prefer, ask, help, expect, beg, mean, intend, e.g.

I want to eat something.
I want you to eat something.
I expect to reach there at five.
I expect him to reach there at five.

Note: *Love, like, hate, mean, intend* and *it wants* (requires) can also be followed by a gerund.

c. Verbs followed by object + infinitive

tell, order, invite, oblige, complete, allow, permit, teach, instruct, warn, urge, advise, tempt, encourage, request, forbid, remind, show:

He told us to remove our shoes.
The police has been ordered to arrest the culprit.

Verbs of sensation like *see, feel, hear* and verbs like *watch, make, let* and *bid* take the infinitive without *to*
Verbs of sensation can also be followed by the -ing form i.e. the present participle, e.g.

I heard her singing.
I saw him walking in.

Allow, advise, permit can be followed by the gerund also.

d. Verbs of knowing and thinking etc.

be sure, think, believe, consider, know, feel, understand and *suppose*, e.g.

He is sure to succeed. OR He is sure that he will succeed.
I think him to be the best person for this job. OR I think that he is the best person for this job.

EXERCISES

1. Replace the group of words italicised in the following sentences with an infinitive or an infinitive construction:
   a. My friend was the last man *who left* the hall.
   b. He passed the examination but was very unhappy *when he found* that he had missed the first position.
   c. It is important *that he should learn* to be self-reliant.
   d. It is better *that he should be* here.
   e. It appears *that the criminal visited* the scene of crime again.
   f. My wife complained that she couldn't go to a movie since she had no good sari *that she could wear.*
   g. Is it likely that India *will make* a nuclear bomb?
   h. If the child had a sister *with whom he could run about,* he wouldn't feel so lonely.
   i. I was shocked *when I heard* that he had gone bankrupt.
   j. I was very happy *when I learnt* that the train was yet to leave.
   k. *He jumped* into the well to save the drowning child, which was very brave of him.
   l. He told me *that I should* do whatever he wanted me to do.
   m. You were the only one *who could anticipate* the result.
   n. Everybody knows *that his wife has* a frightful temper. (His wife ______)
   o. It is better *that we should part* company.

2. Combine each of the following pairs of sentences by using an infinitive of purpose:
   a. He tied a knot to his handkerchief. He wanted to remember that he had to post a letter.
   b. We get up early. We don't want to be late to office.
   c. I am learning Russian. I want to read Russian authors in their own language.
   d. He dyes his hair. He wants to look younger.
   e. I type my own letters. I want to keep my affairs secret.
   f. I am saving up as much as I can. I want to build a house next year.
   g. I walked on tiptoe. I didn't want to wake up my wife.
   h. He rang me up. He wanted to inform me that my brother was reaching Delhi the next day.

i. He changed his house every few months. He did not want to be arrested by the police.
j. He gave me a glass. He told me that I could drink water from the pitcher.
k. The Principal sent my son out of his office. He wanted to discuss with me his performance in the class.
l. He was singing very softly. He didn't want to disturb anybody.
m. He pressed my foot. He wanted to warn me to be very careful while talking.
n. He sent an anonymous letter. He wanted to inform the income-tax authorities that his neighbour was evading tax.
o. I want to take out an insurance policy. I want my family to have a feeling of security.

Note: In some sentences you may have to use *in order to* or *so as to*

3. Combine each of the following pairs of sentences into one sentence by using *too/enough*:
   a. You are very young. You can't drive a car.
   b. It is very hot. We cannot got out.
   c. It was very cloudy. We couldn't even see the sun.
   d. He was very keen to learn. He worked on his own.
   e. He was extremely rich. He didn't care for money.
   f. He was very drunk. He couldn't walk properly.
   g. He is very simple. He can be easily deceived.
   h. Will you be good to me? Please forward my letters while I am away on tour.
   i. I am very tired. I can't stay awake.
   j. The mountain was very high. We couldn't climb to the summit.
   k. You are very young. You cannot be told everything.
   l. He is very clever. He cannot be prevailed upon easily.
   m. The current of the river is very swift. We cannot wade through the river.
   n. This is very strange. It cannot be true.
   o. He was deeply hurt. He couldn't even protest.
4. Insert *to* where necessary before the infinitives given in the brackets:
   a. He made me (show) him how (play) the piano.

b. I felt the earth (shake) under my feet.
c. He told me (try) (come) early.
d. I heard the door (open) and saw a man (walk) out of the house.
e. You should (know) how (make) an omelette, but if you don't my wife will (show) you how (do) it.
f. It is easy (be) wise after the horse has bolted.
g. I was so upset that I dared not (tell) him everything.
h. You need not (bring) an umbrella with you. You can (have) mine.
i. As we appear (have missed) the train we may as well (wait) for the next one.
j. I don't (remember) his telephone number, you had better (look) it up in the telephone directory.

Historic/Dramatic/Graphic Present:

The following sentences have been taken from the story you have just read:

1. It is twilight.
2. The cab-driver Iona Potapov is quite white and looks like a phantom.
3. His little horse is also quite white and remains motionless.
4. It is no doubt plunged in deep thought.

In all these sentences the verbs underlined are in the Present Indefinite tense. The action of the story took place in the past and yet the author has used the present indefinite tense to describe the scene and the appearance of Iona Potapov and his horse.

In English, the present indefinite tense is not used to describe the present alone. It can be used to describe planned arrangement in the future, e.g.

We leave Delhi at seven, reach Agra at 9.30, have tea there and then leave for Gwalior at 10.00.

It can also be used to describe past events, as in the sentences quoted above. This makes past events vivid in our imagination. The events seem to be taking place before our eyes. This use of the present indefinite tense to describe events in the past has earned it the name 'dramatic, historic or graphic present', e.g.

Babar now leads his men through mountain passes.

EXERCISES

Put the verbs in the following sentences in the present indefinite tense.

a. The Commanding Officer called a meeting of the fighter-pilots, briefed them about the details of their mission, their targets and the opposition they were likely to face. The pilots listened to the briefing, asked a few questions, took up their flying equipment and walked towards the planes.

b. The king called his minister and told him that for urgent reasons he wanted to go back to Vaishali at once. The minister, who was opposed to this, explained that the time was not auspicious for the king's return to the capital.

c. The captain led the team to the field. The players looked smart and the stands in the stadium were packed to capacity. Thousands of people were there to witness the clash between the two teams. The referee blew the whistle, the centre-forward pushed the ball back to the centre-half who hit it towards the right-out. The right-out dashed across the field and hit the ball towards the centre-half. There was a scramble near the goal and one of the forwards pushed the ball neatly into the goal.

d. The Hon'ble Minister arrived near the saluting base. A contingent of the local police presented a guard of honour. A band played the national anthem. Everybody stood at attention. The Hon'ble Minister was led to the V.I.P. stand where he delivered a speech. He declared the tournament open. The game started and the spectators loudly cheered the players.

e. Porus looked at the young ambassador of the Greek king and whispered something to his commander. The commander's hand jumped to the hilt of his sword but Porus restrained him. A smile of understanding and appreciation appeared on the lips of the young ambassador.

f. The first to take off were the Thunderbolts which flew past the saluting base in a box formation. There were followed by a squadron of Hunters. Thereafter four Jaguars flew low in an inverted position. A squadron of Mirage fighters followed. These planes flew over pre-placed targets and hit them accurately. A big ball of fire enveloped these targets.

The present indefinite tense is used mainly to:

a. Describe habitual action time/an action or things that happen as a part of a routine, e.g.

I wake up at seven.
We drink tea in the morning.
The Andhra Pradesh Express leaves Secunderabad at 2 p.m.
I always sign my name with a special pen. (It is used with adverbs and adverb-phrases like *always, often, generally usually, sometimes, occassionally, seldom, never, rarely, on Mondays, every day, every week,* etc.

b. To express general truths as in proverbs, e.g.

Man is mortal.
The earth is round.
God helps those who help themselves.

c. To describe the present state of affairs.

His father is a doctor.
This library is well-stocked with books.
His brother is seriously ill.

d. In exclamations, e.g.

Here it goes!
How tall she is!
Here comes the postman!

e. To introduce quotations, e.g.

Oscar Wilde says, "I can resist everything except temptation."

f. To indicate a planned arrangement in the future e.g.

We take off at 7.00 p.m., reach Bombay an hour later and then take off again for London at 10.00 p.m.

g. In commentaries on sports events, certain performative declarations etc., e.g.

Kapil Dev bowls, Imran lifts the ball and Ravi Shastri catches it on the boundary.
I declare the Asiad open.

h. In subordinate clause of time or condition when the principal clause is in the future tense, e.g.

I shall go when he comes.
If he invites me I shall attend his birthday party.

i. To describe the action of a play or an opera, e.g.

When the curtain rises an old man is seen sitting in a chair. Somebody knocks at the door. The old man puts on his spectacles and walks towards the door.

j. The present indefinite tense is used instead of the present continuous tense with verbs which are not normally used in the continuous form, e.g. we can say 'I like you' but not 'I am liking you'.

The following verbs are not normally used in the continuous form:

Verbs of perception:	see, hear, smell, notice, recognise.
Verbs of appearing:	appear, look, seem.
Verbs of emotion:	want, wish, desire, feel, like, love, hope, refuse, prefer, abhor, adore.
Verbs of thinking:	think, suppose, believe, agree, consider, trust, remember, forget, know, understand, imagine, mean, mind.
Verbs of possession:	have (to possess), own, possess, belong to, consist, comprise, be (except when used in the passive or as an auxiliary verb).

Some of these verbs may, however, be used in the continuous tenses with a change of meaning, e.g.

He is thinking (considering the possibility) of migrating to Canada.

I think you are right. *but*

I am thinking of you all the time.

Please note the use of a continuous with *always* and *forever*, e.g

You are *always seeing* unusual things.

He is *forever refusing* to do what I wish him to do.

(This implies *for all times*, especially *now*, at this moment.)

Present Indefinite Tense and Present Continuous Tense:

The present indefinite tense does not describe actions or the situations in present along. The *dramatic present* describes actions that took place in the past and to describe planned actions in the future particularly those relating to a journey.

a. To describe actions taking place at the present moment we use the present continuous tense.

(Said at 10.00 p.m) I take my breakfast at eight in the morning.

(Said during breakfast) I am taking breakfast (now)

(Said on a working day) On Sundays I love to sit in the sun.

(Said when the speaker is sitting in the sun) I am sitting in the sun (now).

(Said on Monday) The ship sails on Wednesday.

(Said while watching a ship sail) The ship is sailing.

(Narrating past events) The security forces surround the rebels and order them to lay down their arms.

(Said while watching the movement of security forces) The security forces are moving into troubled areas to restore peace.

b. The present continuous tense is also used to describe actions happening at present in a general sense but not necessarily now, e.g

These days I am writing the review of a recently published novel.

He is preparing for the I.A.S. examination.

c. Other uses of the present continuous tense:

To describe frequently repeated actions, usually those that the speaker thinks unreasonable or those which annoy him. In such sentences the verb is generally preceded by the adverb *always*, e.g.

He is always forgetting his spectacles.

You are always doing your work.

She is always imagining things.

When used with a first person pronoun it implies accidental (not deliberate) action.

I am always forgetting the right word.

I am always addressing you as Ramesh when you are Mohan.

d. The present continuous tense, like the present indefinite tense is also used to describe a definite and planned future arrangement in the near future.

In such sentences the time of the action is mentioned, e.g.

I am going to the concert tonight.

She is getting married next month.

EXERCISES

Use the correct form of the present tense in the following sentences. You have to use either the present indefinite or the present continuous tense.

a. The earth (*revolve*) round the sun in 365 days.
b. The sun (*shine*) at present.
c. I (*go*) to college at eight in the morning. I (*go*) there now.
d. This time he (*contest*) election as a candidate of the Congress party.
e. You always (*tell*) me his weaknesses.
f. Every Sunday they (*go*) for a picnic. We too (*go*) for a picnic this Sunday.
g. We (*leave*) for Betul tonight. You (*come*) with us?
h. I don't know why I always (*misplace*) the bunch of keys.
i. He (*get*) angry whenever I (*ask*) him for a loan. I (*go*) to meet him today but I (*not want*) to talk to him about any loan.
j. You usually (*not carry*) an umbrella. How is it that today you (*carry*) one?
k. You (*rince*) your mouth after every meal? Why you (*not do*) it now?
l. 'I never (*wear*) woollens before the 15th of November.' 'Then why you (*wear*) them now?'
'I (*wear*) them because I have to watch a night game.'
m. He (*study*) engineering at present. He (*work*) very hard. He literally (*burn*) the midnight oil.
n. My mother still (*cook*) in the kitchen. She (*finish*) her work rather late. My sister (*play*) in the garden. She always (*play*) there in the evenings. I believe that my mother (*pamper*) my sister.
o. You usually (*sit*) at the back of the class. How come that today you (*sit*) in the front row?
p. I (*pass*) the post office on my way to college every day. Today, however, I (*take*) a different route.
q. You (*listen*) to what I (*say*) ? I (*ask*) you where Ravi (*live*).
r. He seldom (*come*) here to discuss an urgent problem.
s. 'You (*watch*) T.V. serials regularly?'
'Our T.V. (*be*) out of order today but I (*not want*) miss today's programmes.'
'Why you (*no call*) a T.V. mechanic to repair it?'

The use of Present Continuous and Present Perfect Continuous Tense

Unlike English, Hindi does not differentiate between actions described by the present continuous tense and those described by the present perfect continuous tense, e.g.

	Hindi	English
1.	Main padh raha hoon.	I am reading
2.	Main pichle do ghante se padh raha hoon	I have been reading for the last two hours.

In English we use the present continuous tense to describe an action taking place at the present moment. It can be presumed that the action started some time ago and is likely to continue for some more time. This tense does not, however, indicate when the action started and for how long it has been continuing.

For such a situation we require the present perfect continuous tense. This tense is used to describe an action which began in the past, has been continuing and is still continuing or has only just finished. An expression of time indicating when the action started is almost always a part of such a sentence., e.g.

He is sleeping.	He has been sleeping for three hours.
I am waiting for him.	I have been waiting for the train for an hour but it has not arrived yet.

EXERCISES

Use the correct form of the present tense in the following sentences. Use either the present continuous or the present perfect continuous tense. (Some sentences require the use of the passive voice).

a. They (*fish*) in the lake just now.
b. We (*walk*) for four hours.
c. My mother (*make*) cakes in the kitchen.
d. She (*not cry*). She (*peel*) onions for the last fifteen minutes.
e. I do have a driving licence. I (*drive*) heavy vehicle for fifteen years.
f. Ever since he joined this college he (*create*) problems.

g. The snow (*fall*) for two days. The roads (*be*) cleared.
h. Someone (*read*) this book. He has put pencil marks here and there.
i. The train (*run*) for quite some time. I should like to get a glass of water at the next station.
j. They (*live*) in this house since 1963.
k. Ashok (*suffer*) from fever for a week. I fear that he (*not treat*) properly.
l. He (*take*) a bath. He (*sing*) in the bathroom for half an hour.
m. You (*attend*) the concert tonight? She (*talk*) to me about it since morning.
n. The workmen (*agitate*) for a week. Just now they (*shout*) slogans.
o. The dog (*bark*) since morning. It might (*feel*) hungry.
p. The engine of this car still (*make*) an unusual noise. I (*try*) since morning to repair it.
q. It appears that birds (*build*) a nest in this room. Since yesterday they (*bring*) twigs in their beaks.

Conditionals and the Use of If-clauses

The following sentences have been taken from the story you have just read:

1. If a whole snowdrift fell on him, it seems as if he would not find it necessary to shake it off.
2. If you were snatched from the plough from your usual grey surroundings, and were thrown into the slough full of monstrous light, unceasing noise and hurrying people you too would find it difficult not to think.
3. Should his heart break and the grief pour out, it would flow over the whole earth.

Three different types of conditions can be expressed using *If* conditional clauses, e.g.

Type 1 — If I go to New York I shall meet him.
Type 2 — If I went to New York I should see him.
Type 3 — If I had gone to New York I should have seen him.

Type No. 1

The 'If clause' describes a future possibility and the likely result. There is a cause and effect relationship between the clause of condition and the clause of result. If the condition described by the 'If clause' is fulfilled in the future, the result/possibility indicated by the result clause will be the consequence. This type of sentence implies that it is quite probable that the action indicated by the 'If clause' will be performed. Please note that English does not allow the use of double future tense, i.e. future tense in the clause of condition or the clause of time.

When he will come I shall speak to him.

When he comes I shall speak to him.

Type No. 2

This type of 'If clause' describes an imaginary and sometimes unrealistic condition.

If I were a king I should make you very rich.

If you were a rat a cat would eat you.

The condition indicated by the 'If clause' may or may not be fulfilled. But if that supposed condition was ever fulfilled the probable result as indicated by the result clause would follow. This type of sentence describes a theoretical possibility.

The past tense in the 'If clause' is not a true past tense but a subjunctive which indicates improbability or unreality.

In this type of sentence we don't expect the condition to be fulfilled. It is also used when the supposition is not in conformity with known facts.

What would you do if you were elected to Parliament?

Type No. 3

This type of 'If clause' describes a condition which was not fulfilled, and since that time is past, it cannot now be fulfilled. Thus the condition is an impossibility and is being talked about only in retrospect and that too as an unrealised preposition, e.g.

If you had gone to the Railway Station you would have met him. (But you did not go there and, therefore, did not meet him.)

He would have advanced you a loan if you had asked for it. (But you did not ask for it)

Note: You have already been made familiar with this type of 'If clause at No. 3 above in Exercise No. 3 of the story 'Bachcha

Lieutenant' by Manohar Malgaonkar. Please attempt that exercise once again to refresh your memory.

In the following exercises we shall limit ourselves to only type 1 and type 2 'If clauses'.

Unless means 'if not'

I shall write to him if he writes to me.

I shan't write to him unless he writes to me.

We won't go out unless it stops raining.

If clauses' of type 1 and 2 can also be structured as follows:

If you should decide to buy a house you would have take the help of a property-dealer.

Should you decide to buy a car you would have to.........

If this machine should fail we shall import another machine.

Should this machine fail we shall import a replacement.

Imperatives can also replace 'if clauses'. e.g.

Lend money and lose your friend.

Marry in haste and repent at leisure.

Buy a car and spend a lot of money on its maintenance.

EXERCISES

Complete the following sentences

a. If he buys a car ______.

b. What will you do if I ______.

c. ______ if you don't do your homework.

d. It will be a great pleasure for us if you ______.

e. He will get very good marks in the examination if ______.

f. If you don't take your meals at regular hours ______.

g. ______ if I don't have an umbrella.

h. He will certainly help you if ______.

i. ______if they don't hurry up.

j. If my telephone is out of order ______.

k. He will surely get this job if ______.

l. Go straight if ______.

m. If you decide to go to the zoo ______.

n. ______ she will marry him.

o. Your mother will be angry with you if ______.

p. ______ you will catch cold.

q. If you handle crackers carelessly ______.

r. If you reach there in time ______.

Complete the following sentences:

a. If I were stronger ______.
b. He wouldn't grow so fat if ______.
c. He could become very rich if ______.
d. If the boat sailed ______.
e. If we went up that hill ______.
f. ______ you would learn English much better.
g. We should go for a walk if ______.
h. You wouldn't make so many mistakes if ______.
i. If you were honest ______.
j. ______ if you wrote legibly.
k. ______ your servant would serve you better
l. ______ if the condition of the workers was improved.
m. Would she marry him if ______.
n. The soup would taste better if ______.
o. Would she buy this book if ______.
p. If I had more money ______.
q. I should punish you if ______.
r. He would not sell his house if ______.
s. We would miss the train unless ______.
t. You would spoil the child if ______.

Definite Articles

Read the following sentences and note the use of the definite article *the* in these sentences:

1. The dog barked, alarmed and frightened.
2. In his head surged all the thoughts that come to one in the face of imminent death.
3. The night was warm, the forest giving out a steamy heat.
4. Two hundred yards away the cat track dipped into the dry bed of the Chaung.
5. (i) He and another scout had been sent out to find out how far down the road the first enemy position was.
   (ii) But after they had gone about a mile Tukaram left the other scout behind.
6. The yelping and whining trailed off into a howl.

Sentence No. 1: The speaker is referring to a particular dog at the Japanese post.

Sentence No. 2: The noun 'thoughts' is followed by a qualifying expression 'that came to one'. Similarly the noun 'face' is also followed by a qualifying expression viz. 'of imminent death'. Other examples of such a use of the definite article are:

The hand that rocks the cradle rules the world.

Uneasy lies the head that wears the crown.

Sentence No. 5: In sentence No. 5(i) the scout is first referred to as 'another scout' but when he is mentioned again if 5(ii) he is referred to as 'the other scout'. When a singular noun is referred to for the first time it is preceded by the indefinite article 'a' or 'an' but when it figures again and thereafter it is preceded by the definite article.

Ordinals like 'first', 'second', 'third' when followed by a noun take the definite article.

He was the first person to arrive.

He is the fifth swimmer to have swum across the Palk Straits.

EXERCISES

Use the definite article 'the' in the following sentences wherever necessary. (Some sentences may not require the definite article)

a. He was advised to go to a specialist but wanted to see _____ family doctor.

b. I must go to _____ college today to meet _____ Principal.

c. I have to go to _____ college to attend an extra class.

d. He was badly injured and was taken to _____ hospital.

e. She went to _____ hospital to meet her friend who worked there.

f. You must carry oxygen with you if you wish to climb _____ Mount Everest.

g. _____ Ganges is a sacred river for _____ Hindus.

h. Do you know who was _____ first man who landed on _____ moon.

i. Throughout _____ year _____ Himalayas remain covered with snow.

j. _____ gentleman with a bundle of books under his arm is our professor.

k. _____ supervisor is not in his office.

l. _____ book lying on _____ table is yours.

m. _____ people of the Kashmir valley welcome tourists.

n. There was not a cloud in _____ sky.

o. _____ road was deserted except for a dog who sat in _____ middle of it. _____ dog was an ordinary brown dog.

p. Can you hear _____ soft murmur of _____ wind?

q. We went to Bombay by _____ car.

r. _____ patient is in _____ bed.

s. When I entered _____ room I found my dog Jimmy sitting on _____ bed.

t. She put _____ kettle on _____ stove while her husband glanced through _____ pages of _____ newspaper to find out what was on _____ T.V. that afternoon.

Past Indefinite Tense, Present Perfect Tense

Note the use of the past indefinite tense in the following sentences.

He *wrought* at one great work for years.

The world *passed by* with a lofty look.

His wife and child *went* clothed in rags.

The past indefinite tense is used to describe what happened in the past, e.g.

He *jumped* over the fence.

The ship *sailed* two days ago.

It describes habitual actions in the past or actions that took place with a pre-determined regalarity:

He always *went* out for a walk in the morning.

He usually *came* at ten.

It describes a state of affairs at a given time in the past. (The past tense of the verb *be* is used in such sentences.)

He *was* at that time in Amritsar.

He *was* a prosperous businessman.

A hundred years ago there *were* dense forests in this area.

A tense that is often confused with the past indefinite tense is the present perfect tense. The present perfect tense is used to describe:

An event that has just taken place:

My father *has just* arrived.

The rain *has stopped*. Now we can go out.

The completion of an action at the present moment:

I *have written* ten letters since morning.

Thank God, I *have succeeded* in tracing this missing document.

An action that took place in the past but is in some way connected with the present. This association with the present may be purely psychological or real, e.g.

The debate *has been held*. (So you need not prepare for it now).

It *has rained*. (You can see that the earth is wet.)

The present perfect tense is basically a present tense. It has a very strong connection with the present moment even when it describes something that happened in the past. This tense does not, therefore, permit the use of an adverb of time indicating time is already over e.g.

He *has arrived* yesterday. To correct this sentence we can recast it as:

He has arrived.

He arrived yesterday.

EXERCISES

Put the verbs given in brackets in the present perfect tense or the past indefinite tense as required in the blank spaces in the following sentences:

a. The ship _____ for London last week. (sail)

b. I _____ several attempts to meet him but _____ till now. (make, not succeed)

c. He is a prosperous businessman. He _____ what he deserves. (get).

d. He _____ for a licence last year but he _____ in getting one only this year. (apply, succeed)

e. He _____ to his new house. He _____ it two years ago. (shift, build)

f. It _____ heavily last night. The rain _____ the long spell of drought. (rain, end)

g. The case _____ in his favour. He _____ the complaint six months ago. (decide, file)

h. "I _____ much for you," I said to her. Neverthless, she _____ me most heartily. (not do, thank)

i. There _____ ruins of a temple here. They _____ the temple now. (be, rebuild)

j. The monsoon _____ this year. It _____ last year as well. (fail, fail)

k. These experiments _____ earlier too but the desired results _____. (make, not achieve)

l. I am not prepared to lend him any money so I _____ to him about this. (write)

m. Chance _____ him. He _____ only one lottery ticket last year and _____ the first prize. (always help, buy, win.)

n. Labour unrest _____ a constant problem in this factory. The policy of the management to divide the workers _____ during the last strike. (be, not pay off)

Relative Pronouns, Relative Clauses and Subordinate Clauses

Note the use of *which* in the following sentences. They are taken from the poem by Ogden Nash.

1. Or may be a sound like the wind in the trees on the hills,
   Which is the rustling of thousand dollar bills.
2. Most bankers dwell in marble halls,
   Which they get to dwell in because they encourage deposits and discourage withdrawals.
3. And particularly because they all observe one rule *which* woe betide the banker who fails to heed it,
   Which is you must never lend any money to anybody unless they don't need it.

In sentence No.1 *which* refers back to the *sound* and the clause that follows tells us more about the sound of the rustling of thousand dollar bills.

In sentence No.2 *which* refers back to the *halls* and the clause that follows it tells us that bankers get to dwell in these halls.

In sentence No.3 the first *which* refers back to *the rule* which no banker can fail to heed. The second *which* tells us *what that rule is.*

Which in these sentences is a relative pronoun. The following are some of the relative pronouns of the *wh* series.
Personal: *who, whom, whose, whoever;*
Non Personal: *which, whose, whichever, whatever*
In addition to the *wh* series of relative pronouns *that* is also a relative pronoun. It is a general purpose relative pronoun.
A zero relative pronoun is also used identically to *that.* e.g.
The book that/which you are looking for is with Rakesh. =
The book you are looking for is with Rakesh.

EXERCISES

1. Combine the following pairs of sentences by using appropriate relative pronouns, e.g.

   I hired a taxi.

   The taxi broke down after ten kilometers.

The taxi *which/that* I hired broke down after ten miles.

a. He read a book.
   He had borrowed the book from me.
b. I spoke to a man.
   The man is a doctor.
c. This is a theatre.
   I bought this theatre last week.
d. Here is the money.
   You lent me this money last month.
e. Dr. Bhatnagar prepared this plan.
   The Ministry of Health approved of the plan.
f. I was travelling by train.
   The train met with an accident.
g. He thanked the audience.
   The audience appreciated his speech.
h. There is a man outside the gate.
   You borrowed that man's bicycle.
i. Mohan is waiting outside.
   Mohan wants to speak to you.
j. Five men robbed a banker.
   The judge punished all the five men.
k. I drove home with Ramesh.
   Ramesh has a Maruti Car.
l. She heartily dislikes her mother-in-law.
   Her mother-in-law says that she is not a good daughter-in-law.
m. I gave money to my servant to pay the electricity bill.
   The servant did not pay the bill.
n. The doctor advised the patient not to drink alcohol.
   The patient refused to be treated by the doctor.
o. Circumstances compelled him to take up a job in a circus.
   The circumstances were beyond his control.

2. Complete the following sentences by filling in appropriate relative clauses. You may, if you like, use the verbs/adjectives given in brackets. Example: Sentence No. (a) would be: The patient who was admitted to hospital is progressing well.
   a. The patient (admit) is progressing well.
   b. The milk (get) is not pure.
   c. The songs (telecast) are generally songs from new films.

d. Our guests (arrive) yesterday have left for Agra.
e. People (sensitive) feel hurt very easily.
f. My friend (live) next door is an army officer.
g. Students (inquisitive) ask many questions.
h. The factory (supplies) gas lighters has closed down.
i. The lady (carry) an umbrella is my aunt.
j. The baby (wear) a red sweater is my nephew.

Subordinators

Read the following sentences and note the use of *because*:

This is a song to celebrate banks *because* they are full of money.

Most bankers dwell in marble halls,

...*because* they encourage deposits and discourage withdrawals.

And particularly *because* they all observe one rule which woe betides the banker who fails to heed it.

Because in these sentences introduces *the clause of reason* which answers the question *Why*?

Structurally *because* is a subordinator (or more fully a subordinating conjunction.

"They are full of money" is a complete sentence. But "*Because* they are full of money..." is not a complete sentence. The sentence has been reduced to a clause with the addition of *because* to it.

The clause of result must either precede or follow the clause of reason.

When *because* is used, the emphasis is on the reason and the subordinate clause usually comes last. But when the clause of reason has the structure, "It is/was because..." the subordinate clause is placed early in the sentence, e.g.

He succeeded *because* he worked hard.

It was because he worked hard that he succeeded.

In the latter case the clause of reason has prominence.

When the conjunction used is *as, since,* seeing that the subordinate clause is usually placed first. In such sentences there is less emphasis on the cause or reason and more emphasis on the result (stated in the main clause), e.g.

Since I haven't much money, I can't buy it.
As he is working hard, he is sure to succeed.

The following are a few other subordinating conjunctions or subordinators.

Simple subordinators

after, (al)though, as, because, if, once, since, that, until, when, where, while, etc.

Compound Subordinators

(ending with that):	in that, so that, except, that etc. in order that (or to + infinitive clause)
(ending with optional that):	now (that); provided (that); supposing (that); considering (that) seeing (that) etc.
(ending with as):	as far as, as long as, as soon as, so long as etc, so as (to + infinitive clause) so that (+infinitive clause)
(ending with than):	rather than (+non-finite or verbless clause)
Others:	as if, as though, in case.

Correlative subordinators

If ... then; (al)though ... yet/neverthless; as ... as; so ... as; more or less ... than; so ... that; such ... as; no sooner ... than; the ... the; whether ... or etc.

Note: *For, with, without* elsewhere prepositions might be added to the list of subordinators when they introduce the subject of a non-finite or verbless clause, e.g.

For him to interfere______.

With so many people there______.

Some of these subordinators introduce non-finite clauses, e.g.

If a nuisance______.

The subordinating conjunctions that introduce an adverbial clause of reason are: *because, since, seeing that, now that, for* etc.

EXERCISES

Supply the clause of reason in the following sentences:

a. ______ he reached the station in time.
b. ______ he couldn't attempt all the questions.
c. ______ he jumped from the third floor of the building.
d. ______ he is not likely to be very popular.
e. ______ anybody can cheat him.
f. ______ it is unlikely that AIDS can be wiped out in the near future.
g. ______ you are likely to be selected.
h. ______ the judge believed all that he said.
i. ______ he was left far behind in the race.
j. ______ he faced the consequences with courage.

Supply the result clause in the following sentences:

a. As I have already placed the order ______.
b. ______ because he is polite and soft-spoken.
c. Since he cannot afford to join a college ______.
d. Since the population is increasing fast ______.
e. ______ he met with an accident last week.
f. Seeing that his house was on fire ______.
g. Now that we are here ______.
h. ______ for he was in no mood to give up.
i. As he couldn't start his own business ______.
j. Seeing that he wouldn't get a loan from a bank he ______.

Infinitives and Gerunds

Both the Infinitive and the Gerund function as nouns. The 'to infinitive' is made by using 'to + the root or stem form of the verb e.g. *to go, to enjoy, to sleep* etc. With some verbs the 'to' of the infinitive is dropped. A gerund is made by using the root or stem form of the verb + -ing e.g. *smoking, drinking, enjoying, moving* etc. Both the infinitive and the gerund are, therefore, verbal nouns.

The use of the infinitive or the gerund is purely a matter of usage and rules of grammar do not help much in the selection of the one or the other. The choice of the infinitive or the gerund is, therefore an area of difficulty for the learners of English. The following discussion may be of some help to you.

As Subject of a sentence:

Either infinitive or gerund can occupy the place of the subject of a sentence particularly when action is treated in a broad general sense.

It is easier to eat than to cook.
Eating is easier than cooking.

1. Both the above sentences are grammatically acceptable but they do not mean exactly the same thing. The use of the infinitive implies that the speaker is expressing an opinion or propounding a general theory. The use of the gerund, on the other hand suggests that the speaker has had personal experience of the action and has partaken of it, e.g.

   It requires a lot of effort to learn grammar. (An opinion)
   Learning grammar requires a lot of effort. (Personal experience)

2. When the action is presented as a habit it is better to use the gerund, e.g.

   It is impolite to interrupt while somebody else is speaking.
   Interrupting while somebody else is speaking is impolite.

3. The gerund is used in prohibitory orders when not followed by an object e.g.

   No smoking please.

   No talking during prayers.

   But when the prohibition involves an object the infinitive is used, e.g.

   Do not feed the animals in the zoo.

   Do not ask too many questions.

As Object

1. The following can have only the infinitive as object:

afford	endeavour	refuse
agree	fail	seem
appear	get	stand
arrange	happen	swear
be begin	hesitate	trouble
be bound	hope	undertake
care	hurry	to be
chance	manage	to have
come	neglect	ought
consent	offer	used
decide	pretend	prove
determine	promise	

   I hope *to do* well in the examination

   He promised *to go* with me to Trivandrum

   He pretended not *to hear.*

   He failed *to cross* the obstacle (*but* he succeeded *in crossing* the obstacle)

2. The following verbs are followed by the infinitive or object + infinitive construction:

ask	help	like
beg	hate	mean
choose	intend	prefer
expect	love	

I want *you to finish* this work today.
The nation expects *every citizen to do* his duty.
I want *to reach* home before six p.m.
We prefer *to get* up early in the morning.

3. The following verbs are followed by object + infinitive construction:

advise	allow	ask
bid	cause	compel
command	enable	encourage
forbid	force	instruct
invite	lead	let make
oblige	order	permit
persuade	press	request
show	how	teach
tell	tempt	urge
warn		

Verbs of knowing and thinking: (These verbs are never followed by an infinitive alone).
believe, consider, know, feel, think

He invited *me to pay* him a visit.
The teacher told *me to re-write* my composition.
My mother advised *me to speak* the truth.
She showed *me* how *to paint* a picture
Note: (Some of the verbs in group 2 and 3 above can also be followed by the present participle or by the gerund)

4. The following verbs are followed by object + infinitive construction but the infinitives these verbs nearly always have are 'to be' and 'to have' and 'to have been'

acknowledge	find	suppose
believe	guess	take
calculate	imagine	understand
consider	know	feel
declare	maintain	see
deny	perceive	reckon

The teachers consider him to be the best behaved boy in the class.

He is known *to have* the best collection of stamps.

(This form of sentence is not however, very common. It is considered formal.)

A commoner form of such sentences is:

The teachers consider that he is the best behaved boy in the class.

It is known that he has the best collection of stamps.

5. The following verbs are followed by the gerund only.

avoid	not help
confess	not mind
dislike	not stand
defer	pardon
delay	postpone
dread	practise
detest	prevent
drop	recollect
enjoy	resent
excuse	risk
fancy	stop
finish	suggest
forgive	try
hinder	understand
keep (continue)	can't bear
imagine	can't stand
mind (object)	can't help
not bear	worth

After the expressions:

It is no use.......

It is no good......

Avoid *postponing* your work.

I hope you do not mind my *smoking* here.

Please excuse my *coming* late.

She dislikes *replying* to letters from strangers.

6. Gerunds are used after prepositions, e.g.
   He is very good at *inventing* excuses.
   I do not believe in *crucifying* people.
   I am tired of *listening* to such excuses.
   He made a fortune by *investing* in shares.

7. A gerund is used after 'Do + a lot of' or 'Do + a little of', e.g.
   He did a lot of *swimming* when he was young.
   She learnt a lot of *acting* at college.
   She does a little *acting*.
   I still do a little *singing* in the bathroom.

8. The following verbs are followed either by infinitives or gerunds:

attempt	like	forget
bear	intend	recollect
begin	love	remember
cease	neglect	need
continue	prefer	regret
disliked	omit	start
read	propose	try
fear	start	hate

9. Comments on a few specific verbs:
   (a) *'Remember, forget* and *regret'*:
   When these verbs are followed by the infinitive the infinitive refers to an action which takes place after the action — *remembering, forgetting* or *regretting,* e.g.
   Remember *to brush* your teeth before going to bed.
   Don't forget *to wash* your hands before eating.
   We regret *to inform* you that you have not been selected.
   When these verbs are followed by a gerund, the gerund refers to an action which took place before the act of remembering, forgetting or regretting, e.g.
   Do you remember *borrowing* five rupees from me?
   I can never forget his *insulting* me.
   I regret *telling* you my secrets.

(b) Verbs of sensation: *See, hear, observe, watch, notice, feel, smell* etc.

These verbs take the -ing form (present participle) or infinitive without 'to', e.g.

I saw him cross the bridge and run away.
I saw him crossing the bridge.
I heard her come in.
I heard her coming in.
I saw him break open the safe.
I saw him breaking open the safe.

The infinitive is used to describe the completed action. The -ing form (present participle) can be used both for complete and incomplete action. The latter form is therefore more common.

(c) *Want* and *need*:

The use of gerund after these verbs has a passive meaning.

This pencil needs mending.
The furniture wants polishing.
I want to reach home by evening.
He needs to study a lot.

(d) *Try*:

The verb try when used in the sense 'to make an effort' is followed by an infinitive but when it is used in the sense 'to make an experiment or trial' it is followed by a gerund. e.g.

He tried hard to win the election.
Try doing it this way.

(e) *Learn*:

When followed by an infinitive this verb implies a certain degree of success but when it is followed by a gerund it means nothing more than studying or learning something, e.g.

I have learnt *to drive* a car.
I have been learning *swimming* for two months.

(f) *Stop*:

When this verb means 'to cease' it must be followed by a gerund, e.g.

Stop drinking.
Stop coming late.

but when it means 'to halt' it can be followed by an infinitive or purpose, e.g.

I stopped to remind him of his promise.

(g) *Mind*:

When used in the interrogative and the negative it is followed by a gerund. 'Would you mind.........?' is one of the most usual ways of making a request.

Would you mind waiting for me?

Would you mind not smoking in this office?

Would you mind shifting a little to the other side?

I don't mind living in Bombay.

(h) *Love, like, hate, remember, respect,* and *prefer* etc.

The gerund is used to indicate habits and past actions. The infinitive is used for the future. The gerund is preferred in case of general statements, the infinitive is used to refer to special occassions.

I love going to the movies. (Habit)

I should love to spend this evening with you.

I hate to advise him in matters of a personal nature.

I remember meeting him at the club.

I must remember to write to my father once a week. (Future action)

(i) *Permit, allow,* and *advise*:

These verbs are followed by an infinitive if there is an indirect personal object, otherwise a gerund is used, e.g.

I allow my son to smoke.

I do not allow smoking in my drawing room.

I advise you to join an engineering college.

I advise investing money in shares.

(j) Expressions like *It needs, it requires, it wants* etc. are normally followed by a gerund when these refer a thing, e.g.

Your hair needs cutting.

This house requires white-washing.

These expressions can also be followed by a passive infinitive but the gerund is more normal.

(k) *Expect* is followed by an object + infinitive with to or a dependent clause:

I expect to meet him today. (look forward to)

I expect (that) she will come to see me.

I expect everyone in this office to be honest. (look for as due)

(l) *Begin* — when followed by a gerund this verb expresses a deliberate act. In other contexts it is followed by an infinitive.

On reaching America he began studying the science of computers.

Quite unexpectedly it began to rain.

(m) *Cease*:

On account of the strike buses ceased running in the evening. (deliberate act)

Monarchy has ceased to exist in many countries.

(n) *Start* is normally followed by a gerund.

I have lost weight since I started cycling. (to take up).

Gerund, Participles and Prepositions

Gerunds and Participles

Please read the following sentences carefully and note the use of italicised words in these sentences. The sentences have been arranged in two groups — A and B.

Group A (Present Participles)

1. Gracious when all goes to his pleasure but as irritable as a *teething* child when crossed.
   Note: (The words 'He is' at the beginning of this sentence may be understood.)
2. Shall it be one mad man, his head stocked with visions, or forty honest sea-men *pining* for their homes.
3. Today is the 11th of October — more than two months since we saw the shores of Spain *receding*.
4. A light faintly *flickering, rising* up and down.
   Note: (The words 'I see' may be understood at the beginning of this sentence.)

Group B (i) (Gerunds)

1. I thank you for *reminding* me.
2. It is more than a mortal can bear, this endless *sailing* into unknown seas.
3. Juan is on his knees adjusting *rigging*.
4. A blight upon their *singing*.
5. But there is such a thing as being too clever, *prying* into mysteries which were not meant for our eyes.

Group B (ii) (Gerunds preceded by 'the' and followed by 'of'.)

1. The *deepening* of their discontent is ominous.
2. There are men whom God has chosen for the *working* of His will.
3. I heard the *snarling* of angry beasts.
4. I am tired of the *mumbling* and *grumbling* of the crew.

Structure of Participles and Gerunds:

You must have noticed that the underlined words in sentences in both the groups have the structure Verb (stem) + ing, e.g.

Teething	=	teethe + ing
receding	=	recede + ing
flickering	=	flicker + ing
rising	=	rise + ing
reminding	=	remind + ing
sailing	=	sail + ing
rigging	=	rig + ing
singing	=	sing + ing
being	=	be + ing

There is therefore no difference between the structure of a present participle and that of a gerund and yet the two are different parts of speech and perform different functions.

Both participle and gerund are double parts of speech. A partciple is a word which is partly a verb and partly an adjective. It is a verbal adjective. Its structure is that of a verb (stem + ing) but it performs the function of an adjective. The present participle is also used as a constituent of the verb group, e.g.

The baby is teething.
The flood waters are receding.
A light was flickering in the distance.
The temperature has been constantly rising.

On the other hand:

'A teething child' means a child who is teething.

'Seamen pining for their homes' means seamen who are pining for their homes.

'Shores of Spain receding' means the shores of Spain that/which were receding.

'A light faintly flickering, rising up and down' means the light which was flickering (faintly) and was rising up and down.

All these participles have an antecedent noun or pronoun which they qualify. A participle may also qualify a noun that follows it. Since a participle performs the function of an adjective it can be further qualified by an adverb as in the expression 'faintly flickering'.

Please note that most of the stage directions in this play make use of present participles, e.g.

Columbus: (thundering again)

Columbus: (humouring him)

Pepe: (approaching near)

Guillerme: (scowling but sheepish)

Fransisco: (the words springing from him spasmodically)

The examples given above so far are those of present participles There are, in fact, two types of participles in English:

Present Participle: running, sleeping, singing etc.

Past Participle: broken, tired, spent etc.

While the present participle has the structure:

'Verb(stem) + ing, the past participle has the structure:

'Verb -en' or the third form of the verb.

As a constituent of the verb group the present participle represents an action going on or incomplete or imperfect. It is used in continuous and perfect continuous tenses, e.g.

He is writing a letter.

He has been writing letters since morning.

They were writing letters.

They had been writing letters for years.

He will be writing letters tomorrow.

He will have been writing letters for two hours by tomorrow noon.

The past participle as a constituent of the verb group represents a completed action. It is used in perfect tenses, e.g.

We have finished our work.

The train had left when we reached the station.

By tomorrow he will have finished reading this novel.

The past participle is also used in the passive voice. When the past participle is a constituent of the verb group in the passive it is preceded by an appropriate form of the auxiliary 'be', e.g.

This type of work is done only by a plumber.

The prize was won by Ramesh.

This task will be completed by tomorrow.

This tale has been told many times.

The road is being repaired.

The bridge was being built.

Like the present participle the past participle can also be used as an adjective, e.g.

Past participle used as a finite verb	Past participle used as an adjective
1. This tedious journey has tired me.	1. I feel tired at the end of this tedious journey.
2. Who has broken this cup?	2. We have thrown away the broken cup.
3. They have run the race.	3. You need a holiday, you look run-down.
4. A number of shops were burnt by the rampaging mob.	4. A burnt child dreads the fire.

The present participle as a constituent of a finite verb group is invariably preceded by an appropriate form of the auxiliary 'be'.

1. I *am* reading a very interesting story.
2. He *was* walking across the road when he met with an accident.
3. He has *been* practising as a lawyer for years.
4. He will *be* sleeping at four o' clock.

But when the present participle is used as an adjective it is not necessarily preceded by a form of 'be'. It may however be preceded by, 'being', or 'having been', e.g.

1. A rolling stone gathers no moss.
2. It being a very hot day, we decided not to move out.
3. Hearing the noise he peeped through the open window.
4. The work being rather tiring the workers found it difficult to continue with it.
5. Being a sitting M.P., he has every right to speak on behalf of his constituency.
6. Having been an inspiring social worker he had the confidence that he would get electoral support from the people.

The past participle when used as a constituent of a finite verb group is preceded by an appropriate form of the auxiliary 'have', 'be (passive) I or both i.e. 'have been'.

I have seen this movie earlier.
Someone has broken this cup.
The lights had been switched off before I entered the hall.
This play will be forgotten in a few years' time.

His leg was hurt in an accident.

You have been invited to lunch today.

But when the past participle is used as an adjective it need not be preceded by 'have' or 'be'. It may, however, be preceded by 'being', 'having been' or 'having'.

Being tired the traveller decided to rest for a while.

Having delivered the message the messenger left.

Having been provoked the cob started pelting stones.

A burnt child dreads the fire.

A lost opportunity never returns.

The visit being a frustrating experience he decided not to visit that place again.

Please go through the following sentences. These sentences are grammatically incorrect. Can you find out the reason?

1. Being a rainy day I remained in my room the whole day.
2. Entering the room the noise was very deafening.
3. Walking on the road a but hit him.

Since the participle is a verb-adjective it must be attached to some noun or pronoun. If it gets detached or unduly distanced from its subject of reference it becomes a 'hanging participle'. The above sentences are examples of the use of 'hanging participles'. These sentences, therefore, need to be restructured as:

1. It being a rainy day I remained in my room the whole day.
2. Entering the room, I found the noise deafening.
3. Walking on the road he was hit by a bus.
   While he was walking on the road, a bus hit him. (In this construction 'was walking' is a finite verb and not a participle).

An exception to this rule are some participles which owing to the frequency of their use in certain connections are used without any antecedent noun or pronoun for them to qualify: Some of these are;

Barring, bating, excepting, concerning, considering, regarding, respecting, saving, touching, owing (to), according (to) etc.

Considering his youth, his conduct is excusable.

EXERCISES

Correct the following sentences:

a. Being in haste the purse was left behind.

b. For sale a dining table by a gentleman with carved legs.
c. Being a holiday the office was deserted.
d. Standing on the bridge an aeroplane flew above us.
e. Broken into many pieces she picked up the jar.
f. Looking from the fifth floor window the sea looked calm.
g. Not being familiar with the game there was not much to interest us.
h. Having read a part of the story it should now be possible for you to guess the conclusion.
i. Standing on the top of the hill the people below looked like small toys.
j. While cutting grass a snake bit him.
k. Travelling in a train trees and houses rushed past him.
l. Being seriously hurt in an accident the ambulance was for.

Combine the following pairs of sentences into one sentence by using participles. Make such other changes as are necessary, e.g.

a. He shot the tiger.
b. He returned home.
Having shot the tiger he returned home.

1. a. The men were tired.
   b. They went home.
2. a. They won the match.
   b. They entered the final.
3. a. He saw them.
   b. They were polishing pieces of furniture.
4. a. I was walking down the road.
   b. I found a man lying by the road-side.
5. a. Take a turn to the right.
   b. You will reach the railway station in ten minutes.
6. a. He has been a great jurist.
   b. He is respected by members of the bar.
7. a. He passed the Plus Two examination.
   b. He decided to join the National Defence Academy.
8. a. He read the letter.
   b. He tore off the letter.
9. a. He heard a shot fired.
   b. He rushed into the street
10. a. We met a man.
    b. The man was carrying a bundle on his head.

11. a. The angel took pity on the old man.
    b. The angel made him young again.
12. a. Passengers saw the train steam in.
    b. They picked up their luggage.
13. a. He was sick.
    b. He did not feel hungry.
14. a. He was very happy.
    b. He patted the child on the back.
15. a. We started in the morning.
    b. We arrived at dusk.

Gerunds

Read the sentences in Group B (i) and B (ii). There is not much difference in the use of the words italicised in Group B (i) and those in Group B (ii) except that the words in Group B (ii) are preceded by the definite article 'the' and followed by the preposition 'of'. These words have thus been used like ordinary nouns, e.g.

The roads of this city are very wide.

Sweet are *the uses of* adversity.

The teaching of grammar is a challenging task.

A gerund, you have already learnt, like a participle, is a dual part of speech. A gerund is a verb-noun. It has the force of a noun and a verb.

A gerund, therefore, can occupy those places slots in a sentence which a noun or pronoun in the nominative or objective case can occupy. These three places/slots are:

1. The subject position/slot.
2. The object/complement position/slot.
3. The slot/position after a preposition i.e. as object of a preposition. e.g.

1. Flying kites is a pleasant game. (subject position)
2. He enjoys flying kites. (object position)
3. What I like most is flying kites (complement to the verb)
4. He is fond of flying kits (object to the preposition 'of')

Note: Gerunds are also used in formulaic expressions like: How about joinng us? Sentence No. 4 in Group B (i) above 'A blight upon their singing' is a formulaic expression of 'Let there be a blight on their singing'. or 'May a blight be cast on their singing.'

Since a gerund has the properties of a noun, it may be preceded by an article, a possessive or demonstrative pronoun, a noun in the genetive or an adjective or followed by a noun with 'of' (or another preposition), e.g.

All this is his doing.

I was pleased at his coming.

This commuting to Delhi every day is very tedious.

The indiscriminate felling of trees has disturbed the ecological balance in many parts of the world.

Since a gerund also exhibits the syntactic properties of a verb it may be qualified by an adverb or adverbial phrase, e.g.

He began singing slowly and clearly.

I am engaged in carefully revising this lesson.

A gerund may also take an object or a subject, e.g.

I don't like everybody criticising me.

It was no use Ramesh trying to explain to him.

Visiting the Taj was a delightful experience.

EXERCISES

Recast the following sentences using gerunds. Make such other changes as are necessary.

a. It is easy to ask questions, it is difficult to answer them.
b. Don't walk on the grass. (...... not allowed)
c. We played cards and thus spent the whole day.
d. Misers do not like to spend money. (Use 'hate')
e. If you praise everyone, you do not praise anyone.
f. If you read small print you will ruin your eyesight.
g. He comes here much too often and I dislike it.
h. You are not allowed to pluck flowers.
i. He left suddenly and didn't even leave a message for me.
j. If you help someone in need, you get happiness and satisfaction.
k. He invested money in shares and earned a lot of money.
l. The conduct of an examination is not easy.
m. He insisted that I should apply for the job.
n. You can teach a child better if you encourage him.

o. It is dangerous to trust everyone.
p. The engine driver ignored the signal and caused the accident.
q. In this country people like to hunt tigers for sport (..... a favourite sport)

In written English, the gerund should be preceded by a possessive pronoun or a noun in the possessive form. But since non-personal pronouns do not normally have a possessive form there is a parallel pattern which uses the objective case, e.g.

Informal (Spoken) English

1. Do you mind me smoking?
2. Our teacher doesn't like us coming late to school.
3. Please excuse me asking this personal question.

Formal (Written) English

1. Do you mind my smoking.
2. Our teacher doesn't like our coming late to school.
3. Please excuse my asking this personal question.

The use of the possessive case is considered more literary and more elegant.

EXERCISES

Complete the following sentences by using gerunds.

a. Do you object to (she borrow) your book?
b. You should appreciate (he make) an attempt to help you.
c. I don't like (anybody else read) my letters.
d. I can't understand (I forget) to wish her on her birthday.
f. I can't insist on (you leave) today.
g. Would you mind (Ashok see) your photographs?
h. His wife hates (he read) a newspaper at breakfast.
i. Please excuse (Sunil come) late to the class today.
j. I left without my (mother know) it.
k. There is no fear of (this building collapse)
l. There are no chances of (the examination be hold) again.
m. The reports of (the election be hold) this year could be true.
n. I must thank you for (you come) to my help.